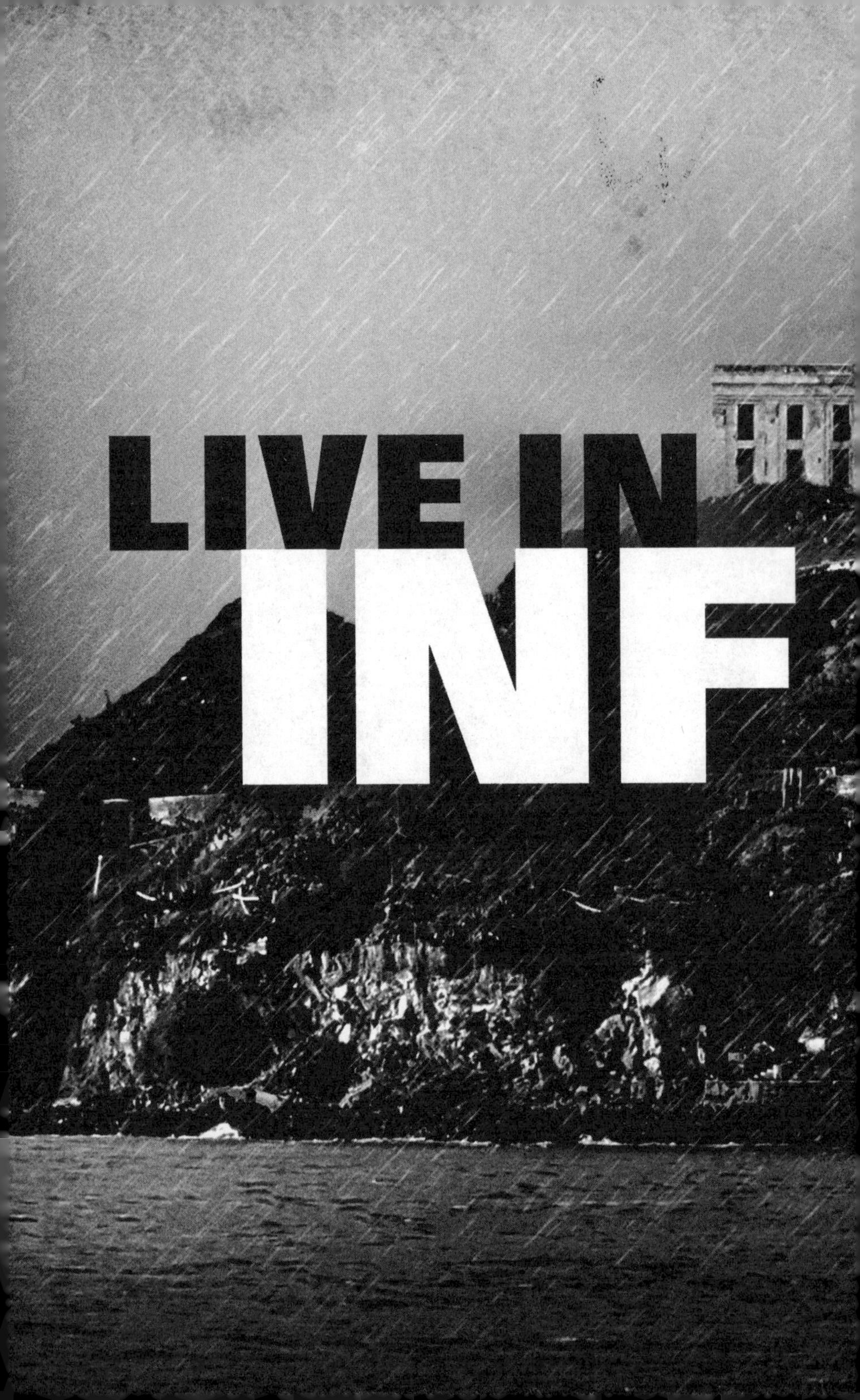
LIVE IN
INF

AMY

BY CAROLINE TUNG RICHMOND

SCHOLASTIC PRESS | NEW YORK

Library of Congress Cataloging-in-Publication Data available

ISBN 978-1-338-11109-5

10 9 8 7 6 5 4 3 2 1   18 19 20 21 22

Printed in the U.S.A.   23
First edition, April 2018
Book design by Phil Falco

To Jody Corbett,
the best editor a writer could ask for

1

By the time he turned sixteen, Ren had witnessed three executions.

The first criminal had been a boy, barely old enough to shave. Ren had been seven at the time and had watched from behind his mother's back as the soldiers dragged the boy up the cliff and pushed him to his knees. But that hadn't stopped the boy from shouting, "Freedom or death! Long live the United States of America!" Until, at last, he was silenced.

The second criminal had been a young father, still dressed in the gray pajamas that he had been wearing when the soldiers first arrested him. His crime? Paying a bribe to free his wife from Alcatraz prison. His sentence? Immediate death. As the winds howled over the Pacific bluffs, the young father had begged for mercy — not for himself but for his children. His three daughters had also been taken into custody, even the youngest, who still sucked her thumb. Rumor had it that the girls were sent to an orphanage on the Oregon coast or driven south to an internment camp near New Tokyo, the city formerly called Los Angeles. Either way, Ren never saw them at school again.

The last criminal had been a middle-aged woman, with bruised eyes and a broken nose but who kept her head held high until the very end. Ren had just turned eleven and was burning with the winter fever that would nearly kill him, but that hadn't stopped him from watching the execution — because attendance was mandatory and because the criminal was his mother.

While the crowd had gathered on the sunny beach, Ren wheezed and leaned on his father's broad shoulder. Forty feet above their heads, the soldiers marched Ren's mom to the lip of the killing cliffs. Ren's father held back tears while Ren almost threw up. Neither of them could do a thing, except watch.

The executioner sharpened his long blade, while Crown Prince Takamado of the Western American Territories lifted a bullhorn to his lips. First came the charges: *treason*. Then the sentence: *death*.

Through it all, Ren's mother never flinched, even though she would soon meet a slow and painful end. She stared out at the cold waves before she searched the crowd for her family. When their eyes met, she nodded at her husband and she gave Ren — her son, her only child — one last smile.

"Don't look," she mouthed to them both.

Ren's father tried to shield his son's eyes, but Ren struggled free.

"Help her," Ren whispered desperately. "We have to help her."

But the sword plunged in fast.

The blood poured in a rush.

And Ren collapsed to the sand.

That would be the last execution in the town of White Crescent Bay — until today.

2

The shop closed early that day for the killing.

At a quarter past two, Ren finished a neat row of stitches on a pair of trousers while his father locked up the cash register. Not one customer had stepped into the Cabots' tailoring and cobbling shop since they opened their doors this Friday morning, and Ren couldn't blame them for that. Nobody was in the mood to buy a spool of thread or drop off a shoe with a broken strap — not with a three o'clock execution looming over their heads.

"Time to go," said Mr. Cabot, glancing out the front window that overlooked East Main Street. "Looks like they're starting the roundup already."

Ren lifted his gaze from the worktable, which was piled high with bolts of low-quality wool and secondhand cotton, and squinted through the window blinds. Beyond the shop door, a dozen soldiers from the Imperial Japanese Army barked orders along the road, each one armed with a pistol on the hip and a rifle over the shoulder. Theirs looked particularly hungry today.

One of the soldiers read from a piece of paper, bellowing: "Attention all! By decree of the Empire of the Rising Sun, every resident of White Crescent Bay must head to the beach for a formal announcement. Anyone found in noncompliance will be fined and face arrest."

Up and down the road, the citizens obeyed. The grocer's lights shut off, followed by the pawnshop. The apartments emptied out, too. The residents hurried onto the sidewalk, forming a row as neat as one of Ren's stitches, but one of them — an elderly woman who sold vegetables around the corner — tripped, stumbling into a soldier's back. She bowed in apology, but not fast enough. The soldier slapped the woman hard and pushed her onto the sidewalk before storming off. After he left, she struggled to her feet, with her knees bloodied and shaking. No one dared to help her.

At the sight of it all, Ren tensed and stood from his worktable. He wanted to make sure that the woman was okay, but his father quickly shut the blinds.

"Leave it be," Mr. Cabot said, a weary warning. "It's not our business."

Ren stood on his tiptoes to get another look, looming a half head taller than his father, thanks to a recent growth spurt. "I just wanted to see —"

"You know we have to be careful. Those soldiers have orders to keep an eye on us."

"I know." Ren sank back onto his heels, and his heart sank with them. "But I had to know if that lady was all right."

"I'm sure she'll be fine. Get the lights." Mr. Cabot turned away from his son. The matter was closed.

Ren swallowed the sour taste in his mouth. Five years ago, his father would've helped that old woman. His mother would have, too. But that was before the Cabots had lost everything — before Ren's mom was arrested and killed on top of the cliffs, and before the patrol cars started lingering outside the shop. Ren had lost count of the times when the soldiers would pop into the store unannounced and stomp upstairs to the Cabots' apartment. They'd kick over the beds to search for contraband: illegal radios, banned newspapers, an old copy of the Constitution, anything that could lead to an arrest. But they never found a thing — Mr. Cabot made sure of it. Losing his wife had changed him. Nowadays, he followed the rules and fell into line and forsook his past, rarely mentioning the rebel Resistance that he had once been a part of and never speaking about the illegal newspaper that his wife had run almost single-handedly. And he expected Ren to do the same.

Ren may have lost his mother to Imperial Japan, but in some ways, he had lost his dad to it, too.

"Can you grab the keys?" Mr. Cabot called from the back room.

Ren was about to do just that when he saw someone approaching the shop. Dread filled every corner of his stomach. "Dad? Looks like we've got company."

His father hurried back into the shop's main room. "Is it a patrol? Or a Ronin Elite?"

Before Ren could answer, the front door was flung open and a single soldier stomped into the store with his rifle swinging. He wore a cloth cap on his head, a rising sun patch on his arm, and a standard gray uniform that marked him as a low-ranking private. Fortunately, he wasn't a member of the Ronin Elite — the most feared soldiers in the imperial military — but Ren's throat still closed like a noose. He would never get used to these visits.

"Why haven't you two left yet?" the soldier asked in Japanese. He looked about Ren's age, but the haughtiness in his eyes was generations older. "Didn't you hear the announcement?"

Mr. Cabot glanced at the soldier's name tag and replied in halting Japanese. "Our apologies, Kawabe-sama. We were locking up."

The soldier didn't seem to like that answer. "Where are your papers?"

Mr. Cabot kept his head down. "In the drawer below the register. License and rental agreement. It's all in order."

While the soldier thrust open the drawer, his gaze narrowed at Ren and his dad, volleying between their faces. "You two related?"

"He's my son, Kawabe-sama," replied Mr. Cabot, taking a protective step toward Ren.

Ren remained quiet. He had gotten used to the soldier's question over the years. He and his dad may have shared blood, but they looked nothing alike. Ren was stick-thin while his father was built like a sequoia, thick around the neck and everywhere else. Ren had inherited his mother's straight black hair while his father had no hair at all, having gone bald years before. And then there was the matter of race.

The soldier stared intently at Ren. "What are you anyway?"

Ren flinched. *American* he wanted to say. He was born here and was just as American as anyone else. But he knew exactly what the soldier was asking — it was another question that he had heard many times before. With a sigh he murmured, "I'm half Chinese."

Ren had never been ashamed of his identity — his dad was white and his mom was Chinese American — but as a kid he had learned where it left him in the pecking order. After the Axis powers won the war and carved up the US into three pieces — the Eastern American Territories, ruled by the Nazis; the Dakotas, run by the Italians; and the Imperial Japan–ruled Western American Territories, which covered the rest of the states west of the Mississippi River — the government had imposed a strict social hierarchy. After all, the Axis powers had long reasoned that they were destined to rule the world because they were superior in every way — mentally, physically, and especially racially.

Here in the Western American Territories, the citizens of Imperial Japan and the Third Reich claimed the very top of the racial ladder while Caucasian Americans (especially those with Western European ancestry) hovered toward the bottom. All other Americans were squished together at the lowest rung, from blacks and Latinx, to Native Americans and non-Japanese Asians. Biracial and multiracial citizens like Ren were looked down upon, too, although children born to one Japanese parent and one German parent were given special status. That sort of logic had never made sense to Ren, but this was how the world was run and he didn't have any say in it.

The soldier dumped out the contents of the drawer and lifted a neon-orange badge from the mess. It was a day pass to enter Fort Tomogashima, the massive military complex up the road. "How did you get your hands on this?" he demanded.

"I have a job interview there tomorrow morning," said Mr. Cabot. "Kato-sama sent me the pass."

"What sort of a job?"

"As a temporary tailor for the upcoming ball."

"Kato-sama sent for *you*?" the soldier huffed.

Mr. Cabot nodded. "A few of his tailors are out sick due to a stomach virus. I'm honored for the invitation."

The soldier studied the badge, and Ren fought off a frown. To be honest, he still couldn't believe that his father had gotten a call-up from Fort Tomogashima. Ever since his mother's arrest, there had been a black mark on the Cabot name. That was why Ren had thought someone was playing a joke on them when they got the request from the fort. But the caller had explained that the facility was very short-staffed for the upcoming Joint Empire Prosperity Ball — the state-run papers had called it "a celebration of our Nazi allies" — and spat out a time and a date for Mr. Cabot to come in for an interview.

After the call had ended, Ren told his father to turn the job down. How could he even stomach the possibility of having his name on Crown Prince Katsura's payroll? But Mr. Cabot had rubbed his eyes and said that he couldn't let a man like Kato-sama lose face. In any case, business had been dragging at the shop all winter and a week's worth of pay from the fort — meager as it was — would help cover next month's rent. They were already behind on their loan payments, and Ren had gone quiet when he'd heard that.

"This badge better not be a counterfeit," said the soldier, still pinching the day pass between his fingers.

Mr. Cabot blinked rapidly. "I can assure you —"

The soldier silenced him with a glare. "Did I ask you to speak, old man?"

Ren's hands tightened into fists. A familiar fury ignited in his gut, a slow-burning rage that had kept him company since his mother's execution, but Ren had trained himself to ignore it. It was a lesson he had learned the hard way. Three years ago, Ren had let his fury boil over. The patrols had ransacked the Cabots' apartment yet again, but this time they'd smashed Ren's mother's music box into pieces.

The old box had long lost the ability to play its song, but it had belonged to Ren's mom, and for that it was priceless.

As Ren had stared at the broken music box, his anger simmered and steamed and burst. He tried to tackle one of the patrols before Mr. Cabot yanked him back — but the damage had been done. The soldiers pummeled Ren hard, kicking his ribs and threatening arrest until Mr. Cabot promised to give them all of the money in the cash register if they'd put away their handcuffs. Ever since then, Ren had done whatever he could to control his temper. He took deep breaths and counted to twenty. He bit his tongue; he gritted his teeth. He never wanted to hear his dad beg like that again, and he had learned firsthand that he'd never beat the Empire with his fists alone. If he wanted to fight back, then he would have to find another way.

"I should take this pass back to Fort Tomogashima for confirmation," the soldier announced.

While Mr. Cabot spluttered a response, Ren took a small step forward. He may have hated the thought of his dad working at Fort Tomogashima, but he hated the idea of losing the shop even more. He didn't think his father could survive that kind of loss.

So Ren did what he had to do, even if it made him cringe. He tucked his narrow shoulders inward and slipped on his usual mask, the one with humble eyes. The one that he wore for the enemy.

"We received the badge from an official courier, but you're welcome to call Kato-sama if you prefer, Kawabe-sama," said Ren, his own Japanese taking off from his tongue on near-perfect wings. His mother had made sure that he'd become fluent — because the more fluency he gained, the easier it would be to put the soldiers at ease. "Can I make you something to drink while you phone the fort? We have Kato-sama's office number."

The soldier's eyes narrowed at Ren one more time. Then he snorted and tossed the badge back into the drawer. "It's not important. It's not like Kato-sama will hire you anyway. You better hurry up or I'm taking you both into custody."

Marching off the way he came, the soldier slammed the front door shut, and Ren released a sigh. When his pulse began to slow, he gave his father a smile. "At least your badge is safe."

Mr. Cabot just sighed. "Let me handle the soldiers next time, all right?"

Ren's grin vanished. "I got him to back off, didn't I?"

"I don't want you getting involved if you don't need to." His father scratched the gray stubble on his chin, looking a decade older than his forty years. "Grab a jacket and let's go. We're already late."

Ren looked down at his work uniform, the usual button-down blue shirt with tan trousers, and shrugged. "I'm okay."

"It's windy down at the beach. You should take your vest."

"I'll be fine, Dad."

"You could catch a cold."

"I'll be fine," Ren said again, this time through tight teeth. *I'm not a sick little kid anymore*, he wanted to say. It was true that he'd almost died from the winter fever that had burned across the WAT five years ago, but he had survived the disease when thousands of others didn't. And yet sometimes Mr. Cabot still acted like Ren was a sneeze away from his deathbed.

Mr. Cabot reached for their coat tree. "I'll bring the vest just in case."

Ren mumbled something but let the matter drop. He wasn't in the mood to fight about this, and they really needed to leave before they got arrested.

The two of them stepped into the winter sunlight, passing underneath the old shop sign that read: CABOT'S TAILORING AND COBBLING, FAMILY OWNED SINCE 1940. Ren's great-grandfather had painted it himself when he was a boy, not long before the US entered the Second World War. Back then, America was still called America, home of the brave and land of the free. The Stars and Stripes had flown in front of every school, and photos of President Franklin D. Roosevelt had graced the morning papers. The old US may not have been perfect — Ren's mother had never minced words about slavery or the Trail of Tears or FDR's internment camps for Japanese American citizens — but there had been progress. There had been hope. But all of that had withered to dust once President Roosevelt signed the official surrender.

Life changed after that. The Axis powers moved in to settle their new colonies, and the Empire had made quick work of installing its military and tossing out the law books and turning the Japanese internment camps into "reeducation centers" for American dissidents. Nowadays, owning an American flag could get you arrested and it was His Imperial Highness the Emperor's face splashed on the evening news. Disobeying a soldier could get you beaten, while speaking out against the Empire could land you a life sentence in the camps.

Home of the desperate, Ren's great-grandfather was known to say, *land of the condemned.*

Ren used to think about who had it worse. Was it his great-grandpa, who had known what liberty felt like but had lost it during the takeover? Or was it Ren himself, who had never tasted it at all? On a day like today, the answer to that question seemed easy.

Ren and his dad made their way toward the beach, joining a mass of townspeople wearing work uniforms or secondhand clothing that had been resewn and patched over the years. Ren's outfit didn't look much different from theirs, but he always stuck out of the crowd like a broken key on a grand piano. It wasn't only his height that set him apart; more than anything it was his ethnicity. Big cities like New Tokyo were more diverse, but a small town like White Crescent Bay — just twenty miles outside of San Francisco — had remained mostly Caucasian. Sometimes, Ren wondered if his mom had felt like an outsider, too. He was sure that she did, but then again she had never experienced what life was like for him. Being biracial meant that Ren had come from two different worlds but never felt like he fit into one or the other. He had often gotten the feeling that people saw him as a curiosity or a question mark — never as a person.

Soon, Ren and his father crossed into the nicer part of town, the part built for the tourists. The scuba shop and souvenir stores had closed for the season, but a few places had remained open, like the posh Boulevard restaurant where Ren's cousin Marty worked and the fancy realty office that boasted a cheery sign filled with photos of oceanfront homes. In the summer months, White Crescent Bay would be crammed full with Japanese families fleeing the hustle and bustle of San Francisco or New Tokyo. They'd come for the soft sand and the sweet air, and they'd stay for the picture-perfect California afternoons.

But right now, no one was smiling and hardly anyone spoke. There hadn't been one of those perfect days since the Axis won nearly eighty years ago.

Down the street the police station loomed ahead, and Ren noticed the latest Wanted signs nailed to the bulletin board out front.

"Looks like they put up new artwork," Ren whispered, but his father only grunted.

Unlike his dad, Ren had always taken interest in the Wanted posters and he looked over the newest ones. Each poster displayed a pencil sketch or a black-and-white photograph of the criminal in question, followed by the charges and reward:

> **JŌSEI TODA:** Wanted for blaspheming the emperor.
> Reward: ¥80,000
> **TIMOTHY ELDRIDGE:** Wanted for approaching Alcatraz
> prison via boat. Reward: ¥240,000.
> **JULIA CHIN:** Wanted for harboring an illegal Anomaly.
> Reward: ¥500,000.

As the rewards rose in price, so did the size of the posters. The last two took up the entire height of the board, both of them taller than Ren himself. The first one showed a photo of a sharp-eyed girl with short black hair. The picture was grainy, but Ren could make out a smudge on the girl's cheek. Mud, maybe? Or blood.

> **ZARA ST. JAMES:** Wanted dead or alive for murder.
> Reward: 10 million reichsmarks, to be dispersed by

the Nazi Intelligence Office in the Eastern American Territories.

Ren raised a brow. They'd upped the reward yet again, but he had been expecting that.

The Nazis would pay any price to hunt down this sixteen-year-old girl named Zara St. James — and for good reason, too. Three months ago, Zara had done the unthinkable: She'd infiltrated the White House and assassinated Dieter Hitler himself, the grandson of Adolf and the Führer of the Third Reich. Following the war, the German Empire had taken over a hefty portion of the globe — from Western Europe to North Africa and across the Atlantic to the eastern half of North America — but the Nazis were struggling to hold on to their slice of the American pie. As Dieter's generals wrestled for power, an insurgent group called the Revolutionary Alliance had rebelled against the Nazis and instigated the Second Revolutionary War, taking over Georgia and Florida and quickly gaining ground. Unsurprisingly, Zara was one of the leaders of the Alliance, and now she was the most wanted criminal in all the Eastern American Territories.

But someone else held that title here in the west.

Ren's eyes landed upon the last poster on the bulletin board, the biggest of the bunch. This one didn't have a photo or even a pencil sketch of the criminal, merely a giant question mark with a bare-bones description:

THE VIPER: Wanted for treason and sedition. Reward for any substantiated tips: ¥550 million.

Ren stared at that staggering amount, 550 *million* yen. That was double the reward money from a month ago, and this reward was only for a *tip*.

The Empire of Japan was getting desperate to arrest the Viper, but Ren doubted that they'd find much of anything. For one thing, no one knew what the Viper looked like. He could have been young or old, short or tall, black or white or brown or a blend of races. Some guessed that he was a she, while others ventured that the Viper was actually a group of people sharing one title.

The Viper's identity might have been anyone's guess, but everyone in the WAT had read his or her writing. The Viper's essays had been printed on pamphlets and dispersed through illegal newspapers. They were shared up and down the coast, memorized, and repeated. They'd been spray-painted on buildings and chanted at strikes, the song of the oppressed:

Liberty unto death.

Together we stand. United we fight.

And most frequently: *In the darkest of nights, we strike.*

Already there were whispers around town about what the Viper would say next. Call for more strikes? Encourage an attack?

An elbow dug into Ren's side. "Move along!" a patrol shouted into his ear.

The wind kicked up and Ren obeyed the command, letting the soldier herd him with prods and barks, walking the path that led down to the beach where sand pelted his forehead and scattered through his unruly hair. Ren tried to shuffle forward, but there was little room to move. The whole town had arrived to watch the execution — two thousand strong — and the crowd had spread so far down the coast that the soldiers had set up digital viewing screens along the shore, mounted against the rocks.

For a few minutes, Ren watched the waves somersault over the shore before he dared a glance at the tallest cliff, the same one where his mother had spent her last moments. Nausea hit him like a punch and he stared back out to sea. He hadn't been here in years, and his first instinct was to run far away from this place and its awful memories.

"Close your eyes if you need to," said Mr. Cabot. He tried to wrap an arm around Ren's shoulders, but Ren shook his head. He wouldn't run away and he wouldn't throw up his meager lunch. If his mother could face death with her head held high, then he could stand on a beach without getting sick. He had to stick this out.

Grinding his teeth, Ren looked at the cliff again. A camera crew stood where his mom had knelt years before, busily checking their equipment to prepare for the live feed on Channel Ten. An execution like this was required watching aross the Territories — it was an actual law — and the WAT would soon grind to a halt. The factory belts would stop rolling, the field laborers would get sent indoors, and the schoolchildren would set down their pencils to turn their heads to the state news.

And Ren envied them for that. They could watch the killing through an old black-and-white TV instead of standing here on the beach, forced to listen to the fresh screams and smell the warm blood. But this is what he got for residing in White Crescent Bay, the nearest town to Fort Tomogashima and home of the killing cliffs. Apparently, this charade made for an excellent backdrop for the cameras — the cliffs and the sea and the silent submissive crowd — and it had turned into a morbid WAT tradition. The first executions had taken place here a month after the war ended and were broadcasted over the radio to stun the Americans into compliance. Later on, the killings were shown on television whenever the Empire needed to remind everyone who was in power — and who wasn't.

"Any idea who it'll be this time?" said a woman next to Ren.

"Probably a murderer," said the man beside her.

"Nah, it'll be someone like Abel Quirk. I'm sure of it," said their friend.

Ren stiffened. He knew that name well, and a memory flooded his mind: a young father up on the cliff, pleading for his three young daughters. Ren had attended school with the Quirk girls — the middle daughter, Tessa, was a few grades above him and the youngest, Hannah, was in Ren's class — but now the whole family was gone. Mr. and Mrs. Quirk were dead, and their girls were never heard from again. They had become a cautionary tale of speaking out against Imperial Japan, just like Ren's mother.

A soldier stood atop the cliff with a bullhorn in hand. "Attention! Crown Prince Katsura will soon make his arrival!"

All conversation halted on the beach. Mr. Cabot stared blankly at the horizon while Ren crossed his arms before uncrossing them, unsure what to do with them. Everything about this day felt so *wrong* — the crowd gathered at the beach, the soldiers with the rising sun on their arms, and the televised execution that he would be forced to watch. But if Ren wanted to protest any of this, he would end up like the Quirks or his mom.

So Ren bit his tongue. He breathed in deep and dug his shoes into the sand and tried not to think about the anger prowling inside him like a caged snake.

Coward, he thought to himself.

But this was life in the WAT.

This was reality under the Axis's thumb. The America that Ren believed in had withered to sand years before.

And now came the wait to see who the Empire would drag to the slaughter next.

3

It was nearly time to start the afternoon events.

Even the winds calmed into a weak breeze, as if the atmosphere itself was holding its breath for what was to come.

The crowd began to fidget, but everyone went motionless again as soon as the beating of propellers drummed into people's ears. Ren spotted a black helicopter rising from the enormous military complex down the coast, built on top of the white cliffs. The Japanese called it Fort Tomogashima, but the Americans had long ago nicknamed it the Fortress.

The Fortress was a hulking thing, perched high on the tallest peak and surrounded by a tangle of barbed-wire fence. Crown Prince Katsura lived inside that metal nest, along with hundreds of young Japanese military cadets. These weren't ordinary cadets, either, who would become the grunts patrolling the beach or badgering shop-keepers for their rental papers. No, these were the cadets of the Ronin Elite, who stood upon the highest shelf of the entire army — because every single Ronin possessed a very *special* skill.

Mr. Cabot leaned into Ren. "Do you see Marty anywhere?"

Ren glanced around them, but the crowd was too thick to spot his twenty-five-year-old cousin. He wasn't worried, though. Marty Tsai had taken care of herself for years, and she preferred it that way, like a scrappy stray cat who refused to be domesticated. She'd come around every few weeks, usually at dinnertime, with a bottle of sake that she had pilfered from the restaurant where she worked. Mr. Cabot had always refused the bottle, and his lips would pull taut whenever Marty inevitably brought up the latest news about the revolution out east. But Ren liked listening to his cousin. She reminded him of his mom, and she even looked like her, too, which made sense since Ren's mother and Marty's mother had been sisters.

The helicopter soared over the beach and released it contents onto a landing pad on a nearby bluff. The crown prince's staff popped out first, followed by his personal bodyguard, Major Endo. Upon her arrival, the crowd collectively shrank back. Endo wasn't frighteningly tall or powerfully muscled; she was just a petite woman in her late twenties, with an ordinary face that would get lost in a crowd. But her blue Ronin uniform set her apart from the others on the cliff, not to mention the absence of artillery on her body. A small black pistol rested on her hip, but aside from that she carried no weapons. No standard rifle. No knives. Not even a can of pepper spray. She had no need for them.

Finally, Crown Prince Katsura stepped into the light. His uniform, a charcoal gray, hung loosely off his slender frame, as if he had stolen the clothes from an older brother's closet. He squinted in the bright sun, looking like a lost tourist rather than the most powerful man in the WAT.

The cameras started rolling, and the television screens on the beach flickered to life. The broadcast began like it always did, starting off with the imperial anthem while images of national landmarks faded in and out of the telecast: the Royal Summer Palace in New Tokyo; the National War Museum in downtown Seattle; the Shinto shrine in Phoenix, which honored the very first emperor of Japan; and finally the Golden Gate Bridge and the rocky prison island called Alcatraz, home to over a hundred American dissidents who would never know what freedom felt like again.

As soon as the anthem ended, the monitors displayed a portrait of the emperor himself, dressed in a military uniform that boasted golden epaulets and an array of medals, even though he'd never stepped foot on a battlefield. The emperor wasn't a military leader and neither were his predecessors — they had their generals take care of that — but the emperor had always been the head of state, the father of all Japanese, and the guardian of the Chrysanthemum Throne. These days he was too frail to leave his palace in Tokyo, but Ren had long felt the emperor's presence across the ocean, especially because his son the crown prince bore a striking resemblance to him.

Finally, the feed went live. The cameras panned over the waves and up the cliffs and came to a stop on Crown Prince Katsura. He was a couple of years older than Mr. Cabot, but his hair lacked any gray and his cheeks had remained smooth, likely due to a healthy diet and a flock of expensive doctors that his subjects could never afford. Given his status, no one would've blamed the crown prince for sending one of his generals to give the announcement today, but he had decided to take a more hands-on approach to ruling than his forerunners.

"To our good and loyal subjects of the Western American Territories, and to those who may be watching this broadcast across the Greater East Asia Co-Prosperity Sphere," said the crown prince into his microphone, "I speak to you today with a troubled

21

conscience." As usual, he wore his round, gold-rimmed glasses, which made him look like the political science professor he had once aspired to become instead of the public figure that he was forced to take on. Four years prior, his two older brothers had perished in a small plane crash over the Tibetan territories (their deaths were later blamed on Chinese nationalists), and the soft-spoken third son had to assume the responsibilities of the eldest, which included overseeing the Empire's most prized colony.

"Since I arrived in the Territories, I've tried to bring change to these lands," the crown prince continued. "I've worked to better our roads and schools. I've built health clinics to care for the poor and the sick. I've also put an end to public executions, choosing to reform our criminals through hard labor in our reeducation centers."

Ren bit back a harsh laugh. Crown Prince Katsura was part of a new progressive movement that promoted harmony between the Empire and its conquered peoples, and his reforms had reflected that, but Ren had always been wary. Take the "reeducation centers." Ren had never stepped foot inside one, but everyone knew there was nothing "reeducating" about them. They were internment camps, plain and simple, with dirty water to drink and rancid rice to eat and hundreds of bedbugs to keep you company at night. The sad thing was, they had first been built by the US to house Japanese Americans during the war, and the Empire had simply reused them after the takeover for criminals and Resistance fighters. Ren had never forgotten this ironic twist in history, but some Americans had been lulled by the crown prince's reforms. They failed to see that at the end of the day, Crown Prince Katsura served the Empire — and the Empire ruled with a fascist fist.

The crown prince pushed his glasses farther up the bridge of his nose. "I undertook such reforms for *our* sake. I was married in the Western American Territories, and my daughter was born here. This is our home. This is our land. But within the last year, I've seen a sharp spike in violence and treasonous acts across the territories. Innocent lives have been lost, including women and small children. The peace we've enjoyed for so long has quickly broken apart.

"Because of this unrest, I will reinstate the nine o'clock curfew, starting tonight," Crown Prince Katsura continued. "The Ronin Elite will also conduct regular sweeps across the WAT. Furthermore, after much thought and deliberation, I've decided to lift the ban on public executions, having no other choice."

Ren ground his teeth at the news, even though he knew it was coming. In the last twelve months, guerilla groups across the WAT — operating under the name the Resistance — had upped their exploits: organizing strikes at state-owned orchards, bombing patrol outposts, and poisoning water supplies that fed into soldiers' barracks — and the Viper's essays had fueled every one of those flames. The Empire had tried to smash each rebellion and hide the attacks from the daily news reports, but the Resistance refused to back down.

"Retrieve the criminal," Crown Prince Katsura said off camera, and Major Endo swept into motion. She returned to the helicopter, where she pulled someone out of the backseat. The camera crew worked fast to zero in on the criminal's face, but a dark hood covered their head.

"To your knees," said Major Endo, depositing the criminal by the crown prince's boots.

The cameras swooped in even closer, as Crown Prince Katsura

yanked off the hood. Whispers thrashed through the crowd at the reveal. Somebody gasped next to Ren and Mr. Cabot muttered something to him, but Ren wasn't listening.

The criminal was a Caucasian girl, not much older than he was. Fresh blood dripped under her nose, trailing splotches onto her gray prisoner's jumpsuit, and a mural of bruises covered her cheeks. Her dark hair whipped in the wind like tumbleweed, reminding Ren of his mother. And just like his mom, this girl didn't whimper.

Whoever the criminal was, she was brave, that was for sure. It was obvious that the soldiers had tortured her for hours before they brought her to the cliffs. Or perhaps the torture had lasted for days. Ire swelled inside Ren like a tide, and he began counting to twenty to calm it.

Crown Prince Katsura addressed the girl directly. "Daisy Montgomery. You have been found guilty of attempted murder and treason against the Empire. Two nights ago, you endeavored to infiltrate my office at Fort Tomogashima. You claimed to commit this act on behalf of the Viper."

Suddenly, Ren lost his balance and he stumbled into his father.

"What's wrong?" his father whispered, alarmed.

"Nothing. Sorry," Ren said quickly. He looked away from his dad and pretended to clear his throat, hoping to hide how the blood had drained from his cheeks.

Around them, another round of murmuring scattered through the crowd.

"The Viper?" someone said.

"Is that girl an accomplice?"

The whisperings multiplied, but Ren could only shake his head.

Daisy Montgomery couldn't have been the Viper's collaborator — couldn't anyone else see that? Some of the Viper's essays encouraged worker strikes and factory walkouts, while others spoke of joining the Resistance — but all of the writings urged unified acts of rebellion instead of a lone-gunman approach. Daisy's crime didn't have the Viper's familiar stamp on it.

But still, Ren's chest hurt for her.

"You all right?" Mr. Cabot repeated. He tried to give Ren his vest, but Ren refused. He wasn't cold. If anything, his collar felt suffocatingly warm.

Crown Prince Katsura went on, this time speaking to the cameras. "For these crimes, Daisy Montgomery, you are sentenced to death."

The crowd went quiet again, but one last question remained: How would Daisy Montgomery die? Over the decades, the overseers of the WAT preferred different methods of execution. One had preferred a slow death by sword. Another, beheadings. And still another had a soft spot for crucifixions in the rising tide.

Crown Prince Katsura signaled to Major Endo to proceed, and the matter was settled. The Ronin Elite would carry out the dirty work today — and their work was often dirty indeed.

At last, Daisy Montgomery made a sound. She spat out a desperate string of words, but they all came out broken.

Mr. Cabot sucked in a breath. "They must've cut out her tongue."

Ren felt nauseous. So *that* was why Daisy hadn't said anything before. He tried counting again, but it was no use stopping the fury — and the fear — from swirling through him. Everyone knew what the Ronin Elite were capable of. Some could turn your insides out with a tilt of the head, while others could drive you insane with a sweet little song. The Japanese scientists who had first engineered these superhuman soldiers had called them Anomalies, for the anomalous gene that made them so prized.

Ren thought another name was more fitting: *killers*.

Major Endo approached her newest victim, and Ren grimaced as he recalled her powers: crushing bones *and* boiling blood with a simple touch. Endo was a rare Dual Anomaly, possessing two superpowers instead of one, which was why she had been selected to protect the crown prince himself. There were very few females in the regular imperial army — Japanese women were expected to marry young and raise children and attend monthly meetings of the Patriotic Women's Association — but the Ronin Elite gladly admitted them into their ranks. Anomalies, after all, were scarce. And so, if a little Japanese girl manifested the ability to bend metal or conjure fire in her small hands, then that couldn't go to waste.

At Major Endo's approach, Daisy struggled against her restraints, but it didn't matter. Endo merely placed her hands atop Daisy's head, and the girl began screaming until her throat went raw. The sound leapt off the cliffs and hammered home into Ren's ears, tunneling itself into his memory.

Ren told himself to breathe. The Empire killed dozens of Americans each week, in the camps or out in the streets. Daisy's death would be no different. Yet Ren's heart kept speeding faster, urging him to run up the path and put a stop to the suffering. But Ren didn't move. Neither did anyone else around him. Maybe it was fear that kept them rooted where they stood, or maybe it was something worse. Like complacency.

A sickening crunch echoed across the beach. Daisy's head lolled to one side, her skull crushed like a quail's egg. Ren shuddered. He couldn't have done anything to save her, but he was disgusted with himself anyway. He had accepted Daisy's fate like everyone else. He had said nothing, done nothing.

Atop the cliff, Crown Prince Katsura wasn't finished yet. "A dangerous cancer is spreading through our lands. The Viper's writing has polluted people's minds and has caused unrest in our peaceful society. Both Americans and Japanese have lost lives, and as steward of the Territories I cannot allow this any longer, which leads me to my newest decree. If the Viper is watching this broadcast, I demand that you step forward and give yourself up." His gaze bore into the camera lens. "If you continue to resist, my soldiers will execute more traitors upon these cliffs. What other choice will you leave us?"

Silence blanketed the crowd. Crown Prince Katsura motioned to the cameraman to shut off the feed before shuffling back to the helicopter with Major Endo on his heels. As soon as they were buckled in their seats, the helicopter took off from the launching pad and headed back toward the Fortress, but this time without Daisy Montgomery.

Down on the shore, it took a minute for anyone to move. Only when the soldiers began barking "Off the beach!" did people begin their trudge back into town, mumbling all along the way.

"Who are they going to kill next?" someone said.

"Just don't do anything stupid and it won't be any of us," replied someone else.

"Wonder what the Viper is going to do now."

The question echoed inside Ren's head, along with Daisy Montgomery's last screams. Her body lay quiet on the cliff, curled inward like a fawn, but this wouldn't be the last time that Ren would see her. Daisy's execution would be broadcasted on the evening news and again on tomorrow's morning reports. The Empire would keep using her death to send the Viper their message: *Come forward or else.*

"Let's go. You don't look too good." Mr. Cabot offered Ren his vest again. "You're shivering."

Ren walked numbly forward, matching his steps to his father's. "I'm *fine*," he said, but that was a lie. Something had cracked inside him. The wall he had carefully built to dam up his emotions was crumbling fast, and he didn't have enough mortar to patch it up. "I need to walk this off."

"Ren, wait!" His father made a grab for his arm. "Slow down, won't you?"

As if that would fix anything.

"I'll be home later. Don't worry," Ren said, slipping into the crowd as quick as a trout. He picked up speed, bumping shoulders with those around him, but no matter how fast he went he couldn't outrun the secret locked inside him. It was the reason why he played nice with the soldiers and tamped down his anger. It was the reason why he knew Daisy Montgomery was innocent of her crimes.

Because they were *his* crimes, not hers.

He was the one who had written those essays. He was the most wanted criminal in the Western American Territories.

Ren Cabot was the Viper.

4

With the killing cliffs behind him, Ren ran back into town. His breathing grew wheezy in the cold sea air, but he had to keep moving. He had to get away from the beach or else he'd replay the execution over and over in his mind, and then his wrath would spike hot enough that he might do something stupid.

So he headed for the one place that might give him some peace.

Hurrying down East Main, Ren passed by his family's shop and Marty's apartment building and left the town behind entirely, walking on a winding road that curled up the side of a pretty bluff. Thirty houses soon came into view, with their cement-and-glass façades overlooking the tumbling seas below. In the summer months, the homes would fill with tourists and their fat pocketbooks, but in the off-season they lay empty and quiet.

Once he reached the Naguchis' vacation house, Ren punched in the code to slip through the gate and skirted along the property's edge. The Naguchi family had made their riches after the war by taking over Californian strawberry farms and shipping the fruit back to Japan and throughout the Eastern American Territories. On paper they were loyal citizens of the Empire, but in secret they'd been sympathetic to the suffering of American workers. The Naguchis were now in their late nineties and had moved back to Japan to live out their days, but they had kept their vacation home for one purpose — and for that Ren was very grateful.

Ren strode past the main house and the guest cottage and made for the gardener's shed. Once inside, he pushed away an old leaking wheelbarrow to expose the splintered floorboards. He ran his thumb along the floor until it caught on a chip in the corner, using it as leverage to pry open the board. A hole opened up before him, with a ladder leading down to the hidden room below.

Ren hopped down, coughed out dust, and switched on a bare lightbulb. A desk was pushed against the far wall, with a single typewriter sitting on top of it. Reams of paper were piled in the corner, unopened. And in front of Ren, there sat a simple printing press.

Resting his fingers on the metal, Ren felt his fury cool, fraction by fraction. For the past year, whenever his frustrations rose, whenever his anger raged, whenever he missed his mom too much, he would visit this room.

The printing press itself had been built in the early 1800s and had spent decades in retirement at the local historical society before gaining a second life after Imperial Japan's takeover. A former newspaper owner had smuggled the machine to this very room, with the Naguchis' permission, and since then it had passed from editor to editor. Some of them had even carved their names onto the press's wooden legs: *Josephine Teller, Luis Medina, Abel Quirk*. Then came Ren's mother's own inscription, *Jenny Tsai*. She had never changed her last name after she married. She may have loved her husband fiercely, but she was also a proud third-generation Chinese American who didn't want to lose that connection to her heritage.

Ren rubbed his thumb along his mother's name. There was a

blank space underneath it where his own name could go, but he hadn't gotten around to inscribing it yet. He had been too busy.

Over a year ago, Ren had revisited the press on the anniversary of his mother's death. The secret room had been abandoned after her execution, and only Ren and his father and the elderly Naguchis remembered its location. Everyone else who had known the press's whereabouts had been killed, including his mother's courier, who was captured and tortured until she gave up the names of her accomplices. That confession was the reason why the Empire had arrested Ren's mom.

On the night of the anniversary, Ren had stood next to the printing press for a long time, with his flashlight flickering, letting himself simply *remember.* As a kid his parents had forbidden him from seeing the press, but once he got older his mom would swear him to secrecy and sneak him down to the gardening shed whenever she needed an extra hand. Ren's very first visit had felt like walking into a brand-new world — the ink on his fingers, the scent of the paper. His mom had put him to work, too, showing him how to typeset the last two articles for the newest issue of her newspaper. The first piece had been an interview with an anonymous Japanese citizen who supported the Resistance, while the second had been an exposé about orphaned American girls forced to become "comfort women" for imperial soldiers. His mother had let Ren read the article, even though its details had made him want to throw up his dinner.

"I know these stories can be hard to read, but we can't live with blinders on," his mother had said as she inked up the press. "Too many Americans have accepted the world around us. They've forgotten how to get angry — and someone has to wake them up."

As Ren sat silent on that anniversary night, his mother's words had resurfaced in his mind, whispering about liberty and the free press and inalienable rights. Jenny Tsai would've seen right through the crown prince's reforms.

His health clinics stayed closed half the time.

His road construction raised taxes across town.

His new schools taught the same curriculum as before — loyalty, obedience, and reverence to the emperor.

Ren's mother would have written article after article about how Crown Prince Katsura may have had good intentions, but those intentions couldn't change an empire. Underneath those reforms, America still bowed to its master across the sea.

Something had shifted inside Ren that night. With his mother's words echoing between his ears, he dusted himself off and left for home with an idea for his own essay planted in his head. The words had dug roots in his thoughts, begging him to put pencil to paper. At first, he had tried to swat them away. His dad had made it clear that they had to toe the line, but words lengthened into sentences and the sentences soon formed entire paragraphs. Ren couldn't stop fighting it anymore. He couldn't drift into complacency like his father had.

And so Ren had started writing. Not on paper — that would be too risky — but in his head. He had written while shining shoes and mending hems. He had written when he should have been sleeping, while the crescent moon rose in the night sky and while his dad snored in the bedroom next to his own.

One evening, against his better judgement, Ren had grabbed a scrap of paper and scribbled down the essay. Then, with shaky hands, he had read the whole thing over. He hadn't expected much — like other American kids, he had only attended school through the fifth grade — but to Ren's surprise his writing hadn't been half bad. He couldn't take all of the credit for that, considering he had piggy-backed on Thomas Jefferson himself. Ren's mother once had an old copy of the Declaration of Independence, and he had memorized a few passages before his dad had burned it after his mom's arrest. Ren had decided to riff on a couple paragraphs, using the original script as his essay's backbone, but updating it to reflect the America he lived in:

We hold these truths to be self-evident, that all people are created equal, that they are born with certain unalienable Rights, that among these are Life, Liberty, and the pursuit of Happiness. But under the regime of Imperial Japan, we the people have lost these very basic rights.

And we must fight for their return.

Governments are instituted among the people, deriving their just powers from the consent of the governed — which the Empire has duly ignored. Whenever any Form of Government becomes destructive of these ends, it is the Right of the People to alter or to abolish it, and to institute a new Government.

Of which we the people now demand.

A strange current had flowed through Ren, part nerves and part thrill. He thought his mom would have approved of his work. She had admired Jefferson, even though she felt he hadn't gone far enough — he didn't give women the vote; he owned slaves and never saw the hypocrisy in that — but she had always believed in what Jefferson had helped found. She simply wanted to improve on it.

In another life, Ren's mother could have been a politician. She had told him once that she would have loved running for Congress if it hadn't been dismantled, but she had been born into this world where a woman like her was forced into a cleaning job by age eleven. But that hadn't stopped her from standing up to fight.

So what was stopping Ren?

It took over a month for Ren to convince himself to get started and gather everything into place: making a short trip to San Francisco to buy the supplies he needed, revising each sentence until he was happy with the whole thing, and relearning how to typeset his work. When he was finished and covered in ink, Ren printed fifty copies of his one-page essay. It was a far cry from the six-page newspaper that his mother had put together, but Ren was proud of what he'd done. Even if his first printing got stepped on or tossed in the garbage, he was carrying on his mother's legacy. He was keeping her alive.

Then a funny thing happened. Ren's essay had plucked a nerve, and his fifty copies were shared and passed beyond the limits of White Crescent Bay. Other underground papers republished his words, and Ren heard whispers around town asking who exactly was this Viper and what was he going to publish next? So he wrote a new issue, this time printing seventy-five copies. Then he penned another one, with a hundred-copy run. He learned over time that he didn't need to print more than that; the local Resistance would pass along his work to bigger newspapers that would reprint Ren's writing, and it grew from there.

Despite the danger he had put himself in, Ren hadn't regretted what he had done. Until this afternoon.

Back in the present, Ren pressed his fingers against his temples and thought again about Daisy Montgomery. He had chosen his pseudonym because vipers were deadly and secretive, but he had done absolutely nothing while Daisy died in his name. Worse still, there'd be more like her to come.

Ren had known since publishing his first essay that his writing might lead some of his readers to get beaten or arrested. Likely even killed. He had grimly accepted this fact by reasoning that the Viper was merely a small part of the equation. A revolution was already simmering across the land, clamoring to break out on the California soil. The Viper was only one shovel trying to unearth it.

The execution today, however, had felt different. Watching Daisy on the cliff . . . Ren still felt dizzy from it. His practical side kept telling him that her death wasn't his fault. He wasn't the one who dragged her to the beach and crushed her skull with his fingertips. Daisy's blood wasn't on his hands. But when Ren glanced down at his palms, they looked smeared just the same.

Maybe I should quit altogether, thought Ren, wincing as a headache bloomed. He could leave the Viper behind and throw himself into working at the shop, toeing the line like his father did. But the thought of that made Ren feel hollow inside — and it wouldn't stop the executions. The Viper's poison had already spread across the WAT, and the Empire was determined to drive him out of hiding. Ren wondered what his mother would have done in his shoes, but he really had no idea. All he knew was that he'd have to figure out his next steps alone.

Ren forced himself to get up. He owed his readers a new essay, a rebuttal against the crown prince's speech, but not today. Right now, he needed to go home and shut off his thoughts for the night. He wanted to bury himself between his sheets and sleep and forget about Daisy, even if it only lasted a few hours.

He returned to the shop in silence, his eyes flickering skyward in case the flying Ronin Elite were out on patrol. He was relieved when he turned onto his block, but that relief wavered when he thought about the lecture his father was going to give him once he stepped inside the shop. He knew exactly what his dad would say: *I was worried sick. You can't run off like that. You know what'll happen if we make even a little mistake.* It almost made Ren turn around and duck into the pawnshop for a few minutes, but then he noticed that the Cabots' shop looked dark and empty. He unlocked the door and quietly made his way upstairs to the apartment.

"Dad?" Ren called out.

There was no response.

Ren gratefully burrowed himself in his room. His dad had probably run out to the grocer's or gone to check on Marty, and Ren decided to pretend to be sleeping as soon as his dad came home. But hours passed, and Mr. Cabot didn't show.

And that's when Ren got worried.

As dusk settled over East Main, Ren pulled on a jacket and headed back outside with jitters in his stomach. He stopped by the corner store, then Marty's apartment, and then to the cemetery, where his paternal grandparents were buried. His dad liked to tidy up the grass around their graves, even though it had been years since his parents passed. Ren's grandfather had succumbed to heart disease a decade ago, while his grandmother had fallen victim to a bad blood transfusion before Ren was born. Most Americans died before the age of sixty, and if they came down with a serious illness before that? Not even the crown prince's free health clinics could help you.

With the curfew looming, Ren had no choice but to return to the shop, except his dad still hadn't come home. He peeked out the living room window, which overlooked the street. Terrible scenarios began playing in Ren's head: his father getting hit by a car, his father having a heart attack, his father getting arrested. This was his greatest fear — losing his dad like he had lost his mom. He and his father might not have been close — there were days when they hardly uttered more than twenty words to each other — but the thought of burying his father made Ren want to curl up in a corner and wrap his arms around his knees.

Ren was ready to head out the door again, no longer caring about the curfew, when he saw two shadows running down East Main, one of them half carrying the other. The duo hunkered down behind a Dumpster while a patrol car rolled past, and when the coast was clear they hobbled toward the shop. Ren backpedaled from the window and catapulted down the stairs. He heard an urgent knock on the door.

"Open up, Renny! It's us," a voice hissed from the other side.

Only one person ever called him Renny. Ren yanked the door open just in time for the two people to stumble inside. Dust covered them both, and a trail of blood dripped in their wake. They looked like they had walked through the middle of a battlefield. Ren's stomach dropped.

"Dad!" he cried.

5

Ren rushed forward to help Marty with his father's weight. "What happened to him?" he demanded.

"Help me get your dad up the stairs first," she replied in her matter-of-fact way.

Ren could only stare at the mangled mess that was his father's right hand. "Was he shot? How did —"

"Just help me get Uncle Paul up the stairs! He's lost a lot of blood." Marty shoved her bangs aside to reveal a startingly pretty face, with wide-set eyes and high cheekbones that could have graced a fashion magazine. Dirt and blood matted her long black hair, but she still could have talked her way out of Alcatraz with a carefully placed pout. Soldiers often went tongue-tied around her — they tended to forget that they were supposed to look down on a Chinese American like her — and Marty had never felt guilty about using her appearance to play them for fools.

Ren snapped out of his haze. Moving fast, he wrapped an arm around his dad's waist and hoisted him onto the worn sofa upstairs, where Mr. Cabot lay back with a groan.

"What happened to him?" Ren repeated, but Marty was quick to deflect the question.

"Grab the first aid kit. I'll get some water and rags." Then she was off to the kitchen before Ren could press her for an answer.

As he dashed to the bathroom cabinet, though, Ren thought about what Marty and his dad had been up to that evening. The two of them had never been close. Seven years ago, Ren's mom had promised her dying sister that she would watch out for Marty after she passed, and that responsibility had fallen to Mr. Cabot after his wife's execution. But Marty was already twenty by then and she didn't want or need Mr. Cabot poking into her business and telling her to stop talking about the injustices in the WAT. That was why their relationship had never graduated beyond lukewarm.

With the first aid kit in hand, Ren returned to his father's side and finally got a good look at his dad's injury. It was ugly — a dark red mass of flesh and blood and shreds of fabric. One of the fingers crooked at a strange angle, too.

"Turn on a light, won't you? I can't see what I'm doing," said Marty, cleaning the wound without flinching. She had always had a tough shell. She never mentioned her father's abandonment of her when she was eight, and she had held back her tears when her mom withered away from kidney failure. Ren knew that Marty had feelings like everyone else, but she liked to keep hers locked away.

Just then, Mr. Cabot's eyes blinked open and he reached for Marty's shoulder with his good hand. "Don't tell Ren. You promised me," he croaked.

"Don't tell me what?" Ren's spine straightened. "What's he talking about?"

Marty ignored Ren's question yet again. "Call Serrano," she told him. "We'll need her to patch up your dad."

"I'm not calling anyone —" Ren said, until his father lurched up with a gasp, crying out from the pain.

Marty struggled to get her uncle to lay back. "Call Serrano now!"

This time Ren listened, not because of Marty, but because he couldn't take another second of his father's agony. Hurrying down the steps, he dialed Serrano's number on the shop's ancient rotary phone. The old nurse agreed to come over, depending on how fast she could dodge the patrols — about thirty to forty minutes — and Ren told her that he'd pay her extra if she hurried, even though the shop's budget was stretched as thin as it was. They'd be lucky to cover her nursing services and even luckier if Mr. Cabot could use his hand again in a month or two. As for the interview tomorrow at the Fortress? That was out of the question.

Ren bolted back upstairs, only to find his dad asleep while Marty wiped a rag over the bleeding wound.

"He shouldn't be unconscious!" Ren lunged toward the sofa to shake his father by the shoulders. He didn't know much about medicine, but he knew enough that his father should stay awake until Serrano could see him. But Marty blocked him with her arm.

"It's all right. I gave him a painkiller to help him rest," she said, as if there was nothing to it.

"How did you even get your hands on something like that?"

Marty stopped cleaning her uncle's wound to glare up at Ren. "You have to trust me. I've done this before."

"What are you even talking about?" The questions began rolling off his tongue, and Ren wanted answers. "What happened to you guys tonight? How did my dad get hurt in the first place?"

Marty blinked away from his prying eyes. "It's . . . a very long story."

"Give me the condensed version."

"It won't make sense if I do that. You'll have to hear the whole thing." Marty elevated her uncle's arm to stanch the bleeding, not even flinching when some of the blood trickled onto her sleeve. "Look, what I'm about to tell you, you can't repeat to anyone."

A shiver worked its way down Ren's neck. "Tell me."

"Swear it to me on your mother's grave."

"What?" Ren said, his gut twisting at her demand.

"People I cared about have died gathering this intelligence and more lives will be on the line if you start blabbing around town." Her gaze hardened at Ren. "Swear it. I need to hear it."

Ren frowned. "Fine. I swear it on my mother's grave."

With a nod, Marty got straight to the point. "I'm with the Resistance."

Ren's breath stuck in his throat. He'd had a hunch over the years that Marty may have been a spy. She worked as a bartender at the Boulevard — she was barred from becoming a server on account of her Chinese heritage — and she must have overheard some very interesting things when the officers got a little tipsy. Yet he never imagined that she had actually joined the rebels.

She continued. "I started out passing along intel that I overheard during my shifts, but I joined the Resistance as a full member five years ago." Marty kept her tone even, but she couldn't hide the pride in her voice. "About eight months back I got promoted to captain of our local cell."

Ren's mouth slid open. "You're in charge of the whole cell at White Crescent Bay?" The Resistance movement had cropped up as soon as President Roosevelt had surrendered, and it had grown to span the entire WAT. The rebels were divided into cells to maximize efforts, and each cell was led by a captain. Ren doubted that there were many captains as young as Marty.

"Don't act so surprised," Marty replied, but she tossed Ren a little smile.

"How'd you rise up so fast to captain?"

"Because I'm that good." Her smile arched, and Ren wasn't sure if she was joking or not. Even if she was, she was probably only half kidding. Marty had never had any problems in the self-confidence department. "We only have about seventy-five members these days, nothing like in your dad's time, when there were hundreds. People got cold feet after your mom was killed, not that I blame them for that." An awkward beat passed between them before Marty spoke again. "But we've had an uptick in recruits ever since the Viper showed up. Every time a new essay comes out, we reprint it and pass it around and that generates even more interest."

Ren flushed, not sure what he should say. No one in the White Crescent Bay cell had ever deduced the Viper was living right next to them. Not even Marty suspected a thing, even here, even now. Ren was both relieved and a little hurt. He had no plans to tell Marty his biggest secret, but he sometimes wished that she saw him as more than her kid cousin. More than *Renny*.

"We used to pick leaders by seniority," Marty said, "but with so many newer members, we do it by vote now. When our last captain stepped down, I figured I'd toss my hat into the ring. I mean, why not? We needed some female blood in the leadership — and people agreed."

This made sense to Ren. The soldiers often overlooked girls like Marty. It wasn't just her pretty face, although that was (sadly) part of the equation. It was the fact that Marty knew how to use her looks like a weapon. Once, during a family dinner, a patrol car had stopped by the shop and demanded to search the apartment. Mr. Cabot had let them in, but Marty didn't look too pleased about it. As soon as the soldiers started shouting at Ren, she had cried like a trained actress, her chin wobbling as she pleaded for her poor baby cousin. Ren wanted to warn her that she was going to get arrested, but the soldiers departed five minutes later — along with Marty's tears. She had returned to the dining table like nothing had happened and asked Ren to pass the rolls. He should've known right then and there that she would've made a great Resistance fighter.

Ren's thoughts shifted back to the present. "Did you send Daisy Montgomery to infiltrate the Fortress?"

Marty wrinkled her nose. "No way. What she did was far too risky."

"Then why did she do it?"

"Hard to say for sure. I've heard that she blamed the crown prince for the death of her parents. They got thrown into an internment camp for unpaid taxes, and they died of dysentery there." Gently, she laid her uncle's arm back onto the sofa and covered it in a thin layer of gauze from the first aid kit. "Either Daisy was deluded or she had a death wish. A one-woman mission to infiltrate the Fortress? I'd never ask my people to do that."

"Right," murmured Ren. Marty probably thought Daisy was a fool, but he saw courage in her last act. While so many Americans had accepted the Empire's rule, she had tried to do something about it, as reckless as it was. But he was getting too off course. "What does all of this have to do with my dad?"

"I'll get there. Patience, Renny," Marty chided.

Ren had always hated that nickname. He was actually named after his dad, but ever since he was little his parents had called him Ren, which was a part of the Chinese name that his mom had chosen for him, Tsai Ren-Kai. Marty, however, had always teased him as Renny, much to Ren's constant annoyance. "Answer the question, *Martine*."

The use of her full name made Marty cringe, then smirk. "Touché. And I really am getting there, I promise. So the Resistance has hit the same problem for years — we'll never match the Empire's firepower, especially when you factor in the Ronin Elite. But what if we could tip that balance a little? What if we could recruit Anomalies with powers like creating tsunamis or hurricanes?"

Ren leaned forward. "But there aren't many of those Anomalies around, and they usually work for the government."

"Not always." Marty seemed to savor her words like a rare cut of beef. "The San Francisco cell got their hands on some interesting info a few months back, and they've built a huge operation around this intel. Over a dozen cells are on board, up and down the coast and pushing inland, too."

Hearing this made the hair on Ren's arms prick up. "What's the intel?"

"It originated from Alcatraz." Her voice became hushed even though Mr. Cabot was still unconscious. "Alcatraz is more than a prison — it's a laboratory. They've been conducting top secret tests on the prisoners for years."

Ren felt breathless. The Empire had never admitted that it had experimented on humans during the war, but everyone knew that it had. How else could it have created the first Anomalies? Most Americans, however, had assumed that those experiments were long over, due to the success of the Ronin Elite. "What sort of tests?"

"Experimenting on the Anomaly gene again. The general public doesn't know this — most military officials have no idea about it, either — but the Empire's Anomaly population has been dwindling for the last decade and no one knows why."

Ren certainly hadn't been expecting that. "How bad is it?"

"Very. Cadet enrollment has been decreasing at the Fortress for years, and the same trend has happened across all of the Ronin Elite academies. Most of these schools are half full, and no one knows why the numbers are so low." Marty began working a crick out of her neck as she spoke. "Some people think that this is nature righting the course because humans didn't develop these powers through evolution. Obviously, the Empire can't accept that, but so far their attempts to create new Anomalies haven't gone well. They keep coming up against the same problem that they did with the first generation of Anomalies — their bodies can't cope with the changes."

Ren found himself nodding along. Those first Anomalies dated back to the 1940s, when the Axis powers raced to create a new generation of super soldiers, and Imperial Japan had barely edged out the Nazis to produce the first viable patient. But due to genetic instability, the new soldiers of the Ronin Elite didn't live very long — they burned bright but they burned out fast. The whole program threatened to cease, but hope arose in the children of the original Ronin. Of those born with the Anomaly gene, most survived well into adulthood. The Empire pounced on this revelation, urging the healthy Ronin to procreate as often as possible, thus creating stable Anomalies who were ready to serve the imperial army. But apparently, this was no longer the case.

Marty spoke faster, a new urgency in her words. "There was a breakthrough at Alcatraz about five years ago. The Empire teamed up with a group of Nazi geneticists who tested out a new gene therapy on a hundred Americans at the prison. Most of the prisoners didn't survive the first few weeks of testing, but there were fifteen who did. They're still living today — all of them with superpowers, too — thanks to this therapy that the Nazis called viral vector 220314, roughly translated. We've shortened it to V2."

"V2," Ren repeated. "Shouldn't that solve the Empire's problem of creating new Anomalies?"

"It isn't that simple. Most patients still die within days of starting the V2 regimen, and you have to remember that the Nazis were the ones who developed V2." She looked at Ren expectantly, but he had no idea what she wanted him to say.

"And . . ."

"And the Nazis aren't stupid. They've been very strategic in how they've shared the details of V2 with the Empire. They'll give the emperor enough to keep him appeased, but they've never shared the exact formula for the injections, and the Nazi geneticists always inject V2 patients directly."

Ren imagined the two empires locked in a cautious dance of diplomacy and silent frustration. "I doubt that has gone over well with the Empire."

"Probably not, but that's the nature of their relationship. They're longtime allies, but they've always looked out for themselves first," Marty said shrewdly. "But when one empire needs help, it's going to start knocking on the other's door. That's why the Nazis have been cozying up to their old friends in Tokyo. They've got their hands full between the Führer's death and fighting off the Second American Revolution, and they need more troops and weapons and supplies." Marty paused and smirked. "You know the Joint Prosperity Ball? It was the Nazis' idea. They need to reassert their partnership with Imperial Japan and put up a united front to scare Zara St. James and her rebels."

Ren had questioned why the Nazis were sending so many ambassadors and dignitaries to the ball when they had a war on their hands. "What does the Empire get out of a fancy party, though?" Then a thought dawned on him. "V2?"

"In a way. The Nazis have dispatched their geneticists to Alcatraz again to test a new batch of prisoners. Essentially, they're giving their allies new Anomalies but still keeping the formula for themselves. Looks like they're saving that gift for a rainy day."

Disgust rolled through Ren's stomach as he thought about those prisoners. He wanted to write an exposé to uncover what they had gone through, but that would mean exposing himself as the Viper to Marty. And he wasn't ready for that.

"How did the San Francisco cell get this intel in the first place?" Ren asked.

Marty pulled her lips together. "We have a source who goes by Bluefin working at Alcatraz as a nurse."

"Why would she want to help the Resistance?"

"Numerous reasons, but she ultimately turned because her fiancé is biracial like you, although he's Korean and Latino. His parents have worked for Bluefin's family for decades, so they've known each other since they were kids. Bluefin's mom doesn't know about her engagement, though. Bluefin would get disowned for that."

"Of course she would," said Ren. His reply came out more harshly than he intended, but it was a sore subject for him. Racism had always existed in America, and it had carried on under the Empire's rule. Ren's own parents had lost friends when they got married, and Ren had learned early on that there were people who'd always scrunch their noses at him simply because of who he was. When he first realized that as a kid, he had buried his face in his pillow and cried. Now it just made him mad. He had published an essay about it, too — *Even in the old United States, some Americans were more free than others* — and nothing had felt so cathartic.

"Tell me more about these Anomaly prisoners," he said, guiding the topic back on track. "I'm guessing the Resistance wants to do something about them."

Marty rewarded his observation with a wide grin, revealing two dimples on her cheeks. "We need them fighting for the Resistance, and that means breaking them out of Alcatraz."

Ren choked. "You're going to do *what*?"

"You heard me. We're going to get those prisoners out of Alcatraz. Many of them were Resistance members. They're our people."

A new round of questions popped into Ren's head and were ready to leap out of his mouth, but that's when someone knocked on the door downstairs. The nurse was here.

"We'll talk more after Serrano leaves," Marty said, rising up to get the door. She left before Ren could reply, leaving him with more questions than he had started with. How exactly did the Resistance plan on breaking into Alcatraz and freeing the prisoners? With what army?

Mr. Cabot moaned on the sofa, and Ren quickly grabbed his father's uninjured hand. His questions would have to wait.

"Ren?" Mr. Cabot coughed.

"I'm here, Dad, and Serrano is downstairs," Ren said quietly. He squeezed his dad's fingers. "We're going to get you patched up."

"I'm sorry. I don't want you to worry."

Ren needed to let his dad rest, but his lips disobeyed him. He had to ask. "What were you doing with Marty tonight? I thought you were done with the Resistance."

"I was but . . ." Mr. Cabot's eyes fluttered open, then closed. He was beginning to go under again. "You need to stay out of this. It's too dangerous. You have to promise . . ."

As Mr. Cabot slipped back to sleep, footsteps came up the stairs and Ren let his hand drop to his side, but he kept his eyes on his father. There was so much unsaid between them.

"What aren't you telling me, Dad?" Ren whispered.

6

At Serrano's arrival, Ren hovered in the shadows to let her do her work. He watched as she plunked down next to her patient and tackled his injury with silent efficiency. Serrano worked as a nurse in the town's health clinic, and she applied her experience here, assessing Mr. Cabot's hand before cleaning it again and stitching it together. Ren slunk into the kitchen when she got out her needle and thread, but Marty sat by the nurse's side, asking questions about what kind of needle she was using and how to stave off infection.

When she was finished, Serrano injected another painkiller into her patient and mummified Mr. Cabot's hand in a new layer of gauze but never asked what had happened to him — and Marty didn't offer her any information. Ren got the feeling that this wasn't the first time Marty had placed a call to the nurse in the middle of the night.

Within an hour of her arrival, Serrano was done. She handed Ren a bag of antibiotics and told him she'd call to check in tomorrow. Ren tried to pay her, but Marty nudged him aside and gave Serrano the contents of her wallet, which was no small amount.

"Always a pleasure doing business with you, Millie," said Marty dryly.

Serrano tucked the cash in her shoe and nodded. "I'm sure I'll see you again soon. I can let myself out."

Once they were alone again, Marty pulled a blanket over her

uncle and headed into the kitchen, gesturing for Ren to come with her. "I'll make us some tea and we can finish talking. I think I saw a few bags of peppermint the last time I was here."

Ren couldn't even think about tea right now. "What about my dad? We'll just leave him on the couch?"

Marty stopped rummaging through the cabinets and glanced at him. "We'll be a few steps away if he needs us. Serrano is the best nurse in town, too. She wouldn't have left if she thought Uncle Paul was in any danger."

As she retrieved the teabags and filled the kettle, Ren adjusted his father's blanket. His dad looked pale and clammy, and Ren doubted that he was in the clear. There was always the chance of a fever or an infection.

"He's going to be okay, Ren," Marty said from the kitchen.

Ren only wished that he could share her certainty.

"Come on and drink some tea. We still have a lot to talk about. Where did we leave off?" Marty said.

Dragging himself to the kitchen, Ren rubbed his eyes. He was dead tired, but he had to hear the rest of what Marty had to say and find out what his father was hiding from him. "You were talking about breaking into Alcatraz."

"That's right." Marty leaned against the counter, crossing her arms, while the kettle heated up. "The plan is already in place. Our objective is to infiltrate the prison and free all of the prisoners there, not only the fifteen Anomalies. We can't let the Empire continue to use them as lab rats."

Ren was in full agreement with that. Freeing the Alcatraz prisoners might not have been a practical idea — the manpower and resources required would be immense — but human experimentation was horrific. His fingers itched for the feel of his typewriter, ready to hammer out a new essay about this very topic. The public deserved to know what the Empire was doing.

Marty wasn't finished. "If we can pull this off, those Anomaly prisoners will be a huge boost to the Resistance. Bluefin has said that one of them can go invisible *and* walk through walls. Another can make fog so thick that you won't be able to see your own hands in front of your face. Think about what that could mean."

Ren didn't have to get too creative to understand what she was implying. American Anomalies were few and far between, not to mention illegal. They were usually children of a Ronin soldier and an American civilian — sometimes these relations were consensual, other times not — and they were taken into custody as soon as they manifested their powers. That was why the Empire required every American child to attend school until the fifth grade. It wasn't to provide a free education, but to keep an eye on illegal Anomalies. Those who managed to hide their powers usually had subtle abilities like hyperflexible joints or underwater breathing.

"How can you be sure that these prisoners will fight for you, though?" asked Ren, unable to stop himself from plucking at the mission details. "What if they've been brainwashed?"

The kettle began to whistle, and Marty moved fast to turn off the burner and pour the boiling water into the awaiting mugs. "It's a risk we have to take, but it'll be worth it even if a few of the Anomaly prisoners are stable enough to join us. They could use their invisibility to spy or create a huge blanket of fog to cause chaos at a place like the Fortress." Marty had obviously thought this through, and she wasn't going to be swayed. "But you have to remember the bigger picture, too. You know how the Viper keeps harping on us to not be complacent?"

Ren's face warmed, and he murmured a quick "I guess."

"What if we blew the whistle on the Alcatraz experiments? That could really wake people up. We could have a real revolution on our hands like what has happened out east."

Marty's eyes glinted in the kitchen lights, and Ren's skin shivered from what she said. The rebels could have new legs to stand on if they had widespread public support.

But one big question still loomed between Ren and his cousin.

"You still haven't told me how my dad factors into all of this," he said.

Marty took a tentative sip of her tea. "I'm getting to that. The Resistance knows that it won't be easy landing on Alcatraz because it's one of the most guarded places in the world. The waters surrounding the island are loaded with bombs that will go off unless your ship has proper clearance."

"Let me guess," Ren said grimly. "Getting clearance isn't easy."

"Exactly. Helicopters and planes are barred from the prison's airspace, which means the only way in and out is by sea. Any ship approaching the prison has to provide Alcatraz's security team with the correct clearance code, which is randomly generated and changes hourly. You get two tries to give the code, and if you're wrong both times? Kaboom."

Ren winced at that image as he warmed his hands on his mug. "Then how do you get around that?"

"Bluefin shared an interesting bit of information." Marty took a

sloppy sip of tea. "Because Alcatraz is so protected, it's also desig-
nated as a safe house for Crown Prince Katsura. Let's say that
the Fortress gets attacked and the crown prince needs to get on the
Rock as soon as possible. The Empire has an exit plan in case that
happens — the crown prince will board a special armored boat headed
for Alcatraz. When it nears the prison, the crown prince can bypass
the clearance code by using a digital fingerprint and retina scanner
on board the ship, which will shut off the bombs and give him
access to the island."

"So you need a copy of his fingerprints and retinas," Ren thought
aloud.

"No, we need the crown prince himself. The scanner requires a
living, breathing human being."

Ren balked. "The Resistance is going to kidnap the crown prince?"

"He's too heavily guarded. But" — a smirk inched up Marty's face
as she set down her mug — "his family members would make slightly
easier targets. Both his wife and daughter can access any safe house
with the proper fingerprint and retina scanners, too. Granted, his
wife has been placed under tighter protection since the Empire
announced her pregnancy."

"Which leaves Aiko," Ren said, the realization dawning on him.
She was the crown prince's only child, called Aiko by her family and
given the formal title Princess Teru. She would never inherit the
throne because she was a girl, and so the emperor had looked into
changing the succession laws — until Aiko's mother discovered that
she was carrying a baby boy. "You're going to kidnap her instead of
her father?"

"That's the plan. The Resistance already bought a military-grade fingerprint and retina scanner. The royal family has been using them for years, and every so often one of them pops up on the black market. Anyway, this is how we've plotted things out: We kidnap Aiko from the Fortress, we smuggle her on board a stolen Coast Guard ship that the San Francisco cell has been refitting, and we use our stolen scanner to get onto Alcatraz."

Ren knew that would be very risky, but it just might work. The tough part would be getting their hands on Aiko herself. She lived a cocooned life inside the Fortress; Ren didn't know much about her aside from what he had read in the state newspapers, which fawned over her ink-black hair that was as thick as a painter's brush and her pale skin that had been perfectly preserved underneath a layer of sunscreen. The society columnists also loved chattering about her odd fascination with French art and murmuring about her potential suitors now that she had turned seventeen. Soon, she would be expected to fulfill her female duties — to marry, to bear children, and to raise a new generation that would carry on the imperial line.

"This is where your dad finally comes in," Marty announced, and Ren almost knocked over his tea. "We're going to kidnap Aiko on the night of the Joint Prosperity Ball. Security will be tighter, but the soldiers' attention will be splintered among all of the dignitaries they have to keep safe. We have two accomplices already embedded in the Fortress who will carry out the kidnapping — code names Beetle and Bird. Basically, they'll slip Aiko a drug that will give her flu-like symptoms and knock her unconscious for a few hours. Once she's asleep, Beetle will head up to the royal apartment with a laundry cart to clean up after Aiko's 'flu' — with Bird hiding inside that cart. From there, Bird will smuggle the princess down the laundry chute. We're almost ready to install a secret pulley system in the chute to bring Aiko safely from the twelfth-floor penthouse and out to the getaway car."

As Marty gulped down her tea, Ren tried to wrap his head around the details she had spat out at him. There was one puzzle piece missing. "Again, what was my dad's role in all of this?"

Marty wiped her mouth with the back of her hand. "You know that drug I mentioned that'll knock Aiko out? It's a liquid chemical compound that has to be absorbed through skin. That means I need someone inside the Fortress who will have access to Aiko's wardrobe — and her outfits will probably remain in the sewing room for her last-minute fittings right before the ball."

Finally, everything clicked into place. "You needed a tailor."

"Bingo. I asked Beetle to pull some strings to get Uncle Paul a job interview, and I was talking everything over with your dad tonight in one of our safe houses." Marty looked over to the couch where Mr. Cabot lay sleeping. She pressed her lips together and sighed. "We were almost finished when some of my team members returned from a supply run. They had a box of explosives with them and I told them to be careful, but one of the sticks of dynamite went off. Most of us got out with scrapes and bruises, but a piece of shrapnel hit your dad's hand."

So *that* was what had happened. Ren digested this information slowly, but something still didn't add up for him. "How did you convince my dad to go along with this mission in the first place? Ever since my mom died, he hasn't wanted anything to do with the Resistance."

"Uncle Paul is a rebel through and through," Marty said a little too quickly.

Ren wasn't buying this, but before he could press her on it, she plowed onward.

"Listen," Marty said. "Your dad is out for this mission. There's no way he'll get hired at the Fortress with his hand bandaged up. That means I need to find a replacement."

Seconds passed before Ren understood what she was saying. "You want me to take his place?"

"You're the only who has the experience, *and* you're someone I can trust. Plus, the visitor's pass that the Fortress sent to your dad only says 'Paul Cabot.' There's no Senior or Junior. That's your in."

Ren couldn't believe that she was asking this of him. Marty had always treated him like her baby cousin, but she was going to take a chance on him to pull off one of the biggest missions in Resistance history. He wanted to say yes, and yet he hesitated.

Marty seemed to catch what he was thinking. "I'll take care of your dad if you get hired at the Fortress. I'll even pay Serrano to stop by every day. As for the shop, you'll survive closing it for a week. You'll get paid by the Fortress, and the Resistance can cover your rent next month."

Ren glanced over at his father. Mr. Cabot's wounds may have been cleaned and dressed, but there was a chance of an infection — or worse. He knew Marty would take good care of his dad, but he wished he had a little time to think this over.

Marty, however, didn't have any minutes to spare. "Look, the interview is tomorrow morning, and the Fortress is expecting a 'Paul Cabot.' I need you." She pushed her empty mug aside and leaned toward Ren from across the table. "You're right that your dad wanted nothing to do with the Resistance. I approached him about this mission a couple of months ago, but his answer was always no. I even started lining up other candidates — but that was before I got a piece of intel that made Uncle Paul change his mind."

Ren's palms went damp with sweat. The room seemed to shrink around them, narrowing upon Ren's ears and Marty's next words. "What sort of intel?"

"A partial prisoner list from Alcatraz. Only the prisoners' initials were listed, along with a few personal details, and one in particular got my attention." Marty drummed her fingers on her thigh. She looked nervous as she repeated what she had seen. "Female. Early forties. Gray hair, about five feet six. Ethnicity: Chinese. Admitted five years ago." Her eyes climbed upward to meet Ren's. "Her initials were J.T."

Ren felt kicked in the gut. He pushed away from the table. "It can't be her."

"That was my reaction, too, but what if it is?" She let her question hang in the air between them, wedging a hope into Ren's heart.

"I watched my mother die. I saw the sword go into her stomach. She couldn't have survived that."

"Probably not, but the possibility was enough for your dad to agree to this mission."

Ren's face plummeted into his hands. His mother was gone. Whoever this "J.T." was, it couldn't have been Jenny Tsai. She died five years ago, and Ren had mourned her ever since.

But what if?

Ren didn't want to get his hopes up, but he couldn't ignore what Marty had told him.

If his mother was alive, if she had become a prisoner at Alcatraz, if all of these "ifs" turned out to be true — then how could he turn this mission down?

Ren looked over his shoulder at his dad, wanting to hug him and shake him at the same time. "Why didn't he tell me?"

"He wanted to protect you in case our lead didn't go anywhere, so he made me promise not to say anything." She stared down at the table guiltily, but when she looked up again her face was wiped clean of expression. "Obviously things have changed, and I need you on this mission."

Ren hated her a little for dangling in front of him the possibility of his mother being alive. He didn't want to open himself to that idea, but it had already rooted itself deep in his heart. Marty's manipulation had worked.

Ren downed his tea in a single swallow. "I'll go to the interview tomorrow. Tell me what to do."

Come daybreak, the Viper himself would knock on the front doors of the Fortress.

7

Early in the morning, as the first rays of Saturday sunlight spread across the sky, Ren stepped into the cold shadow of Fort Tomogashima and wondered if the soldiers above him would shoot. He counted five of them atop the concrete wall, with their rifles pointed at the softest parts of his body. But he forced himself to step forward anyway, even though an American like him would make excellent target practice: helpless, weak, and easily disposed of.

Ren was tempted to turn around and run away, but the Resistance needed him. The prisoners at Alcatraz needed him. And, most of all, his mother — if she was alive — needed him. If she had somehow clung to life these last five years, then he would do anything to get to this interview on time, even if it meant staring down those menacing black rifles.

In any case, it was too late for him to escape now.

"You there! State your business," one of the guards called out, his voice echoing down to the gravel that Ren stood upon. A flag waved next to the soldier, bearing the red sunburst of the Empire. Even that flag seemed to be watching Ren's every move.

Ren summoned his voice and dialed it to its meekest setting, which wasn't hard to do. He wasn't even inside the Fortress yet, but his hands were already shaking. "I'm here for an eight-thirty appointment with Kato-sama."

Ren had done this twice already at the preceding checkpoints, first at the main gate and then at the secondary fence. Marty had briefed him about the Fortress's security the night prior, but hearing her describe it had been much easier than experiencing it for himself. At every checkpoint so far Ren had to lay out his ID card and visitor's badge before he turned over his shoulder bag for inspection. He had hoped that the guards would have let him inside by now, but he wasn't surprised by their caution, considering Daisy Montgomery had tried to infiltrate the Fortress less than seventy-two hours ago.

"Wait there," the soldier told Ren while he murmured into his radio.

Seconds bled into minutes. The morning air crept down his collar and bit at Ren's skin, but he didn't dare zip up his vest. He worried that any sudden movement would be his last. Finally, the metal door in front of him cracked open an inch.

"Go on inside," the soldier shouted. "Slowly."

Ren slid through the door, and his pulse doubled speed. He had gotten past the checkpoints. He was *inside* the Fortress.

Though not quite.

"Up against the wall!" a new soldier shouted into Ren's ear, pushing his nose against the cinder blocks. "Legs apart!"

Gritting his teeth, Ren complied. Apparently, they weren't through with him yet.

The soldier patted Ren down yet again and shoved him through another metal detector. While Ren waited for his bag to finish the security screening, he glanced around the lifeless holding room, his eyes drawn to the TV mounted on the wall. The morning news report played on the screen, showing stills of armored vehicles driving up to the Fortress and depositing foreign officials at its front door. Dignitaries from every corner of the globe were arriving in the WAT to attend the Joint Prosperity Ball, including the Italian prince of San Marino and an elderly emissary from Vichy France and even Deputy Führer Fabian Forst himself. The silver-haired forty-something Forst was rumored to succeed Führer Dieter Hitler and take over the reins of the Third Reich until Hitler's young son came of age. Ren couldn't help but notice how Forst entered the Fortress without a single pat-down or luggage screening. These checkpoints were only meant for Americans like Ren.

"You're the one who Kato-sama sent for?" the soldier asked, a laugh right under his tongue. "He must really be short-staffed if he's asking someone like you for help."

"Hai," murmured Ren, even though he had a few other choice words picked out. He couldn't let this soldier get under his skin; he needed to focus on what lay ahead. So he went over the details that Marty had drilled into his skull, from what to say to Kato-sama to the secret code name of the mission (*Callipepla californica,* alluding to California's state bird). He didn't want to forget anything.

The soldier thrust Ren's bag into his arms. "Follow me."

They exited the holding cell and stepped back into daylight, where Ren got his first look inside Fort Tomogashima. A small city unfurled before him — a crisscross of roads and belching trucks, soldiers' barracks, and other squat buildings. Even at this early hour, the Fortress stood at attention. A troop of soldiers marched past in orderly formation, while a few Ronin Elite launched into the sky to start their patrol down the coast. They looked almost majestic, like eagles taking flight, but Ren knew what they'd do if they found out why he had *really* come to this interview.

Soon, they approached the heart of the Fortress, where a magnificent nineteenth-century building rose regal and proud, a complete contrast to its dull surroundings. With its red roof and half-moon balconies, it looked like a Spanish castle that had been picked up with a crane and airdropped onto the California coast. It was once called the Mission Hotel and was built over a hundred years ago as a lavish resort. After the war, though, the general overseeing the WAT's transition period had been so charmed by the hotel that he had taken up residence on its top floor and built Fort Tomogashima around it.

The soldier bypassed the hotel's front entrance and opted for a tucked-away side door for the staff. *Very fitting,* Ren thought dryly. The original hotel had accommodated only white guests, so he never would have been allowed through the main doors, either then or now.

They walked into a windowless hall, lit by cold fluorescent lights. Dozens of workers whizzed by: maids carrying dusters, janitors pushing carts, cooks tying aprons, and gardeners donning gloves. Ren couldn't help but notice how most of the maids and servers were white, whereas most of the janitors and gardeners were people of color. There seemed to be a clear racial line that separated the front of the house from the back.

As the soldier led them past the boiler room and numerous supply closets, Ren tried to memorize their path, but everything blurred together with the same linoleum floor and their same cream-colored walls. But once he spotted the laundry facility ahead, with the smell of bleach sneaking up his nose, he let his eyes linger on the door.

Check the escape route, Marty had instructed him last night. The laundry chute. Bird would soon install the pulley system to kidnap Aiko, and Marty needed to check that the chute was still viable. If Ren got hired, he would make his way back here as soon as possible.

With a turn here and there, they left behind the workers' wing through a set of double doors and entered a different world entirely. The cheap linoleum turned into polished marble underfoot, and the scent of bleach gave way to the smell of chlorine, which drifted inside from the swimming pool in the courtyard. The old hotel lobby had been turned into a sitting area for the cadets, and Ren noticed a few of them on the chesterfield sofas, studying for tests that they'd take later in the day.

The Mission Hotel had been converted into an academy for the Ronin Elite decades before. The ballrooms had been separated into classrooms, the conference rooms into offices, the guest rooms into bunkrooms. Most cadets entered the fort after they manifested their power, and then they would remain there until they turned eighteen, once they had passed their exams and mastered the art of killing people like Ren.

"Stop here," the soldier ordered Ren as they approached the cafeteria. The room was massive — a former ballroom from the looks of it, with crystal chandeliers that twinkled in the morning light and rows of clean tables set with cloth napkins and chopsticks. Ren wasn't sure why they had stopped until he spotted the line of cadets walking in his direction, ready for their breakfast. The cadets walked in unison, wearing the same black slacks and the same pressed shirts. They even had the same haircuts for boys and girls alike. Ren figured they were around seven or eight in age. Children.

But these cadets weren't just kids.

As they filed into the cafeteria, Ren kept his head bowed, but he could feel one cadet's curious eyes land upon him. Her lips tightened into a smile, and that's all it took before Ren found himself floating three feet above the floor, his arms windmilling as his legs dangled helplessly. The children giggled until their instructor ordered the little girl to behave.

The girl bowed to her teacher and released her hold on Ren, whose feet landed hard on the floor. He had to steady himself against the wall to keep from falling. Within a minute, the cadets filed into the cafeteria like a school of fish — piranhas, more like it — but the girl gave Ren another smile. It wasn't a friendly sort of grin, either.

"This way," the soldier said, prodding Ren in the back.

Ren hurried along and waited for his pulse to slow down. Before today he had crossed paths with only a few Anomalies around town, but each incident had left him feeling jittery. And now they surrounded him, with all sorts of powers at their little fingertips. Thinking about that made his heartbeat speed up again.

They made a few more turns until they reached a cluster of offices, and the soldier shoved Ren inside one of the rooms. "Kato-sama should arrive shortly," he said before departing.

Ren looked around the small office. A table sat low to the floor, surrounded by plump sitting pillows, and a circular mirror adorned the wall opposite him. Ren glanced at his reflection and combed his hair, which was sticking up in different directions thanks to his many pat-downs. He was in the middle of re-tucking his button-down shirt into his pants when the door whooshed open.

Ren stood up straight, readied a bow, and was about to launch into his prepared introduction — *Good morning, Kato-sama, it is an honor to have this opportunity* — but he didn't see a middle-aged Japanese man standing under the doorframe. He found a young Caucasian woman instead, immaculately dressed in a silk blouse and a pressed pencil skirt, finished off with a pair of black heels that looked more expensive than the Cabots' yearly food budget. At first glance Ren guessed that she was in her mid-twenties, but when he snuck another look he figured she might have been nineteen or twenty. She simply carried herself as someone older.

"Are you Paul Cabot? I'm Greta Plank, Kato-sama's assistant. He has been hospitalized due to an illness, so I'm taking over his duties for the time being," the young woman said brusquely. She addressed Ren in Japanese, and Ren had to admit that her accent was better than his own.

Greta Plank, Ren thought, turning the syllables over in his mouth. She must have been a Nazi citizen with a name like that. Her honey-colored hair and papery-white skin would certainly be prized back in Germany, but Fräulein Plank's face didn't look like the rosy-cheeked blonds that graced the Third Reich propaganda posters. Her features were too angular, from her sharp cheekbones down to her pointed chin, but her loyalty to the homeland was still on prominent display — her suit jacket lapel boasted two pins, one of a rising sun flag and one of a golden swastika.

There were thousands of Nazis living in the Western American Territories and enjoying their special status in an ally nation. Most of them were government officials; others were retired expats; and still others were businessmen, with an emphasis on *men*. Nazi women, much like their Japanese counterparts, were expected to marry young and stay home with their brood, so it was a little odd to see someone like Fräulein Plank working for Kato instead of settling down. And it was even more odd that Plank looked vaguely familiar. There was something about the cut of her cheek, the arch of her brow . . .

Ren dared another glance at the *Fräulein*, only to find her staring back at him. Her eyes scrutinized him behind a pair of emerald-green-framed glasses.

"I was under the impression that you'd be older," Fräulein Plank sniffed. "Not a little tadpole who still has to grow legs."

Ren let the insult slide and remembered the story that he and Marty had rehearsed earlier. "You did speak with my father, *Fräulein*, but he unfortunately broke his wrist and sent me in his place this morning. I've trained with him since I was little. I brought —"

"Look at me when you speak," she interrupted, her words like a slap.

Ren shifted and uncomfortably lifted his gaze. His parents had taught him at a young age that he should never look an imperial soldier or official in the eye. That sort of direct contact could be seen as disrespectful, so Ren had trained himself to always keep his chin down. But maybe the Nazis were different.

"Tell me," said Fräulein Plank, "how did your father break his wrist?"

Their gazes clashed, and Ren saw that her irises were a shocking blue. They weren't a pretty color, either, like the ocean at dawn, all soft and welcoming waves. They were icy and bright, like the hottest part of a lighter flame.

"He tripped down the stairs," Ren said, and offered nothing more about it. Marty had warned him that the more he embellished a lie, the more trouble he could get into. So he kept his mouth shut.

Plank looked doubtful. "I see."

Ren decided to switch the topic before she could dismiss him. Digging a hand into his shoulder bag, he presented her with an olive-green tie that he'd sewn a year ago. "I brought a sampling of my handiwork." Then he unfolded a men's dress shirt, made from crisp cotton. And then he grasped his humble masterpiece, a lace handkerchief that he'd finished when he was twelve. "I can do embellishments as well."

Fräulein Plank gave the shirt and tie a passing glance and held up the handkerchief to the light. The Cabots didn't handle much lace at the shop, but his father had taught Ren lacework anyway, just in case a rich tourist had a fancy commission for them.

"Passable." Plank practically tossed the handkerchief back at Ren. "Though I've seen better."

Ren's thoughts jumbled together. Marty had assured him that the handkerchief would be his in, and he had to wonder if Fräulein Plank was judging him by the color of his skin rather than his talents. It wouldn't be the first time that had happened.

If he wanted this job, though, he had to ignore his frustrations.

Ren hunched his shoulders forward. "*Fräulein*, please give me a chance."

Fräulein Plank sighed, and Ren was sure that she'd dismiss him with a snap of her fingers. Would he have to beg for the job? But then she told him, "The truth is that we need an extra tailor and we needed one yesterday. You're hired, Cabot, but not because of your experience." She clicked her tongue at him like he was a workhorse. "You'd better come along with me."

Ren couldn't believe it, but he wasn't going to complain. "Thank you —"

"I said come along. You need an ID badge, and I'll show you around the sewing room and the workers' bunkrooms. We have one week until the ball and there's plenty to do, and Kato-sama doesn't want you squandering time on your commute."

Ren's eyes leapt upward to hers. Getting locked inside the Fortress wasn't a part of Marty's — or his — plans. "That's very generous, but there's no need to waste a bed on me. I live nearby, a few minutes' walk."

"You don't understand. This job will require overtime hours. Most of the staff was told this morning that they'd have to remain at the fort until the ball is over. The sewing team isn't exempt from that." Plank raised a carefully plucked brow. "Will that be an issue?"

Ren felt blindsided by what she was demanding, but he had to think fast. "I'm honored to take the position, but there are a few things I should grab from home. My personal sewing kit. A change of clothes —"

"You'll find everything you need here. Are we in agreement, then?"

For a few seconds, Ren struggled for a reply, but he couldn't say no to Plank, either. He had to take this job, no matter the terms.

"Yes, we're in agreement, *Fräulein*," Ren said, defeated.

With a curt nod, she charged out of the room and Ren forced his legs to follow her. He tried to stay calm despite the emotions tearing through his chest — relief at getting hired and a growing sense of alarm. He was supposed to meet with Marty right after the job interview to talk about their next steps and check on his dad, but now Ren wouldn't be returning to the shop at all. He was trapped inside the Fortress, with the weight of the mission balanced on his narrow shoulders.

He would be on his own from here on out.

8

Ren told himself to count to ten, like his mother had taught him before she died. She had given him so many lessons over the years, from tying his shoes to mixing dumpling dough to what he should do if he was interrogated. That was where the counting came in — to clear his head so that he could stay calm in whatever circumstance. But when Ren reached the number ten and continued on to twenty, he wasn't feeling much better.

If he just had a moment alone to think and regroup —

Fräulein Plank came to a full stop in the middle of the hallway. Ren almost crashed into her back, but Plank didn't seem to notice. Her whole being was fixated on the soldiers who had rounded the corner, flanking a teenage girl at their center.

It was Aiko herself, here in the flesh. Ren bowed and shrank back toward the wall, not wanting to draw attention. Next to him, Fräulein Plank bowed as well, and her whole posture changed, shifting from her role as an authoritative assistant into a meek and modest servant.

"May I be of assistance, Your Imperial Highness?" Plank asked.

"Perhaps," Aiko replied. She looked like the epitome of royalty, thanks to the army of servants who helped her get ready every morning. Those servants had masterfully played up the innocence of her doe-like face, framing her dark eyes with a touch of mascara, and her soft yellow dress only added to the girlish look. And yet when Aiko spoke, her voice registered lower than Ren expected, each word punctuated with authority. "Do you know what happened to my order of canvases? They should have arrived yesterday, but I haven't seen them."

Fräulein Plank tapped a finger on the arm of her glasses. "Ah, yes. Your mother asked me to put the package in a storage room until after the ball. She knows your schedule will be very busy this week."

"I see." Aiko's pleasant façade seemed to crack, and her spine tightened until it went completely straight. "What about my phone call tomorrow with the admissions office at the Institute of the Arts — has that been confirmed?"

Fräulein Plank dipped her head. "Your mother asked me to cancel it."

"Was it rescheduled?"

"I haven't been notified if it has, Your Imperial Highness. Shall I speak to your mother about it? I could —"

"I can reschedule the call myself," Aiko said, interrupting Fräulein Plank so abruptly that her etiquette teachers would have chided her. Ren was pretty sure that those same teachers would never approve of a princess attending a school like the Institute of the Arts down in New Tokyo. As a young woman of her stature, Aiko was expected to fulfill her family duties, no matter how progressive her father's reforms might have been. The map of her life had been drawn long before she was born.

"As you wish," Fräulein Plank demurred with a prim smile. "And might I offer you an early congratulations? Your mother told me the good news yesterday."

Aiko's mouth puckered like she had taken a bite of a lemon, but she managed a quick thank-you. "There's a call I have to make," she said before making her exit.

Ren bowed again at the princess's departure, but he let his head bob up right before Aiko rounded the corner, her billowing yellow skirt barely keeping up with her pace. He had no idea what Plank had congratulated her about, and he had no clue, either, that Aiko could be so forthright. He had expected a princess like her to be spoiled and sheltered, spending her time picking out new clothes, but Aiko didn't seem to fall into that stereotype. He found that surprising and, if he were being completely honest, a little admirable.

Of course, it didn't matter what Aiko's personality was like. What mattered was that Ren had to smuggle her out of the Fortress and into the hands of the Resistance.

As soon as Aiko was out of eyeshot, Plank resumed her role spitting orders at Ren. "Let's go. I have a busy schedule, so don't fall behind."

Ren walked behind her in silence, grateful for a few minutes to gather his thoughts. He had to reassess the mission now that he wouldn't be able to talk to Marty after his shift every night. There was also the issue surrounding Bird and Beetle. Ren had asked Marty about their identities, but she wouldn't disclose their names until he got hired, arguing that she had to keep them safe in case his job interview turned into an interrogation. Because of that, Ren had let the matter drop — but now his job would be even harder. Panic began climbing up his throat, but he took a breath and told himself to focus. He'd find a way to talk to Marty. Until then, the mission had to move forward and he had to think about the next step: *Check the escape route.*

"Cabot!" said Fräulein Plank, turning around just long enough to scowl at Ren. "How hard can it be to keep up with me?"

Ren made his apologies and upped his pace. Their first stop was the security office, a cave-like space filled with dozens of television monitors. While the security guard prepared Ren's employee badge, Ren glanced over at the screens. The monitors displayed live feeds from the video cameras scattered throughout the Fortress — from hallways and exit points to classrooms and the cafeteria. The Empire had its eyes everywhere.

"Clip this on and don't take it off." The security guard tossed the finished badge to Ren. "Or else you'll give the soldiers a reason to shoot."

Their next stop was a massive storage closet full of service uniforms, where Fräulein Plank plucked two white dress shirts and a pair of slacks for Ren, explaining that his pay would be docked to cover the price of the clothes. She waited for him to change in the bathroom before ushering him to their last destination.

"Here's the sewing room," she said. The room was narrow and long and windowless, more like a hallway than an actual work space. Ten sewing machines took up a good chunk of the room, each one sitting upon its own wooden table. A couple of the machines lay quiet, but the others sang a mechanical tune, operated by a chorus of female seamstresses. At Plank's arrival, the staff stopped working and stood out of respect, even though most of the seamstresses were decades older than Plank. The *Fräulein* told them to keep working.

"You'll find everything you need in this room," Plank told Ren.

She opened a cabinet to reveal its contents. "Thread, needles, buttons, zippers, scissors. Be careful, though. If you break anything, it'll be taken out of your pay as well."

Ren battled the urge to roll his eyes. The Empire's coffers may have run deep, but apparently not deep enough to cover a pair of spare scissors.

"Your main responsibility will be altering the cadets' dress uniforms and having them laundered and pressed. The crown princess wanted new uniforms made for the ball, and we had them bulk-ordered and shipped from Tokyo. But the first two shipments got lost, and by the time we received the third order over half of our sewing team got sick."

"That's awful," Ren lied. The truth was that Beetle had secretly canceled the "lost" orders while Bird had poisoned the staff's breakfast soup, just enough to knock them out of commission. This had all been a part of the Resistance's plan.

"We're racing against the clock now, and we need every cadet properly fitted in less than a week," Plank continued. "Each uniform comes with a dress shirt and tie, a formal suit jacket, and trousers."

"Understood," Ren said, even as his stomach sank. Fräulein Plank had been right about one thing — he would definitely be working overtime at this job. He'd have to use his precious free time very judiciously.

While Plank showed him yet another storage cabinet, Ren's gaze wandered toward the back of the room. A flock of seamstresses hovered around six dress forms, and on each of those forms was an exquisite kimono or a Western-style ball gown. Hours of work had gone into each piece, from hand-beading to lacework to painted silk. Ren didn't need to ask Plank who these outfits belonged to — they were Aiko's and her mother's wardrobe for the ball.

"You won't be working on those," Plank said sharply as she walked back toward the door. "Before I go, you'll be staying in Bunkroom Eight until the ball. Ms. Clarke can get you settled after your shift." She called out to a white-haired woman clucking over a silk kimono patterned with flying cranes. "Claudette? This is Cabot, the new tailor we've hired."

That said, Plank left the room with a turn of her heels, and before Ren could thank her, Ms. Clarke had besieged him.

"Cabot? Like the shop in town?" said the older woman, gripping Ren's arm with cold, bony fingers. She was about half Ren's size, but her grip felt stronger than his. And she didn't wait for him to reply. "How old are you, son? Have you ever used a Brother HC1450? Because that's the model you'll be using here, and I don't have the time to give you a primer."

Ren's head spun at her rapid-fire line of questions. "You won't have to worry about me, Ms. Clarke. Just show me what you need me to do."

Ms. Clarke looked doubtful, but she led Ren to a workstation by the door. "You can use Ernesto's machine. He should be back in a week or so, I hope." She drew out a sigh. "I'm blaming the breakfast soup for this stomach virus outbreak. It smelled a little fishy to me, but that didn't stop people from eating a bowl of it anyway." She squinted at Ren. "You better stick to toast for breakfast, do you hear?"

After Ren assured her that he would, Ms. Clarke rolled a dress rack toward him. Twenty child-size uniforms hung from the rack, each one pinned with a name tag. "Let's start with your first task. I'll make it easy. These are the uniforms for the six-year-old cadets, and we finished them last night. Now they need to get starched and pressed down in the laundries. Tell them we'll need these back by tomorrow morning for delivery."

Ren brightened. A trip to the laundries? "I'd be happy to do it."

Ms. Clarke gave him the directions, and Ren pushed the dress rack out of the room. A left here. A right there. Down the hall and then some more. At last the smell of detergent snuck into his nose, and the steam from the boiling linens misted his forehead. Inside the laundries, the growl of two dozen industrial washing machines traveled into Ren's ears. A crew of workers scurried around the massive space. Some folded linens. Others bleached towels. And still others starched and ironed. Ren wondered if one of them could've been Beetle or Bird while he searched for a certain laundry chute, but his search came up empty.

Ren approached an old woman with rough hands and jack-o'-lantern teeth. She was hunched over a washbasin, scrubbing a stain on a tablecloth. "Pardon me, I work in the sewing room, and Ms. Clarke needs these uniforms starched and pressed."

The woman didn't look up. "You can leave that here. I'll get to it when I can."

"She said that we'll need them back by tomorrow morning."

That's when the woman snorted. "You tell Ms. Clarke that we're running at half speed ever since the maintenance crew started banging around here last night." She waved a hand farther down the laundries toward a section of the space that had been roped off. A few workers in construction hats stood beyond the rope, hammers and nails in hand. "They've cut power to half our machines and they're bricking in the chute, and *that* means I have to send two of my girls up and down the elevator to grab every dirty towel and sheet from the hotel's upper levels."

"What?" Ren spluttered. He must have heard her wrong. "The laundry chute is closed?"

"Didn't you hear me the first time? They're bricking it up and installing new washing machines and dryers on the top floors." She returned to her scrubbing, muttering about how she would have to head all the way upstairs every day to do even more laundry, but Ren was no longer listening.

Ren forgot to thank the woman for her time. He simply left, too stunned to say a word. Once he exited the laundries, he leaned back against the double doors. He felt punched. Slapped. Knocked down flat. Marty had been so sure about the escape route but her intelligence must have been a couple of days behind.

Because the chute was now compromised.

And with it, maybe the mission entirely.

9

The clock on the cement wall stared at Ren with a stark white face. 3:30 a.m., it read.

Ren had been up for hours. With every minute that ticked by, he felt more lost and lonely. He had never spent a night away from home — there had never been enough money for a family trip — and he ached for his apartment and he really missed his dad. But he was stuck inside the Fortress, and the strikes against him were coming fast. He couldn't even talk to Marty, and the lone escape route had been shut down. The mission had taken a huge hit, and Ren wasn't sure how to fix it.

But somehow he *had* to fix it — for the sake of every prisoner on Alcatraz. And for his mother especially.

So Ren had to think instead of freak out. He had to utilize every second very carefully if he wanted the mission to succeed, and that meant finding a new escape plan, even though locating one would be far from easy.

Ren considered asking his bunkmates a few veiled questions, but most of them had gone straight to bed after their shifts, their souls wrung dry after another hectic day of cleaning or cooking or gardening or whatever else the Empire demanded. After their shift, Ren had noticed them dragging their tired bodies to their cots, some of them nursing colds and others weathering more serious injuries like broken fingers or sprained ankles. It didn't help that the bunkroom's lone heater had broken, making all of their teeth chatter in a bone-crunching chorus.

If Ren had known about these conditions two days ago, he would have brainstormed a new essay that tackled his bunkmates' long hours and workplace injuries. He would've written how most of these men were shaving years off their lives in the service of an empire that treated them no better than dogs. The words would have flowed out of his fingers so easily, and Ren wished that he had a pencil and paper to jot down some notes. But his readers would have to wait. He had to figure out this mission first, but when it was done — and if he survived — he'd return to his typewriter to expose the Fortress's work conditions along with the experimentation happening at Alcatraz. Maybe his mother could even help him with the piece, and Ren felt a flutter of hope at the idea.

Don't get ahead of yourself, Ren thought. There were no guarantees that his mom was even alive, but it was hard to contain his hope after Marty had sparked it. But if he wanted to keep this flame flickering, he would have to find a new escape route.

Ren's mind roamed over the possibilities, and he tugged at a promising thread. He needed to look at the Fortress's blueprints or a facility map — something that would help him figure out if there was another secret exit out of the fort — but those types of documents would probably be locked away in a top secret file cabinet.

In other words, Ren's chances of success were slim to nonexistent, but those chances could improve if he wasn't working alone. So that was what he had to tackle next. He needed to find Beetle and Bird, the sooner the better.

And to do *that*, Ren had to get in touch with Marty.

As sunlight stretched over the dark sky, a wake-up alarm blasted through the loudspeakers, but Ren was already dressed. He asked his bunkmates if there was a way to get a message out to his family, like a pay phone, and once he got an answer he was ready to go.

But leaving the bunkroom wouldn't prove easy that morning.

Three of the Empire's watchdogs barged into the room and barked at everyone to line up against the wall.

For a moment, Ren's heart seized. Had the soldiers somehow figured out his secret Resistance plans? But the rest of his bunkmates merely shuffled toward the wall like this was no big deal, so Ren lined up with the rest of them. He didn't have any other choice, really. With his hands over his head, he watched as the soldiers overturned cots to search for contraband. Ren's jaw clenched at the mess they made: the ripped-off bedsheets, the emptied toiletry bags, the tossed-aside clothes. What did they expect to find aside from toothbrushes or combs or a worn photo of a worker's family? But Ren couldn't say a word, just like he couldn't say a thing when this happened at the shop.

Biting hard on his tongue, Ren tried to concentrate on the morning news report that flickered on the ancient television mounted against the wall. Technically, everyone in the WAT was supposed to watch the morning and evening news reports. Ren had been subjected to them when he attended school, and he remembered how he had to pledge allegiance to the emperor every morning and absorb the nationalist form of Shintoism that Imperial Japan had promoted since the 1940s. After he "graduated" from the fifth grade, however, Ren never bothered to watch the reports again. Here inside the

Fortress, though, he wouldn't be able to escape from this daily dose of propaganda.

The news report started like the execution the day before, with the image of a rising sun flag and the musical notes of the Empire's anthem. As soon as the song ended, a portrait of the eighty-year-old emperor came onto the screen, and everyone bowed to the image. Then the live portion of the report started up, and a newscaster gave a rundown of current events, including a glowing report on the surplus of almonds on state-run farms and the new libraries that Crown Prince Katsura had funded. Ren frowned when he heard that. He doubted that any American could patronize those libraries. Then the news report showed a few clips of Crown Prince Katsura with Deputy Führer Forst as they broke ground for a munitions factory outside San Francisco.

Suddenly, one of the soldiers waved a thin book of poems in the air, and Ren jumped. "Who does this belong to? Speak up!"

Ren's bunkmates glanced nervously at one another. No one came forward.

"I said speak up!" the soldier demanded. He opened the book and plucked out a folded piece of paper, which he unfurled and raised up for everyone to see. At the sight of the paper, Ren's knees turned to jam — it was an essay by the Viper. He recognized it immediately. It was one of his more popular pieces that picked apart Crown Prince Katsura's reforms one by one, starting with the infrastructure that raised taxes, to the health clinics that were only open half the week, to the new textbooks that went to waste because American children could never gain higher than a fifth-grade education. "Who sleeps on cot number five?"

More seconds ticked by until some of the bunkmates nudged a gardener forward. The man looked about fifty, with a skeletal frame and hollowed-out cheeks that were a testament to a lifetime of malnourishment. He was shaking when he said, "That's my cot, but I promise that paper isn't mine! I—I—I barely know how to read!"

His plea fell on unmerciful ears. "Bring him in for questioning," said the soldier to his comrades. To the rest of the room he said, "Half of your pay will be docked for the week — that goes for all of you." He approached the wall and waved the paper at the men. "If you suspect one of your bunkmates is reading illegal material, then you turn him in. It's that simple. If you choose to turn a blind eye, then you'll all be punished. Is that understood?"

The men nodded in unison.

And Ren nodded with them. He didn't know what had possessed the gardener to bring a copy of the Viper's essay inside the Fortress. Who would take such a risk? But then he realized how ridiculous he sounded. Here he was, the Viper himself, willingly embedded in the crown prince's own house. He could never let his guard down in this place.

"I'm telling the truth!" the gardener cried out. His desperate gaze clung to Ren. "What about him? That boy's mother was a traitor. He could've planted the essay on me!"

Ren felt every pair of eyes leap in his direction. He didn't think that his bunkmates had connected him with his mother — she had died years ago and he didn't share her last name — but White Crescent Bay was a small town, and the town's memory was longer than he had hoped. His forehead began sweating.

Ren had to quash this accusation fast. "My loyalty is pledged to

Crown Prince Katsura and our emperor. You can look through my belongings again if you'd like. I'm on cot number fourteen." He flicked a furious glare at the gardener, whose hands were trembling.

While two of the soldiers marched toward Ren's cot, the third stalked toward the wall and Ren. This soldier had a lean yet muscled frame, but baby fat still clung to his cheeks, making him look even younger than Ren. His name tag bore the surname Sasaki.

"Who was your mother? What did she do?" said Sasaki.

Ren tried to keep his voice even but was failing. He wanted to punch that gardener for turning the spotlight on him. "She was charged with treason, Sasaki-sama. She was executed."

The room went absolutely silent before Sasaki said, "You didn't tell me her name."

Ren swallowed. "Jenny Tsai."

"*Tsai.*" Sasaki's lips curled sourly around the syllable. "Was she Chinese?"

"Yes, Sasaki-sama." Ren grew anxious at what was left unsaid. The Empire had long viewed the Chinese as inferior, and anti-Chinese sentiment had brewed since the days of the Meiji Restoration. In recent years, those feelings had spiked after Chinese nationalists killed the crown prince's brothers, and patrols were sent out regularly to police Chinese American communities.

"I remember your mother now. She groveled for her life on national television, like a coward. How did scum like you get a job at the fort?"

Ren's jaw twitched, but he kept his eyes trained on Sasaki's boots. His mother wasn't a coward; she never begged for mercy. "I'm only here temporarily. The sewing room is short-staffed, and Kato-sama hired me."

"Kato-sama, eh? I bet he didn't realize that your mother was a filthy traitor."

Wrath burned in Ren's heart. Usually, he could ignore it, but hearing Sasaki insult his mother made that fist eager to hit something. Thankfully, the soldiers had to move on and they hauled the gardener away for questioning. But on his way out, Sasaki jammed his shoulder into Ren's chest. "See you tomorrow."

As soon as the soldiers left, Ren's bunkmates scattered out of the room, none of them looking or speaking to him. Breathing in, Ren gave himself a minute to pull it together. He did a little ritual every time the patrols left his apartment, and he did the same routine now: rolling his shoulders, clenching his hands, and then punching his pillow hard. He imagined it was Sasaki's face. *Call my mother a coward again*, Ren thought as he hit the pillow. After that, he forced himself to head to work. He had a job to do, and he wouldn't let some arrogant soldier get in the way of that. It'd all be worth it in the end anyway — helping the Resistance, saving lives, maybe seeing his mom again. That would be the best revenge against the Empire, and he needed to remember that.

Ren hurried out of the bunkroom. He was already running late, but there was one thing that he had to do first. The corridors were clogged with workers heading to their shifts, but Ren managed to spot the janitorial closet that he was looking for. He peeked through a crack in the door to see two janitors crammed inside, both of them dressed in navy coveralls. They were shuffling a deck of cards on an overturned mop bucket and finishing off their bowls of breakfast rice porridge. One of them noticed Ren and abandoned his cards to make a quick exit, while the other remained where he sat, sweeping up the cards in one smooth motion. He was skinny and looked a handful of years older than Ren.

Without looking up, the young man said to Ren, "Nothing to see here. Just an innocent game of Go Fish before my shift." He glanced up finally, a grin tickling at the corner of his mouth, showing off a single dimple. "Unless you're here for an early round?"

"Gambling is illegal," Ren said, the first thing he could think of. Then he flushed because he realized how uptight he sounded.

The young man grinned wider and ran a hand through his buzzed hair. "Sure, gambling might be illegal, but playing cards isn't." He dealt himself a hand, and it definitely didn't look like a game of Go Fish. "You new around here?"

Ren nodded but didn't elaborate. "I'm looking for Jay. Do you know where I can find him?"

"What do you need Jay for?"

"I heard that he could get a message to my cousin. She lives in White Crescent Bay."

The young man spooned some porridge into his mouth. "Do you have cash on you? Jay works for a fee, you know."

Ren frowned. "Tell him that I can pay. He can look for me in the sewing room or in Bunkroom Eight."

"No need for that. I'm Jay." He reached for his ID badge when Ren looked doubtful. "See for yourself."

Ren studied the badge. It did indeed belong to a Jay Park, and the photo matched the Korean American man in front of him. "Why didn't you say you were Jay before?"

A smile tilted again on Jay's mouth, easy and relaxed. Ren got the feeling that very few things rattled Jay, otherwise he wouldn't be gambling inside the Fortress. "Where do you need this message delivered to?" Jay asked.

"To Cabot's Tailoring and Cobbling, over on East Main. There's an apartment above the store."

"I know the place. I heard old man Cabot was going to take a job at the fort."

"That's my dad." Ren grimaced as he thought about his father again. He really wished that he could check on him. "He got hurt, which is why I'm here."

Jay's grin made a fast exit. "He got hurt? How?"

"Fell down the stairs," Ren said warily. He wondered why Jay seemed alarmed at this news. He didn't remember seeing him at the shop before. "Do you know him?"

"My mom buys thread from your store sometimes."

"Oh. Anyway, my cousin Marty will be staying at the shop to watch after my dad. You can give her my message."

Jay stretched out his legs and crossed them at the ankles, his easiness returning. "Sure, sure. How much yen do you have on you?"

Ren sighed and dug his hand into his pocket, holding up a few bills. "I can pay you this much now, and the other half after you give me a response."

"Hard bargainer, eh? Okay, if that's how you want to play it. What's the message?"

Ren paused to choose his words. He couldn't say anything outright about the mission, of course, but he had to pick a message that Marty could decipher. "Tell her that I'm stuck here for the week, so I wouldn't mind getting introduced to some of her friends. Aren't you going to write this down?"

Jay tapped a finger against his temple. "I got it all right up here. What else?"

"Tell her that she'll need to find a new place to ... um ... wash her clothes. She'll understand." He noticed Jay's confusion but barreled on. "How can I be sure that you'll pass along the message?"

"I'm a man of my word." Jay stood up and patted Ren on the shoulder. "Plus, I want to get the rest of my payment. I'll come find you tomorrow, tailor boy."

"My name's Ren."

"I think I like the sound of 'tailor boy' better. Maybe TB for short." Pocketing the money, Jay slid out of the janitorial closet and said over his shoulder, "Close the door behind you, TB."

Ren rolled his eyes, but he wasn't going to fuss about a stupid nickname when he had a mountain of work to tackle. Back in the sewing room, he murmured an apology to Ms. Clarke and started ticking off tasks on his to-do list, which had been left there earlier that morning by Fräulein Plank. Her handwriting was unsurprisingly neat and it instructed Ren to finish up the fourteen-year-old dress uniforms and to get that done by lunch. Before long, Ren was elbow-deep locating the appropriate thread, loading his bobbin and top spool, and tackling each trouser cuff and jacket sleeve and shirtwaist to Plank's exact specifications.

As the morning drifted by, Ren fell into a rhythm of sewing new seams and snipping soft threads. The hum of the machines droned like the buzz of bees. Across the room, Ms. Clarke and her assistants moved between the dress forms that held Aiko's and her mother's wardrobes. Both of them had three separate outfits for the event — one for the cocktail hour, one for the banquet dinner, and one for the dancing that would close the night. Ren wished that his dad could see all of these outfits in person. Mr. Cabot may have looked like a boxer, but his hands were as nimble as a potter's, and he would have appreciated the handiwork in the sewing room.

Aiko's mother had taken the traditional route for the ball, favoring three *tomesode*-style kimonos made from the finest of fabrics that flowed as smoothly as a summer stream.

Aiko, on the other hand, had made more modern selections. She would don the formal *furisode*-style kimonos with long swinging sleeves for most of the night, and then she'd change into a fitted European-style gown for the dancing. The gown had elbow-length sleeves and a flowing skirt — modest enough for even the most old-fashioned of dignitaries — but Aiko had chosen a bold black-and-white fabric that looked like traditional brushwork calligraphy.

Ren quietly eyed Aiko's wardrobe. Like Marty had said, it would be his job to take the tiny bottle of the sleeping drug and apply it onto Aiko's outifts. The timing would have to be perfect. Apply the drug too soon, and it might lose its potency. But apply it too late, and the serum wouldn't have enough time to seep into Aiko's soft skin. Either Beetle or Bird was supposed to pass along the drug to Ren, and now he could only hope that Marty would send them Ren's way. This mission would splinter and break if he didn't have that sleeping drug.

Once the evening arrived, the sewing staff finished their work and departed one by one, but Ren couldn't budge. He still had four uniforms to finish off, and he couldn't risk having Plank fire him for not meeting his quota. It was going to be a long night, and Ren thought about loading up on strong black tea when a knock on the door jolted him from his work.

Fräulein Plank stood in the doorframe, her blond hair locked in a neat bun and her back ever straight, making her look even more severe than yesterday. Ren scuttled to his feet.

"*Fräulein!*" He hurried to bow and hoped that she wasn't here to actually fire him. She seemed like the type of boss to dismiss an employee if she was having a bad day. "I'm nearly done with this batch of uniforms."

But Fräulein Plank didn't give the uniforms a second glance. "Where's Ms. Clarke?"

"Off to dinner. I can go find her —"

"Then you'll have to do. Come with me." She was already out the door when she looked back and said, "Bring a sewing kit. And pliers!"

Ren knew better than to ask questions, so he grabbed the supplies and jogged out of the room, dodging a half dozen gardeners heading for the showers and a flock of launderesses pushing carts full of soiled towels. Fräulein Plank marched straight out of the workers' wing and into the hotel lobby, leading Ren toward a formal tearoom that Ren hadn't seen before. The tearoom was decorated simply, with two enormous woodblock prints taking up residence on the far wall. There was nothing gaudy or showy about the place, which kept in line with classical Japanese aesthetics, but Ren could sense the money that was spent here. The potted orchids flanking the entrance could've belonged in a historic garden while those woodblock prints were probably more expensive than a seaside estate.

Inside the tearoom, dozens of people chatted and smiled and plucked hors d'oeuvres from silver platters. The men wore military dress uniforms, both for the Imperial and Nazi armies alike, while the women showed off their finest silks and velvets, flitting around the room like prized peacocks, which made Ren's uniform look like drab pigeon feathers.

Ren blinked at the splendor, knowing how out of place he must have looked. Crown Princess Katsura was known for hosting beautiful dinners and receptions, and this party must have been one of them. The timing was right, too, considering the number of foreign guests arriving at the Fortress ahead of the Joint Prosperity Ball.

Toward the back of the tearoom, Ren spotted the crown princess herself, the folds of her kimono unable to hide her growing belly, which held the future male heir to the Chrysanthemum Throne. The crown prince stood nearby and was locked in a conversation with Deputy Führer Forst. Forst himself looked like a walking Nazi stereotype. Along with his jewel-blue eyes and his red swastika armband, he had the same rectangular mustache that Adolf Hitler had made famous. Ren wouldn't have been surprised if Forst clicked his heels together, raised his arm shoulder-high, and barked out a crisp "*Sieg heil!*" just for kicks.

Fräulein Plank pulled Ren toward the butler's pantry adjacent to the tearoom. "Cabot! Don't keep her waiting."

Her?

The pantry was packed with extra champagne glasses and serving platters, along with two beverage refrigerators stocked full of white wine and club soda. But Ren didn't notice any of that. His gaze had fixed on the person waiting for them inside.

Drawing a shaky breath, Ren bowed and said, "Your Imperial Highness. May I be of service?"

10

The princess stood facing the wall, her hands fighting the back zipper of her tea-length dress. The dark red gown boasted a strapless neckline and looked vintage to Ren — European in style, likely French, and dating back to the 1940s or 1950s. He had to admit that Aiko looked radiant in the color, and the dress itself appeared in excellent shape considering its age. But its zipper had gotten stuck a couple of inches from the close.

Aiko glanced over her shoulder at Ren's arrival, and she pressed her lips together at the sight of him. Ren almost apologized for his presence but blushed instead. It wasn't exactly proper for a male tailor to attend to a princess in a butler's pantry, but she didn't tell Ren to leave.

"This is the staff tailor. I'm very sorry, Your Imperial Highness, but none of the seamstresses were available," Plank said to Aiko by way of introducing Ren. Then she glared at him. "Can you fix the zipper?"

"I think I'd rather change into something else," Aiko said, twisting what must have been the dress's matching bolero in her hands.

Plank quickly switched back to a gentler tone. "Please, let the tailor try. This dress belonged to Deputy Führer Forst's grandmother, and your parents would very much like you to wear it tonight."

Aiko sighed. Every inch of her looked impecabble, from the

French twist in her hair to the glittering teardrop diamonds swinging from her earlobes, but she seemed ready to yank out the pins and toss aside the earrings and throw the whole outfit to the floor. She looked like a kettle full of steam.

But Aiko didn't lose her cool. She swallowed a few deep breaths, like Ren did whenever his ire ignited; and she banished the frustration from her face, slipping on a mask of calmness, like Ren did in front of the soldiers. The transformation spanned mere seconds. She must have had a lot of practice.

Ren didn't find this surprising. Royalty like Aiko were trained early on to obey their parents and follow societal rules. Gift-giving was a delicate art, and if Forst had given Aiko his grandmother's dress and if her parents expected her to wear it, then she would insult them all if she refused. To be honest, Ren thought Aiko was a little childish for huffing about a dress — it wasn't like she would have to wear it forever — but this was probably the sort of "problem" that a princess had to deal with.

Aiko stopped fidgeting with the bolero and stood still. "Go on," she said to Ren.

Fräulein Plank promptly shooed Ren forward; he gripped his pliers and assessed the stubborn zipper, careful not to touch Aiko's skin. Ren may have been sixteen years old, but he had never stood this close to a girl his age. Of course he *thought* about girls — he thought about them quite a lot. But minding the shop took up most of his time, and writing his essays took up any leftover minutes. Besides, even when he struck up a conversation with a girl at the grocer's or the park, he always got tongue-tied. He found writing much easier than talking — he could always start an essay from scratch if he messed it up — but he couldn't do that with girls. That was why he often avoided them completely.

But as Ren started to tackle the zipper, he found it hard to concentrate. His thoughts alternated between worrying that Aiko would dismiss him and ignoring the scent of her perfume, which smelled like an orange grove.

Get a grip, Ren told himself. There was far too much on the line for him to be thinking about citrus fruit. Aiko could order him put to death with the snap of her fingers and no one would bat an eye. It'd be Ren's own fault if he forgot that.

Fräulein Plank came up behind Ren. "Can you fix the zipper or not?"

Ren fumbled for a reply. "Unfortunately, no — not quickly anyway — but I can sew the dress closed. That way Her Imperial Highness could rejoin the party sooner."

"Very well," Plank said, repinning a strand of hair that had defiantly slipped from her bun. "We can't keep the guests waiting, and I need to update the crown princess before the first toast. Work fast, Cabot." She turned to speak to Aiko. "I left your mother's pearls by the faucet behind you. She noticed that you forgot to change your necklace before the party began."

After Plank's departure, a hush fell inside the pantry. Ren rooted in his sewing kit to find some scarlet thread, and snippets of conversation drifted in from the party.

"They'll make a fine couple, aside from the age difference," said a woman in Japanese. "I've heard that the empress herself had a hand in the matchmaking."

"Do you think the princess will move to Berlin?" asked her companion.

"I'd assume so." The woman laughed softly. "She'll move wherever her husband wishes."

The conversation tapered off, but Aiko's shoulders remained tense.

Finally, Ren realized what was going on.

This wasn't an ordinary party. It was an engagement celebration to toast Aiko and Forst's upcoming nuptials.

And that was big news. This union was obviously a political move, judging by Aiko's reluctance, but she probably hadn't been given any choice in the matter. Her opinion was secondary because the Empire had *something* to gain from this wedding.

What, exactly, Ren wasn't sure.

While Ren continued sewing, he noticed Aiko touching the beaded necklace that currently hung at her throat. It was a simple strand of glass beads, each one the size of a marble, but when Ren took a closer look he realized that the individual beads were hand-painted. Half of them were adorned with swirls of blue while the other half bore tiny Japanese characters, so small that Ren had to squint to read them. Even then he could only make out a few.

Higuchi Ichiy

Yosano Akiko

Ito Noe

Ren almost dropped his needle. He had seen these names before. They were feminist Japanese thinkers — considered enemies of the state. All three had died before the war even broke out, but the Empire still used them as examples to fight "worldly" ideas like women's suffrage or women seeking advanced degrees. Aiko had no business wearing a necklace like this. It wasn't merely a rebellious act — some would see it as treason.

"Are we almost finished?" Aiko asked, breaking the quiet.

Ren hurried with the last few stitches. "I'm done, Your Imperial Highness."

Aiko turned around. There was no mirror for her to look into, but she didn't seem to care. Her eyes were blank as she said, "Hand me the pearls."

Ren reached for her mother's double strand of white pearls, which weighed heavily in his hand. No doubt one of those pearls could feed an orphanage for a week. He had planned on writing an essay about the distribution of wealth for months, and now he held the evidence in his palm, but he would have to return to the idea later. Until then, Aiko was waiting.

Ren held out the pearls while Aiko tried to take off her glass-beaded necklace, but she struggled with the clasp.

"May I help, Your Imperial Highness?" offered Ren.

"*No.*" Aiko's response came with a bite, and Ren automatically stepped away from her, wondering how he had offended her.

"My sincerest apologies —" he started to say.

"There's no need for that," Aiko interrupted him, but her tone had softened. "I've changed my mind. You can put the pearls back where you found them." Her fingers drifted back to the beaded necklace that she was wearing, and a smile ghosted on her lips.

Ren found himself saying, "It's a lovely piece."

Aiko's eyes brightened through her royal mask. "I made it myself," she said so quietly that he almost didn't hear her.

Ren didn't know what to say. Who exactly was this girl in front of him? She should be offended by someone like Ito Noe, but Aiko had painted the woman's name on her necklace instead — which she planned on wearing to her own engagement party. She had to have known that her family would never allow her to break her engagement, and so Ren wasn't sure what she wanted to accomplish. To make her parents angry? To exercise what little independence she had? Or was there something more at play, something deeper?

Ren had no idea, and he told himself it didn't matter. He had a mission to see through. Who cared if Aiko was wearing a scandalous necklace? And yet, he kept thinking about it anyway.

Aiko put on her bolero and regarded Ren coolly. "This conversation never happened," she said, her tone abruptly sharp. "Understood?"

"I — I understand, Your Imperial Highness," Ren stammered.

Aiko left without another word, leaving Ren to slump against the pantry's countertop, his head spinning at what had happened; but he couldn't linger here. He had a to-do list to tackle. Ren gathered his things and was about to open the door when he heard voices on the other side. He paused, waiting for the guests to move on, but they stayed planted where they stood and their exchange soon floated into Ren's ears.

"What a lovely party. The Bavarian dessert buffet was absolutely divine," said a voice that belonged to Deputy Führer Forst. His Japanese was heavily accented but passable. "I must thank the crown princess for such a thoughtful evening."

"We're honored to host you in our home," replied the soft tenor of Crown Prince Katsura. Ren held his breath, shivers tingling all over him at what he was overhearing. "I believe my daughter picked out the buffet options. She wished to pay homage to your heritage."

"Then I will thank her, too. Might I add that you've raised such a poised and graceful young woman?"

Ren shuddered on the other side of the door. It sounded like Forst was talking about a show horse on his personal estate, not his future wife.

"I can assure you that she'll have every comfort imaginable once she moves to Berlin," Forst continued. "I hear that she enjoys art galleries and museums?"

"It's a hobby of hers, yes. Her tutors have praised her talents," Crown Prince Katsura admitted. There was a flare of pride in his voice, but there was slight disapproval, too. Maybe he had discovered Aiko's plans on interviewing for the Institute of Arts.

"Every girl should enjoy a hobby, certainly. My niece has become an accomplished rider and has her own stable of thoroughbreds. It's a harmless enough pursuit until she settles down with a husband. Then she'll set aside such fancies."

There was a pause, but if the crown prince disagreed with such a sentiment, he didn't voice it. "I trust your visit so far has been comfortable?"

"Oh, very. My staff has settled in and we've been in touch with our main office since we landed, thanks to your assistance. In fact" — excitement curled into Forst's next words — "right before the party began, my office briefed me on an interesting development. Our military intelligence has been tracking Zara St. James as she moves toward our shared border along the Mississippi. If all goes well, we may be able to remove her Wanted signs."

"That's very good news."

"No word yet on your little Viper problem, though?"

"Not yet but hopefully soon," the crown prince said.

Ren broke into a cold sweat. He didn't know if the crown prince had told a white lie or if his intelligence officers were getting closer to unlocking the Viper's identity. He had to hope that it was the former. Ren had been more than meticulous about covering his tracks, but he'd always figured that his days were numbered. And wouldn't the Empire rub its hands with glee if it captured him here inside the Fortress?

"Ah, before I forget," Forst said, shifting topics. "I meant to tell you that we'll ship the vials from Neuberlin tomorrow morning and that the case will arrive here that evening. I do regret that I couldn't bring it with me, but our team of scientists wasn't quite ready. I was hoping to present it as an engagement gift."

"There's no need to apologize. My father and I both are thankful for it."

"I've instructed the team to come to the fort directly from the airport, or shall I tell them to meet us at Alcatraz instead?"

"We can rendezvous at Fort Tomogashima before driving north to the city. My personal yacht will await us at the dock to take us into San Francisco Bay. My staff will take care of everything."

Their dialogue shifted again, this time to the fruity undertones of the red wine being offered, but Ren had stopped listening. If he had heard everything correctly, the Nazis would soon bring vials of *something* to Alcatraz. Vials of V2? That would make sense. It would indeed be the perfect engagement gift.

Now Ren understood why this marriage was so important. The Nazis needed help — their Führer had been assassinated and they were fighting a full-on revolution against Zara St. James's Revolutionary Alliance. Morale was low, and troops were spread thin. There were whispers that the mighty Third Reich could tumble and fall like ancient Rome.

Imperial Japan, on the other hand, was faring better than their allies, at least superficially. The royal family remained intact, with the emperor heavily protected, and so far the WAT had snuffed out any flames of rebellion. But there were cracks splintering under the surface. The Resistance wasn't backing down, and the prized Ronin Elite were dwindling in numbers. If the Empire didn't solve these problems soon, they'd become like the Nazis.

And that was where Aiko and Forst's engagement came in. The old allies needed to make a trade — Imperial troops and supplies in exchange for Nazi vials of V2 — and what better way to cement that than with a royal marriage?

Ren's thoughts spun faster. The Resistance, however, couldn't let this trade go through. The rebels had long struggled to take down the Goliath that was the Empire, and they would have no chance at all for independence if they had to take on a unified front of Imperial Japan and the Nazis.

But what if the Resistance could cut this engagement short *and* get their hands on V2? Kidnapping Aiko would take care of that first part, and the attack on Alcatraz could possibly ensure the second. If they could pull this off . . .

Ren's heart glowed with the possibilities.

After another minute of chatting, both Forst and Crown Prince Katsura headed off to give yet another toast and Ren swiftly slipped out of the pantry, hurrying back to the workers' wing. He had a new item on his to-do list.

He needed to find Jay.

He had to send out another message.

11

Ren jolted awake the following morning before the alarm went off. His pulse was already accelerating, ready to sprout wings and rocket into the sky. He hadn't been able to track down Jay the night before, which meant Ren had to find him before their shifts started. After all, it was already Monday morning, with the Joint Prosperity Ball coming up fast on Friday night. There was too much to be done — finding a new escape route, figuring out Bird's and Beetle's identities, and passing along the intel he had overheard at the engagement party — but Ren could do none of that without Jay.

And the soldiers weren't helping him much, either.

Just like the morning before, they stormed inside Bunkroom 8 before Ren could head out for the day. Once again, Ren and his bunkmates lined up against the wall, and Ren tried not to move as the morning news report played on the television. The newscaster went over current events (this time praising a plentiful crop of cocoa beans at the Empire's holdings in South America) before seguing into the upcoming union between Princess Teru and Deputy Führer Forst. The engagement had been officially announced the night prior during a three-hour international telecast, but even that sort of coverage wouldn't be enough. A big event like this one would occupy the news reports for days to come, and it would build up to the Joint

Prosperity Ball, where the happy couple would make their first public appearance.

While the newscaster speculated about possible wedding sites — perhaps a ceremony in Tokyo and then a reception in Berlin? — the TV screen filled with photographs taken at the engagement party last night. The first few pictures showed Forst greeting ambassadors from the Nordic Territories and the Canadian Zones, while Aiko hung a few steps back, dressed in the red dress that Ren had mended. But the last photo showed Aiko with her parents. Her mother and father looked stiff, but the slightest of smiles tilted on Aiko's mouth as her fingertips trailed along her necklace. Ren wondered if anyone else had noticed the writing on her beads. Apparently not.

As soon as the report was finished, Sasaki cracked his knuckles and gestured for Ren to step out of the line. Ren stifled a groan and did as he was instructed.

"I did a little research on you," said Sasaki, closing the distance between them. "I heard you shine shoes in town."

Anxiety churned in Ren's belly. The Cabots' shop specialized in tailoring and cobbling, but he and his father would shine shoes, too, if a customer requested it. This didn't mean that Ren wanted to shine Sasaki's boots, though. The thought made him nauseous — stooping down to an imperial soldier while the bunkmates watched in silence.

"Let's see how good you are." Sasaki took a clean rag from his pocket and dropped it to the floor.

Ren bent down and got to work, telling himself that he didn't have to smell Sasaki's breakfast breath anymore at least. His cheeks flushed as he heard the other soldiers snickering, but he pretended he was back at the shop and attending to a picky customer.

"You missed a spot on the left boot," Sasaki said halfway through the cleaning. "Here, let me help." Then he spat onto his shoe, but half of it landed in Ren's hair instead. That got another laugh from the soldiers.

Sasaki's spit seeped into Ren's scalp, which made his skin crawl with disgust. Worse, he couldn't stop to clean himself up. He had to ignore the saliva and the chuckling soldiers and his staring bunkmates. And somehow he did. By the time Ren was finished, his hands were quivering and he wanted to quit right then and there. But he had to smother that impulse. He told himself that the Alcatraz prisoners had been tortured and experimented on for years, and if they could survive that — his mother included — then he could endure Sasaki for a few days.

But that did little to rein in his anger.

The soldiers left and dismissed everyone from the bunkroom, and no one asked him if he was all right. It didn't matter. Ren was too busy sprinting into the bathroom to rinse his hair. He turned the hot-water faucet as far as it would go and then doused his scalp with the scalding water, but no matter how hard he scrubbed Ren didn't feel clean. Humiliation coursed through him, and it was soon joined by a white-hot fury. He breathed and he counted and he clenched his eyes shut, but when none of that worked, Ren wrapped a towel around his left hand and punched the wall hard.

Falling to his knees, Ren blinked back tears and stared at his throbbing knuckles. Four and a half more days until Friday. He had to stomach this treatment for that long, but it would be worth it. He would make it worth it.

He couldn't fail the Resistance. He wouldn't let his mom down.

After splashing some more water on his face, Ren took off running. He was already late to his first appointment in the cadets' changing rooms. Weaving in and out of the morning foot traffic, Ren grabbed a dress rack of uniforms from the sewing room and dragged it toward the indoor gymnasium. The class of seven-year-old cadets was already lined up outside of the changing rooms, awaiting Ren's arrival before their first training session of the day, and Ren got an earful from their instructor for his tardiness.

"My deepest apologies," Ren said while catching his breath and trying to hide the residual frustration in his voice. He had to put Sasaki out of his thoughts and work quickly to make up for his lateness. He couldn't let this get back to Fräulein Plank. With flying speed, he doled out each uniform to its corresponding student and waited for them to change before he started each fitting, pinning new pant and sleeve hemlines, marking where a waist should get taken in, and noting if a collar gapped too much around the neck. He moved from cadet to cadet, and when he reached the last student, he had to stretch his cramped fingers before measuring the length of her skirt. This cadet, however, kept yawning and fidgeting and making Ren's job almost impossible.

The instructor regarded the girl with a frown. "Did you stay up too late again, Hata?"

The girl bowed her head, her bangs hiding her eyes. "The trucks woke me up."

"What trucks?"

"I saw them outside my window. Emi did, too! We counted five of them."

"I'm sure it was nothing. They were probably delivering supplies."

"Yes, but —"

"But what?" pressed the instructor.

The girl kept her chin down. "I apologize. It's nothing."

"Tell me what you were going to say," the instructor said with a sigh.

"We . . . we saw the soldiers taking someone out of one of the trucks." She whispered, "In *chains*. It looked like a prisoner."

The instructor's mouth pinched. "It was probably nothing but a training exercise. The next time you hear something at night, shut your blinds and go back to sleep."

The girl looked chastened. *"Hai,"* she said softly.

The girl remained quiet and still for the rest of her fitting, making it easy for Ren to finish his work, but his fingers went clumsy because his thoughts had leapt elsewhere. As far as he knew, the Fortress didn't take any prisoners — that was what internment camps and Alcatraz were for. Most likely the girl was mistaken.

But Ren's paranoia sank teeth into his skin. He never liked giving in to his nerves, but his isolation inside the Fortress made him more anxious than usual. What if the Empire had arrested Marty? Or his dad? The patrols were always looking for an excuse to take Mr. Cabot into custody.

Stop, Ren told himself. He couldn't panic. Right now, he had only heard a rumor of a prisoner at the Fortress. From a seven-year-old.

Ren needed to stop worrying, but the idea had been planted in his head and it was hard not to dwell on it.

Mercifully, the morning passed quickly from there, and the afternoon flew by even faster. Ren left two more notes for Jay, but aside from that he didn't take a break from his worktable. There were too many alterations on his plate to even grab a bowl of rice from the cafeteria.

A little past nine o'clock at night, Ren had started on another pair of trousers when he heard footsteps thudding toward the sewing room. Ren groaned. It was probably Plank coming in to check on him and tell him that he wasn't working fast enough.

"Thought I might find you here, tailor boy," said Jay, leaning over Ren's worktable. "Got a minute?"

"Where've you been?" demanded Ren, the day's frustration coloring his words. They were alone in the sewing room; the other staff had left over a half hour ago. "Didn't you get my messages?"

"Whoa, there. You're not the only one working around the clock. And yes, I got your messages." A slight smile danced across Jay's mouth. "Felt like I had a secret admirer."

Ren ignored that and stood from the worktable, flinching as his back muscles cramped from sitting in one place for too long. "Have you heard about a new prisoner at the Fortress?" he whispered, unable to contain the question for another second.

"Prisoner?" Jay said, baffled. "The Fortress has a couple of holding cells, but it's not a jail. What exactly did you hear?"

"That a bunch of trucks dropped off a prisoner late last night. Supposedly, in chains." Ren realized how far-fetched this must've sounded, but he had to ask. He had been sitting alone with his thoughts for too long.

"I guess I could ask around, but this is the first I've heard of that."

"I'd appreciate it." Ren relaxed, but only slightly. The prisoner in chains was probably a rumor, but he couldn't put his guard down yet. "Were you able to stop by my family's shop?"

"Yes, finally. I couldn't leave the Fortress without a pass, and I couldn't get my hands on one until my boss sent me to pick up a few packages after dinner. I just got back."

"How's my dad doing? How's Marty?"

"They're fine. They're safe. But let's talk somewhere else."

"Why? Do you have bad news?"

"Your family is *fine*, TB, but I don't like talking out in the open." He headed back toward the door. "I know a place where we can go."

Ren wasn't sure what Jay meant by that — every corner of the Fortress was always being watched — but Jay was already in the hallway and striding to the last door at the end of the hall. He opened the door for Ren, allowing a brisk wind to pummel their chests.

"After you," said Jay. "Welcome to the employee lounge."

Ren stepped outside into a small courtyard that looked nothing like a lounge. The little terrace was fenced in by a six-foot-high concrete wall. A metal table and chairs wobbled in one corner, currently unoccupied, but Ren did notice a video monitor poking out from one of the walls. He didn't know why they couldn't have stayed in the sewing room. There were cameras everywhere.

"It's not much to look at, but we shouldn't be bothered out here," Jay said. "Don't worry about the camera. There's no audio, just visual, and we'll be out of eyeshot if we talk at the table. Care to take an uncomfortable seat with me?"

They moved to the table, where they sat upon rusted chairs. Jay began shuffling a deck of cards to keep his hands busy while Ren threaded his fingers together on his lap. He was ready for an update from home. There were times when Ren had felt boxed in and suffocated by his life at the shop — the never-ending work, the nitpicking customers, the *smallness* of it all — but he ached for it now because it was home. And he really missed his dad. For years their relationship had grown silent and chilled, but deep down Ren had always known that his father loved him. Maybe Mr. Cabot didn't vocalize that much, but he showed it by making sure Ren was never cold and by tiptoeing around the apartment every weekend so that his son could sleep in. Ren wished that he would've thanked his dad for that, but he honestly hadn't noticed it until he came to the Fortress.

"How's my family doing?" Ren said.

"I'll be honest. Your dad isn't too happy that you're gone." Jay shifted until he found a comfortable position, leaning forward slightly with his elbows resting on the table. Then he dealt them both a fresh hand of five-card stud, even though Ren didn't play. "He wants you to quit and come home. I believe he added a *right now.*"

Ren had to chuckle. At least that meant his dad was recovering. "He's holding up okay?"

"Marty said that he sleeps most of the day, but he should be healed up in a couple of months." Jay picked up his cards and scanned them quickly. "Don't you want to see your hand?"

"Not really." Ren wasn't one to gamble; he didn't have the money for it. "Did Marty say anything else?"

Jay pushed Ren's cards closer to him and jutted his chin at the video monitor. "Indulge me."

"I thought you said the camera couldn't see us here."

"The soldiers might be able to see a part of you because of where you're sitting. In case they get curious, pretend you're playing cards with me. They won't bother us if they think we're doing that."

Ren sighed and went along with this charade. It never hurt to be too careful, and he really wanted Jay to finish passing along the message. "What did Marty say?" he asked again.

"She told me to tell you something." Jay leaned forward, and his gaze flicked toward the video camera. Then he uttered two words so softly that Ren barely heard them before the wind snatched them away. "*Callipepla californica.* I'm with the Resistance, too."

12

Ren drew in a cold breath of air. "Did you say . . . ?"

Jay grinned like a purring cat. "Don't look so shocked." He ran a hand over his close-shaven head. "You know, your cousin was the one who came up with my little nickname."

Ren still couldn't believe what was happening, and he had absolutely no idea what Jay was talking about. "What nickname?"

Jay rubbed his scalp once more, his fingers gliding over the short hair. It looked soft to the touch, like a newborn chick's. "I'm Bird."

"Wait. You're —"

Jay whistled a little tune. "Tweet, tweet."

Ren had to give himself a minute to let this revelation sink in. His first thought was that he wished Jay had told him sooner. And his second thought was wondering if he could really trust Jay. The Fortress had made him very paranoid, but Ren had to be extra vigilant.

"So how long have you known Marty?" Ren said, trying to sound casual but failing.

Jay tossed down his hand and reshuffled the deck. "Not ready to trust me, eh?"

"I'm just asking some questions."

"Yeah, Marty said that you might be a hard-liner. I get it. Let's see . . . I've known your cousin for years. Our moms lived on the same block growing up. We lost touch for a while, but then Marty showed up at one of my poker nights last year. Those nights are invitation-only, but she had heard about it somehow and dropped by to ask me something."

Ren stared at his newly dealt cards — he had a pair of nines, which seemed like a decent hand — although his attention was solely concentrated on Jay. "Ask you about what?"

"About becoming a donor to a little group she was affiliated with. She called it a charity fund." Jay rubbed his stubbled jaw and laughed. "You should've seen how she dolled herself up that night. I saw right through it, but the rest of the guys were reaching into their wallets to donate."

Ren smiled. It sounded like Marty, all right. "Did she try to recruit you?"

"Of course. She wanted another insider at the Fortress, but I couldn't risk losing my job. My poker nights bring in good cash, but it's not steady pay and I have my mom and little sisters to think about." Jay plucked a new card from the deck. "Don't mention my extracurricular evening activities to anyone, okay?"

"Not a word." Ren knew how to keep a secret. Gambling was illegal in the Territories, but the soldiers might turn a blind eye to it if you gave them enough cash. But running a betting ring was another crime entirely — one that came with severe consequences.

"What made you change your mind about Marty's offer?" asked Ren.

The smile slipped from Jay's face and he tossed down his cards, showing triple queens, but he looked the opposite of triumphant. "Let's say that one of my sisters had a bad run-in with her old boss."

Ren winced as he thought of the possibilities of what happened. None of them were pretty. "Is she okay?"

"She still has nightmares and has to sleep next to my mom, if you call that 'okay.'" Jay gritted his molars hard. "She worked as a maid at one of those vacation houses. Her drunk of a boss dropped in on her one day and made a pass. When she tried to run for it, he cornered her and beat her unconscious." He began shuffling his deck, his fingers gripping the cards. "We got worried when she didn't come home that night. My mom was the one who found her."

Ren clutched the armrests of his chair. It was hard enough to be an American living in the WAT, but being an American *female* made everything that much tougher. There were more rules that women had to live by: avoid going out alone, know your exits at all times, keep your eyes down always. It was an unfair map that girls had to learn to navigate early on. "I'm sorry."

"Don't feel sorry for me. Feel sorry for her." Jay shuffled the deck again before glancing up. Were there tears in his eyes? Ren wasn't sure. "She's fourteen years old."

Fourteen, thought Ren, *just a kid*. It reminded him of something his mother had murmured to herself years back, after she'd picked him up from school and they had crossed paths with the Quirks. *I don't know how Abel does it*, she had said on their way home, *raising three little girls in a world like this*.

"My sister is the reason why I changed my mind about Marty's offer. And she's also the reason why I got this." Jay angled his back from the camera and motioned for Ren to scoot closer before he pulled at his bottom lip to reveal the soft pink flesh — and something else.

Ren leaned in, studying the black marking. "Is that a tattoo?"

Jay nodded and shut his mouth. "I had to put it in a spot where the soldiers wouldn't see it."

"What does it say? The lighting out here isn't great."

Jay's smile reappeared, tugging one side of his mouth upward. "It says: *We strike.*"

A shiver traveled down Ren's spine. He recognized those words. He had written them. *In the darkest of nights, we strike.*

"It's part of my sister's favorite quote. She has most of the Viper's essays memorized because we obviously can't keep them around the house. Her favorite one was about the new America. Did you read that?"

Ren picked up the deck of cards and shuffled them like the amateur he was, but it was better than sitting there and stammering. Of course he remembered that essay. It had been one of his more philosophical pieces that envisioned an America built upon the Founding Fathers' ideals but making it better. It would be a nation based on liberty and inalienable rights and the pursuit of happiness — come one come all, no matter the color of your skin or what deity you worshipped or whom you loved. It would be a country where his mom wouldn't have been murdered and where Mr. Cabot wouldn't have to worry about patrols. It would be a place where Ren no longer had to write his essays.

Jay drummed his fingers on the table. "What do you think? Have you deemed me trustworthy yet?"

Ren found himself nodding. Jay had uttered the passcode for the mission, which was no small thing. And he had gotten a traitorous tattoo that could get him killed. So Ren decided to go along with this Bird who'd flown into his path. If Marty trusted Jay, then Ren would, too.

"What did Marty say about" — Ren chose his words with care — "our plans for the ball?"

Jay rubbed his palms together. "We're talking business now? Great."

"Did you give her the message about the laundries?"

"Yeah, and it just about killed me telling her that." Jay placed a hand on his heart and winced. "It took me weeks to even scout out the chute. Almost broke my neck a few times, too. I was about to install the pulley before you told me the news."

"Bad timing," Ren said with a sigh. "Do we have a plan B in place?"

"Not exactly. We were betting our chips on that laundry chute, so we're back to square one. We have to look through the Fortress's schematics and find a new escape route."

This wasn't good news at all. In fact, it was even worse than Ren was expecting. He really thought Marty would've had a firm alternate plan. "Do we even have a set of these schematics?"

"Nope." Jay plucked a card from the deck, still playing for the cameras. "We'll need to sneak into the security room to get them, which won't be easy. The office is staffed around the clock: three guards during the day shift and two taking the graveyard. I've cleaned that place more times than I can count."

"We don't have much of a choice at this point. It's already Monday."

"I know. That means we'll have to sneak into the security room tomorrow night."

"*Tomorrow?*" Ren whispered.

"That's when I'm scheduled to clean the security office again, and we need to get this ball rolling."

Ren went quiet, but he knew Jay was right. Getting those schematics was only the first half of the equation. The other half was scoping out each new route and making sure that they weren't blocked or heavily guarded. There was a lot of work to get done and not much time to do it. "Can the two of us pull this off?"

"I doubt it, but that's why we have Beetle to help us."

Ren's head jerked up. "You know him?"

"Do you mean if I know *her?*" Jay said with a smirk.

"Oh," Ren said, chastened. If his mom were here, she'd have a few choice words with him for jumping to the conclusion that Beetle was male. "Who is she, then?"

"She's Kato's assistant. Greta Plank."

Plank? Ren felt the breath knocked out of him all over again. Jay must have been kidding, and yet he wasn't grinning. "Tell me you're joking. How could my cousin trust a Nazi like her?"

"Look, I was skeptical at first, too, but Marty vouches for the good *Fräulein*. She trusts her."

"But Plank could be a double agent."

"There's always that chance, but she has passed on good intel to Marty. Plus, she was the one who helped me scout out that laundry chute."

Still, Ren wasn't convinced. "Why would she want to help us?"

"Apparently, Plank's best friend was dating a Japanese soldier, but the soldier had a temper and put Plank's friend in the hospital. After the friend died of a blood clot, the Empire covered the whole thing up because the soldier's uncle is a general or something." Jay's face darkened the same way as when he had been talking about his little sister. "That's why Plank has a bone to pick with her employers."

This big of a bone, though? Becoming a traitor was no small decision.

Jay slid the deck of cards back into its box. "We should head out."

"Wait. When can you see Marty again?"

"Maybe around noon tomorrow. It's shrimp chowder day at the diner in town, and my boss's boss usually sends me out to pick up a bowl for his lunch." Jay regarded Ren warily. "Why do you ask?"

"I have another message for her." Ren leaned over the table, grateful that the video monitor didn't catch any audio — because both he and Jay would get executed tonight if someone was eavesdropping on them. "I overheard something at the engagement party."

Jay raised a brow. "Oh?"

Ren proceeded to fill him in about Forst's engagement present to the Empire — the precious vials of V2 that would soon arrive at Alcatraz. When he was finished, Jay looked dazed.

"This is big," Jay said finally.

"It's huge. I haven't been able to stop thinking about it. If we can pull off this mission and if Marty can get inside Alcatraz, then she could destroy the Empire's new stash of V2. The Nazis will probably send them more, but that might take time and it will delay the crown prince from making new Ronin Elite. At least for a little while." Ren realized that he was talking too fast, and he forced himself to slow down. "That's why I need you to tell Marty this information. The Resistance has to add it to their plans."

"I know," Jay said quietly. His eyes glittered with the possibilities of this development. "I'll find a way."

Suddenly, a voice behind in the doorway startled them both. Jay almost dropped his box of cards.

"Hey, lights out," another janitor called out to them. "I have to lock up."

"No problem, Benny. We were finished with our game anyway," said Jay, recovering smoothly.

They left for Ren's bunkroom, where the lights had already been turned off. Jay continued on toward his own assigned room. His easy gait had returned, as if they really had spent the last hour playing cards instead of discussing how to overthrow the Empire.

"Sweet dreams, tailor boy. See you tomorrow," Jay said.

The weight of the day pulled Ren toward his bed and didn't let go until he was settled on his cot. He lay on his back in the darkness, with his hands clasped on his stomach and his blanket neatly pulled over his waist. All he had to do was fall asleep, but he doubted that he would drift off anytime soon. Not tonight. He had hours of thinking and planning to tackle instead.

At least now he wouldn't have to do it all alone.

13

By 9:45 the next night — a mere seventy hours until the ball — the plan was set. The pieces were in place. The players were ready.

Almost ready, that is.

Ren was going through the motions, but he wasn't sure that they could actually pull this operation off. There was a decent chance that they'd all be arrested within the hour and tortured for information. If that wasn't bad enough, Ren still doubted Plank's trustworthiness. He couldn't help it. Maybe Plank had passed Marty's vetting process, but she wouldn't be the first double agent that the Resistance had dealt with. Ren had wanted to talk to her earlier, but she hadn't stopped by the sewing room and Ren didn't have time to seek her out. Now he would have to trust her with his life, even if he didn't quite trust Plank herself. But if Ren wanted to free those prisoners and if he wanted to follow the bread crumbs that might lead to his mom, then he needed Plank's help.

With that in mind, Ren slipped into the janitorial closet where Jay had promised to meet him. Holding his nose, Ren climbed inside the rolling garbage can that occupied the closet's corner, squishing himself against the dirty paper towels and empty bleach containers inside.

Minutes ticked by until the door swung open again. Someone tapped a fist against the side of the garbage can.

"Knock, knock," whispered Jay. "Comfy in there?"

"Let's get this over with," Ren whispered back.

"What are you complaining about, tailor boy? You get to sit there and wait for my signal while Plank and I do the talking and string-pulling. Sounds simple enough to me." Jay's words were teasing, but Ren didn't hear any playfulness in them. He had a hunch that Jay was thinking the very same thing he was — how if this plan didn't go well, then they'd likely be dead before the night was over.

"Where's Plank?" Ren said, shuddering as Jay dumped three more bags of garbage into the can.

"She's on her way. You know, she was a little skeptical about you joining the mission so late in the game when she had been expecting your dad. But Marty vouched for you, so she's completely on board."

Ren huffed at the thought of Plank not trusting *him*. He wasn't the Nazi. But if she truly believed in the Resistance and in the mission itself, then he couldn't really blame her for doubting a "tadpole's" abilities.

Jay placed a lid on the garbage can. "Showtime. Sit tight and don't make a peep."

Whistling a little tune as he went, Jay rolled the garbage from corridor to corridor until he slowed it to a stop. They must have reached the security office. Ren held himself absolutely still as Jay knocked on the door and one of the security guards on duty answered.

"I'm here to clean the office," Jay said, using a humble voice that Ren had never heard before. "I also brought your new uniforms to change into. My supervisor sent out a notice about them earlier."

"We didn't get any notices," the guard said gruffly. "And we don't need new uniforms."

"My sincerest apologies. The notice might have gotten lost." Jay's voice lowered a decibel. "If you haven't heard already, there has been an outbreak of Rocky Mountain lice on the first floor. Just to be safe, we need to bleach the floors and wash your uniforms in boiling water."

There was a pause. "Rocky Mountain lice?"

"They're like regular lice except they're much harder to get rid of. Not to mention the bloodsucking part," explained Jay, somberly serious. He was lying through his teeth — there was no such thing as Rocky Mountain lice — but Jay delivered his lines with such earnestness that Ren almost believed him, too. "We have to keep the infestation hush-hush because the ball is coming up so soon, which means we're bleaching the floors in every room. If you don't mind changing out of your uniforms, I can take care of them after I'm finished."

Soon, the second security guard on duty joined the conversation at the door. He sounded strangely familiar to Ren. "What if the lice got to us already?"

"A hot shower can definitely help. The bugs don't like that," offered Jay.

A cramp spiked in Ren's calf while the guards murmured about what they should do. One of them even whispered how he had felt a little itchy since lunchtime.

"Watch my station," the first security guard said to the second. "I'll shower and change first, and then we can switch out."

The first security guard hurried out of the room, and Ren silently cheered. Now there was only one left to get rid of, but that was where Plank was supposed to come in — whenever she decided to show up.

Ren counted the seconds, waiting for her arrival. Jay had said not to worry, but Ren was already plotting what-ifs. What if she had gotten held up? What if she had gotten cold feet? What if she was turning them in right this moment?

A new set of footsteps came down the hall, the click-clack of heeled shoes. Ren dared to hope that it was Plank.

"Oh, good. You're here," said Fräulein Plank to the remaining security guard. She sounded a little breathless. "I could use your help, Sasaki-sama."

Ren resisted a groan. That was why this security guard had sounded familiar to him — it was his old friend Sasaki. He and Plank must have known each other if she called him by name.

"Is something wrong, *Fräulein?*" said Sasaki. His polite tone couldn't have been more different from how he barked orders to Ren in the bunkroom. Ren's hands fisted as he thought about polishing Sasaki's boots and getting spat upon. It took a few seconds for him to calm himself.

"I have to drop off these files on the sixth floor, but I'm having trouble with my security card at the elevator. Could you swipe me in?" Plank said sweetly.

"I can't leave this room unattended, *Fräulein.* Could you wait until my partner gets back?" said Sasaki.

"This won't take long, I promise." Fräulein Plank's voice lowered. "These files are meant for Crown Princess Katsura, you know. They came straight from Tokyo and I *really* need to bring them upstairs. Won't you help a girl out?"

Ren braced himself inside the garbage can. That was another lie they were using tonight, and if Sasaki sniffed it out, they would definitely get hauled in for an interrogation. There were no urgent files sent from Japan — Plank was merely using a manila envelope filled with old office paper.

"Please, Sasaki-sama?" said Fräulein Plank, her words dripping with syrup. "I'd be so grateful. It'll only take a minute, and after your shift we could grab a cup of tea."

Ren waited for Sasaki to turn her down. How could Sasaki fall for this? But then —

"I suppose if it'll only take a minute . . . ," Sasaki said.

Ren could almost see the smile radiating from Plank's face. "You're such a lifesaver," she gushed. "It won't take us long at all. I promise."

Their voices trailed off as they left the security room behind, and Ren felt a hearty knock on the side of the garbage can.

"You're up, TB." Jay removed the lid and helped Ren out of the can. Blinking under the fluorescent lights, Ren saw over thirty video monitors in front of him, capturing every angle of the Fortress and switching every few seconds from feed to feed. But there, tucked in a corner, he spotted three file cabinets and made a beeline for them.

Mop in hand, Jay strode to the open door. "I'll keep watch. We'll have a couple of minutes at most."

Ren didn't even bother replying; he didn't want to waste a second. He opened the first drawer and thumbed through the folders, his eyes scanning for any key word that he and Jay had discussed earlier. *Floor plan. Blueprint. Map.* But nothing popped up.

"Find anything?" Jay whispered.

"Still looking." Ren opened the bottom cabinet and started the search again, but his fingers only landed on criminal records and tech manuals and endless spreadsheets that had nothing to do with what he needed. By the time he reached for a new drawer, his hopes were shriveling fast.

Until his gaze snagged on a phrase. *Facility Plans, circa 1989.* He cocked his head and pulled it out.

It was a map. Jackpot. But soon Ren's brows knitted together because this map showed nothing that he recognized. He didn't see the hotel lobby or the ballroom or the workers' wing. Instead, the diagram showed something else completely — small rooms labeled *Storage*, with a few stairwells and a crisscross of narrow hallways. Tunnels, maybe? His eyes zigzagged across the paper, and there in the corner he saw the phrase *Access Restricted.*

Ren's neurons fired fast. He noticed that there weren't any windows on this map, either. Could this be a sublevel of the hotel? An underground facility? He'd never heard of such a thing, but this might be what they were looking for — if there was an exit to the outside.

"Did you find something?" Jay whispered.

"I think so."

"Good," said Jay, sweeping his mop furiously around the door, "because one of the guards is heading back right now."

"Stall him."

"You kidding? Get inside!"

But Ren lingered. He was so close. Too close. He needed another minute, maybe half of that if he hurried. He stared at the diagram, searching desperately for an access point to get down to this sublevel so that they could explore it.

A hand fell on Ren's shoulder. "I said come on!" said Jay.

Ren barely had time to shove the map back into place, shut the drawer, and fold himself into the garbage can before Jay slammed the lid back on. Just then, footsteps marched into the room.

"I'm finished here," said Jay. Ren could hear the nervous twinge in his voice. "Let me take your old uniform and I can be off."

"What happened to Sasaki?" said the guard.

"He went to help Fräulein Plank with her security card, but he'll return in a minute." Jay spoke fast, probably too fast, but he was ready to get out of the security office. And so was Ren.

Before the security guard could pepper Jay with more questions, Jay wheeled the garbage can the same way they had come. It felt like hours had passed before they returned to the janitorial closet, and even then Ren waited for the door to shut before he dared to breathe.

Jay removed the lid and offered Ren a clammy hand. "We're clear."

Ren brushed himself off, although he couldn't get rid of the sour smell clinging to his uniform, but a quick change and a hot shower would fix that. What mattered was that they had breached the security room without getting caught. They'd beaten the odds. "We did it."

"We almost didn't. You really put our necks on the line, Ren." Jay crossed his arms — and he looked mad.

"I'm sorry. It was stupid of me, I know, but I was so close," said Ren.

"It better be worth it. What did you find?"

"The Fortress has a sublevel or a basement that was closed off at some point. I found a map of a network of tunnels that might lead outside. It'll take some work, but we could take Aiko from the top floor and down to the basement and out to the car."

Jay chewed on this information. "How do we get to this basement exactly?"

"I don't know. That's why I needed more time." Ren watched Jay's face fall, and it hit him like a punch. "But I did notice something called Stairwell Fifteen. If we could locate that, it should lead us underground."

Jay shook his head. "I've swept all sorts of stairwells, and I haven't seen any with numbers."

"Maybe they had them at some point."

"Maybe. I guess."

Ren could hear Jay's frustration, and he swelled with guilt. Both Jay and Plank had done their jobs. It was Ren who had misfired. If he wanted to salvage this mission, he needed to fix it.

"I'll find a way to the basement," Ren said firmly. "I'll figure something out."

"We'll keep trying. Don't have much of a choice." Jay pinched the bridge of his nose, his usual easiness nowhere to be found. "Right now, though, I could really use a deck of cards."

This was news to Ren. "You're playing poker tonight? How are you getting out of the Fortress?"

"I'm friendly with one of the checkpoint guards, and I could use a little relaxation. I can't disappoint Marty, either. I lost a bet with her a while ago, and she's making me donate half of my earnings to her little Resistance fund."

"Could you get me out, too?" Ren said, the question spilling out of him. Even if he only got an hour with Marty and his father, it would be worth it. He wouldn't even mind if his dad spent the whole time lecturing him.

"Not this time, TB." Jay sounded genuinely apologetic but like he wouldn't budge on the matter. "It'll be too risky to sneak us both out."

"Oh. Right." Ren coughed to hide his disappointment. "Be careful out there."

"I do have a little good news, though. I saw your cousin at lunch today and relayed your message about the vials. She's going to pass that on to the San Francisco cell, and she told me to tell you that she's proud of you and that your dad is doing fine." Jay shifted his head from side to side, working out a crick in his neck. "Anyway, I should go. Stay here for a few minutes after I leave. I don't want anyone seeing us heading out together."

Ren nodded. "Good luck with your game."

"I'll need it. Good night, tailor boy."

For the first time in days, Ren saw a glimmer of hope on his horizon. There was just a glint of it, but it was there, all shiny and golden and ready for the picking.

Little did Ren realize how fleeting that hope would be.

14

After a solid night of sleep, Ren tackled the Wednesday workday with yesterday's hope glowing inside him. There was a lot of work ahead, but they had gotten the mission back on track — and that was no small feat. Now he and Jay and Plank had to figure out how to get to the Fortress's sublevel and scout out another escape route. And with only two and a half days before the ball, they'd have to make every minute count.

Ren slipped out of his bunkroom a full hour before the alarm went off, hoping to avoid Sasaki and his friends, and luckily his early rising paid off. Not only did Ren evade the soldiers, he bought himself a little time to search for Stairwell 15. With the hallways almost empty, he peeked inside a few cleaning closets, then the kitchens, then a couple of storage areas. In case anyone asked him what he was doing, he had slung a bag of dirty laundry over one shoulder so that he could claim he was looking for the laundries. Fortunately, Ren didn't have to explain himself to anyone. Unfortunately, though, he didn't find any secret stairwells.

Ren's scouting trip came to a quick end once his shift started, but as he readied a rack with the ten-year-old class's dress uniforms he kept thinking about the escape route. Even if he found a new way out of the hotel, that still left the problem of sneaking Aiko's unconscious body out of the penthouse. Jay had brought up the idea of hiding the princess in a cleaning cart and simply wheeling her down to the elevator, which might work. But they would have to move Aiko from the cleaning cart and into the sublevel and out to the getaway car that Plank would be driving. She had swiped the keys to a company car.

There were so many details that Ren needed to get right, and the weight of it sat heavily on his shoulders. He had one chance to pull this off . . . or the mission would be a bust and the prisoners would remain stuck at Alcatraz — and he'd lose his chance of finding out what had happened to his mom.

Ms. Clarke clapped her hands to get everyone's attention. "Finish your stitches and let's get going."

The rest of the team nodded and stood at their workstations, but Ren had no clue what was going on. He was supposed to head to the cadet changing rooms in fifteen minutes.

Ms. Clarke noted his confusion. "We have to go to the common room, remember? There was an announcement at breakfast."

"I didn't go to breakfast. What kind of announcement?" As soon as he asked that, fear spread through Ren's insides. There was only one kind of announcement that the Empire usually made.

"We'll find out soon enough," Ms. Clarke replied, elbowing him out.

When Ren reached the common room, he found it already crammed full with people. The ratty sofas had been pushed to the walls to make room for everyone around the lone black-and-white television. Some of the maids had sat down on the couches, with a few gardeners leaning against the armrests. No one stood close to the television. Nobody wanted a front-row view to this show, even though they were spared from watching it on the beach. With the ball looming so close, the Fortress couldn't waste any time by sending its workers to the shore.

The room hushed as three soldiers entered the room. One of them clicked on the television and turned the dial to the state news channel. The anthem had already started, and the soldiers gestured for everyone to join in. Ren pretended to sing along while he looked around for Jay, wondering if his friend had wiggled out of watching the broadcast.

The cooks next to Ren began whispering. "Who are they going to kill this time?" one of them said.

"Just be glad it isn't one of us," another replied.

Ren stood silently as they talked, and he was sure the Empire would have smiled at their exchange. For years, the Empire had made Americans believe that if they obeyed the laws and ratted on their neighbors, then they would be safe. This line of thinking had pitted American against American, dividing communities and possible allies while the Empire did whatever it wanted. It was a smart strategy, and Ren relished the thought of dismantling it one day. Hopefully, one day very soon. He never wanted to attend another one of these broadcasts again.

The anthem concluded, and the cameras swept across the rough seas and up the cliffs and zeroed in once again on Crown Prince Katsura. His makeup looked heavier than the last time — more foundation on his cheeks and more concealer covering the underside of his eyes. It looked like something was keeping him awake at night, perhaps the Viper's whereabouts. Ren felt no remorse about making the crown prince lose sleep, but his stomach churned over what this meant for the WAT. As long as the Viper remained at large, the

Empire would keep slaughtering Americans who didn't deserve to die. There would be more Daisy Montgomerys, and every one of them would weigh on Ren's conscience. A tangle of emotions hit him hard in the chest — hopelessness and desperation and a hot spike of wrath. He began counting to twenty before he lost it in front of all these people.

"Citizens of the Western American Territories, I speak to you again from Fort Tomogashima. I had hoped that our last meeting would have encouraged the criminal known as the Viper to come forward, but the Viper lacks both dignity and honor. He hides in the shadows while his treacherous ideas infest the minds of innocent civilians. Until the Viper is caught, I have no choice but to continue broadcasting from these cliffs."

So much for your "reforms," Ren thought bitterly. Maybe the crown prince had once believed in bringing change to the territories, but now he was like any other minion of the Empire — as soon as he began losing face, he was quick to curl his fists.

"As guardian of the Western American Territories, I will not tolerate the spread of the Viper's vile disease." Crown Prince Katsura signaled to Major Endo. "Bring them forward."

Them? thought Ren.

Major Endo escorted not one but three prisoners from the helicopter and toward Crown Prince Katsura. Hoods covered their heads, and handcuffs restrained their hands behind their backs. Ren leaned forward, trying to figure out who these "criminals" were. None of them looked thick enough to be his father, but he couldn't rule out Marty just yet.

Crown Prince Katsura ordered the criminals to kneel before lifting the hood of the first prisoner, revealing a young Caucasian woman with auburn hair and a broken nose. She wasn't Marty, though, and Ren released a pent-up breath.

"Alma Palmer, you are charged with offering refuge to members of the Resistance. For these crimes you are sentenced to death," said the crown prince. Then he said to Major Endo, "Go ahead."

Major Endo stepped behind Alma and pressed her fingers against the young woman's scalp. Alma opened her mouth, but whatever she planned to say never exited her lips. There was a crunch and a spurt of blood, and her body slumped onto the cliff. It was over within seconds.

The proceedings carried on. The Empire didn't want to waste any time.

Crown Prince Katsura un-hooded the next victim, a quivering lump of an elderly Asian man with precious few teeth. He cringed in the sunlight, as if he hadn't seen the daytime in weeks.

Ren stared at the man until something clicked in his head. It was the gardener from his bunkroom, the same one who had called Ren's mom a traitor. Ren paled at the realization. He never thought the old man deserved to die.

"Harold Nguyen, you are charged with redistributing the words of the Viper. For this crime you are sentenced to death," said Crown Prince Katsura.

Harold wheezed. "My wife —" he began, right as Major Endo placed her hands atop his head. Harold made a gurgled sound and a gasp, and then his face broke from within, like a puzzle shattering.

Ren felt ill at the terrible sight. He didn't even know if the charges against Harold were true. The old man had been caught with one of the Viper's essays, but that didn't mean he had been distributing them. Hugging his sides, Ren hoped he could slip out of the room, but one of the soldiers was blocking the door.

The cameras panned back to the crown prince, who looked a little green himself, but that didn't stop him from moving on to the last criminal. Ren shut his eyes. He was done with this broadcast. But his eyes flew open as he heard multiple gasps in the common room.

The crown prince had pulled off the last hood, revealing the third criminal.

Ren went cold all over. *It can't be him. This can't be happening.*

It was Jay on the screen, dressed in a gray jumpsuit like the one Daisy Montgomery had worn. Bruises covered his face, and his bottom lip was swollen and bloodied.

The room tilted sideways, and Ren stumbled into the maid in front of him, who threw him a frosty glare. He leaned back against the wall, his chest constricting. He'd seen Jay just hours before, down the hall from here. They were supposed to rendezvous after dinner with Fräulein Plank and discuss their next steps.

But now Jay was on the cliffs and he was going to die. And there was nothing Ren could do to save him.

Crown Prince Katsura continued. "Jay Park, you are charged with supporting the Viper and funding his efforts." He turned to Major Endo. "Open his mouth."

Major Endo forced Jay's mouth open and yanked his lip downward, showing the tattoo that marked Jay a traitor. Somehow the soldiers had discovered it.

A sudden fear cloaked Ren's heart. The crown prince's men had likely spent hours questioning Jay last night, and Jay could have leaked intel about the mission — or coughed up Ren's or Fräulein Plank's names. Trembling, Ren glanced at the soldiers in the common room. Would he be next on the cliffs? But the soldiers weren't paying Ren any attention. For now.

"I sentence you to death for these crimes," said Crown Prince Katsura.

Jay raised his blackened eyes to the camera. There was no trace of his usual smirk. He looked like a bombed-out shell of his old self, which made Ren want to curl into a ball on the floor. He didn't want to watch what would happen next, but Ren didn't want to hide while Jay met his end. He owed this much to him — they were allies, they were friends.

Major Endo walked behind Jay, but before she could rest her fingertips on his skull, Jay cried out.

"The Viper lives on! In the darkest of nights, we strike!" he shouted, his voice hoarse from the effort. "In the darkest of nights —"

Major Endo wrapped her hands around Jay's neck, and within seconds Jay started gurgling. Soon, his face changed color from pink to a burning red, and his eyes turned a gruesome scarlet, the color of an open wound.

Ren realized in horror what was happening. Major Endo wasn't crushing Jay's bones. She was using her dual power, the more gruesome one by far — boiling blood.

In the end, Jay didn't scream, but the sounds he made were ones that Ren would never forget. The muffled moans of pain. The last splutters of life.

The broadcast went quiet before Crown Prince Katsura spoke one more time. "To the Viper, come forward and account for your crimes. The blood of those who perished today is on your hands and yours alone. And those who support you will continue to die until you turn yourself in."

The television screen slowly faded to black, replaced by the Viper's Wanted poster. Nobody said a word while they exited the common room. Four public executions in less than a week — that hadn't happened since Imperial Japan's takeover after the war. As Ren shuffled along with the others, it took him a minute to realize that he was walking in the wrong direction, but he didn't care.

Keep moving, Ren told himself. He wandered from corridor to corridor until he saw the janitorial closet where he had first met Jay. That was when his shock twisted into guilt, and a spark of anger ignited inside him. Before it could spread, Ren barreled toward the employee lounge outside. He needed fresh air. He had to clear his head.

"There you are," a voice slithered into Ren's ear. "I've been looking for you."

Ren froze in the middle of the hall. Before he could turn around, Sasaki grabbed his arm and yanked him across the bleached linoleum floor. It took everything inside Ren not to twist away and make a run for it. He couldn't deal with any more of Sasaki's taunts, but Sasaki was hauling him toward the hotel lobby.

"Don't drag your feet. There's someone who wants to talk to you," said Sasaki, tightening his grip until pain shot down Ren's arm.

Ren's wrath gave way to fear. "Who wants to speak with me, Sasaki-sama?"

"Just shut your mouth."

Ren almost tripped. This was bad news. *Very* bad news. Had Jay let something slip during his interrogation? And yet Sasaki didn't drag Ren into a back room for questioning. They marched toward the lobby elevators instead, which soared skyward to the hotel's upper levels. Sasaki swiped his ID on the card reader, and the nearest elevator doors pinged open. After shoving Ren inside, Sasaki punched his knuckle on the button that accessed the twelfth and highest floor of the Mission Hotel, the penthouse.

Ren began to sweat. Where was Sasaki taking him? The penthouse was the royal apartment. Did the crown prince have his own interrogation room up there?

As the elevator whooshed upward, Ren felt dizzy. Something wasn't adding up. If Jay had mentioned Ren's name during his interrogation, then the soldiers should have arrested Ren hours earlier. The Empire would have sent a troop of soldiers to take Ren into custody, too, instead of Sasaki alone.

The elevator opened into a small foyer, covered from floor to ceiling in white marble. There was a set of heavy doors opposite the elevator, but to walk through them Ren would have to deal with the four armed guards who blocked his path. They demanded to see his employee badge before they roughly patted him down. Sasaki watched the proceedings with a satisfied sneer.

"He's clean," a guard announced, and knocked twice on the double doors.

Seconds passed, and Ren couldn't feel his fingers. He didn't know what he'd find on the other side of those doors. It could've been an interrogation room or a torture chamber or something worse, like a locked room with only Major Endo to keep him company.

One of the doors opened, and the soldiers all fell into a bow. Ren couldn't believe who stood in the crack of the doorway. He almost forgot to bow himself.

Aiko regarded him coolly. Then, with a slight tilt of the head, she opened the door farther to let him in. Ren stood dumbly for a few more seconds until Sasaki gave him a push from behind.

With no other choice, Ren stepped into the royal apartment.

15

As soon as Ren stepped over the threshold the guards shut the door behind him with a thunk. Ren's head whipped around, ready for an attack, but there were no interrogators waiting for him in the large white room. From what he could see, it was only Aiko and himself. No soldiers. No servants. And that was very odd.

Aiko stepped toward a hand-carved table at the center of the room, surrounded by plump sitting pillows. Ren hurriedly took off his shoes, as was customary. He didn't see any slippers to slide his feet into, though — even if he did, those slippers wouldn't have been meant for the hired help like him — so he shuffled forward on socked feet.

The room was sparsely furnished, but each piece of art and furniture looked meticulously selected and incredibly expensive. The table and *tansu* cabinets must have been centuries old, and the scrolls of calligraphy hanging on the walls could have belonged in the national museum in Tokyo. Warm sunlight splashed through a bank of windows overlooking the Pacific, offering a view so blue and vast that Ren couldn't tell where the sea ended and the sky began.

This had to be the royal family's receiving room, where the crown prince and crown princess would entertain visiting relatives or their most distinguished guests. The family's private apartment probably lay beyond the closed wooden door, where only close family and servants could gain entrance.

"You must be wondering why you're here," Aiko started off. She wore a casual silk blouse and a floor-length skirt, but Ren still felt woefully underdressed next to her. "I know it's unusual, but I wanted to thank you for fixing my dress the other night."

"It was my honor, Your Imperial Highness," Ren said, still baffled. Royalty like Aiko didn't have to thank a worker personally, much less invite Ren to the royal receiving room. This had to mean that Aiko had summoned Ren for another reason — but what? Ren resisted the urge to chew his nails and said, "May I offer my congratulations on your engagement?"

Aiko didn't reply. Instead, she glanced out the windows. "It's a little warm. Let's get some fresh air." She stepped toward the glass door and threw it open, with her skirt billowing around her legs. It was clear that she expected Ren to come with her.

Ren had no idea what was going on. All he knew was that he had severely underestimated Aiko. To the cameras she looked and acted the part of royalty, but that was only a mask that she had learned how to wear. There was something simmering beneath her surface. What that was exactly, Ren didn't know.

They entered a half-circle balcony overlooking the sea. The wind thrashed against their skin, but Aiko didn't seem to care or notice. She walked forward until her waist hit the metal railing, but Ren hung back by the door. Down the coast he could see the white killing cliffs, where Jay had died not even thirty minutes before. Jay's body was still warm, and yet here was Ren now, standing in Crown Prince Katsura's private apartment. Pain sliced through his chest. If the crown prince stepped onto the balcony right now, Ren didn't know what he would do.

"Are you unwell?" said Aiko.

Ren shook his head, realizing that his fury must have shown on his face. "I'm not the best with heights."

"We don't need to stand so close to the railing." She retreated from the rails and drifted into the corner of the balcony where an artist's easel stood. A watercolor was clipped to it, a swirl of bold blues and moody grays and an angry black line. It was an abstract piece, but it reminded Ren of a sea storm.

"I forgot to take that in," Aiko said absently. She started to unclip the paper, but a gust of wind swooped onto the balcony and yanked the piece from her fingertips. Ren made a grab for it, but the paper tumbled through the air like a lost kite before disappearing below.

Ren watched the paper fly out to sea. "I'm so sorry, Your Imperial Highness."

Aiko, however, didn't appear alarmed. She looked defeated. "I've been meaning to pack up that easel anyway."

Ren considered what she meant by that. Was she packing it away for her pending move to Berlin? Or was she packing it up because she had to become a proper wife?

Aiko turned to stare at the ocean, her eyes as stormy as her watercolor. "There used to be an art conservatory a few miles down the coast, but it was closed after the war. Have you heard of it?"

"I don't believe I have, Your Imperial Highness," Ren said. He glanced nervously at the glass door. If Aiko's parents discovered them out here, there would be a lot of questions and accusations that he wouldn't be able to answer. But he couldn't leave until Aiko dismissed him.

"It was an art conservatory that only accepted female students. Women from all over the old United States would study there. Figure drawing. Oil painting. Watercolors." Hope laced through her words, but then the corners of her mouth tightened. She returned to the railing and gripped the cold metal, reminding Ren of an animal stuck inside a cage. "You know, I've heard all my life how backward America used to be, but when I learned about this conservatory I had to wonder."

"Wonder what?" Ren said before he could stop himself. He started to apologize for being so forward, but to his surprise she answered him.

"About a lot of things," she said vaguely.

It sounded like Aiko was speaking another language. She shouldn't be praising the old America, and she shouldn't have painted dissidents' names onto a beaded necklace. And she never should have revealed any of this to a tailor. More questions popped into Ren's head. Would she try to break her engagement? What was she hoping to accomplish? And if she didn't see the US as a backward country, then how exactly did she view it?

Ren, however, couldn't ask her any of that — and what did it matter? He had a job to do at the Fortress, and he would have to kidnap Aiko no matter what. But guilt tugged at Ren for the first time. Aiko was no longer a faceless princess — she was a girl made of flesh and blood and bone who painted dangerous names on glass beads, who was bound to a duty she didn't want, and who had been a pawn to be married off since the day she was born. Ren couldn't rummage a heart full of sympathy for her situation — Aiko had never gone hungry and she never had to fear the killing cliffs — but his guilt stubbornly remained. For some reason, Aiko had opened up to him, but he was going to use her like a pawn, too.

Aiko turned around and stared straight at Ren. He shifted nervously under her eye contact, but she wouldn't let go. "I summoned you here because I am commissioning a dress."

Ren blinked. "Pardon?"

"I need you to make me a dress," she said again. "I've already chosen the fabric and sketched out what I want." She reached for a small paper bag under the easel and held it out for him to take. "I have everything you need right here, including my sketch and measurements."

Ren stared down at his socked feet. This was the last thing he had expected to hear out of Aiko's mouth. He wondered all over again if this was a trick, and he struggled with what he should say. "I'm only a temporary hire. Ms. Clarke has more experience than I do and —"

Aiko ignored his protests. "I need the dress finished by tomorrow evening."

"*Tomorrow?*"

"Yes, tomorrow *evening*," she repeated, her tone brooking no argument. "When you're finished, put the dress back into this bag and leave it in Classroom Five B. That room isn't being used, and I'll have one of my staff pick it up." She spat out her directions as if she had been rehearsing them. "I think it's understood that this conversation stays between us?"

"But, Your Imperial Highness —" Ren started, then stopped. He began to realize that Aiko was serious about commissioning a new dress from him — this wasn't some ploy — but even then he had no time to create an outfit by her deadline. Why did she need another outfit right before the ball? And yet he couldn't turn down a royal request, no matter how preposterous the terms. Aiko could have him jailed for insubordination, and Ren felt foolish for feeling sorry for her a minute ago. He gave a small nod.

And then Aiko went and surprised him again. "Thank you," she said. "I know this request is unconventional, but I had no one else to ask." She reached for the door handle. "I can see you out."

Ren left the penthouse the same way he had come in, out the apartment's double doors and through the foyer, but it felt like he had aged a year. As the elevator doors closed, Ren slipped a hand into the bag and pulled out a corner of fabric wrapped in delicate silver paper. It was yard upon yard of creamy ivory silk. No pattern, no design, merely a blank canvas.

Resting his forehead against the elevator wall, Ren sighed. He didn't have time to make Aiko a dress from scratch, but he had to do it. He didn't know why she needed it by tomorrow evening, but he didn't have another choice. And he couldn't figure out the princess at all — what she was planning or what she wanted to accomplish. All he knew was that she had dragged him into her plans, and like it or not, he could only hope that it wouldn't backfire on him.

The day marched on and Ren tried to march along with it, but he couldn't find his rhythm. His thoughts were too crowded with Aiko's sketch and Stairwell 15 and Jay's execution, and if he could, he would shut off the lights and sleep for a week. But he had to push forward and he had to keep his hands busy, so he tackled the dress uniforms at his workstation one by one, taking in shirtwaists and shortening pant hems until the rest of the workers left for the night.

Ren didn't leave his own station, though; he had to start on Aiko's secret dress. She had sketched a simple enough design — a sleeveless A-line gown that cinched at the waist before flowing into a skirt that reached the floor — but it would take days of work that Ren didn't have. Figuring he would have to forgo sleep for the night, Ren wheeled out a spare dress form and marked out a silhouette with drape tape before he began pinning the muslin. If his dad were here, he would chide Ren's sloppy work, but Ren wasn't worried about perfection. He needed to get this dress done and refocus on the mission. There was so much to adjust now that Jay was gone. Just remembering the afternoon execution made Ren pinch the bridge of his nose to fight off tears. He couldn't believe that only twenty-four hours had passed since he heard Jay call him "tailor boy" and wish him good night.

Ren jumped in his chair when someone cleared their throat behind him. He had been so busy with the muslin that he hadn't heard anyone walk in.

"Didn't you get my note?" said Fräulein Plank, tapping the toe of her velvet shoe against the floor. "I left it at your workstation this afternoon."

Irritation sliced through Ren and he set down his pins. "No, I didn't get your note."

"I asked you to meet me in my office half an hour ago. There's a

145

lot we have to talk about." She peered at his dress form and frowned. "This isn't a dress uniform. I know you can't be finished with the cadets."

Ren's annoyance doubled while he shoved the dress form into a rarely used closet. His day had dragged on far too long, and he didn't have a scrap of patience left. "You wanted to talk? Let's talk."

Plank regarded him coolly, and Ren realized that this was the first time they were speaking to each other not as employer and employee, but as collaborators within the Resistance. But after Jay's death, Fräulein Plank was all he had within the Fortress.

"Did you watch the broadcast?" Plank said finally.

"Of course. It was mandatory." Ren tasted bitterness on his tongue. He would never forget Jay's last moments. "Do you know how Jay got arrested in the first place?"

Before Plank replied, she walked over to a nearby dress rack to examine a uniform hanging there, inspecting the collar of the shirt and putting on a show for the security guards who might have been watching. "From what I heard, the soldiers raided his poker game last night. They probably ransacked the place and did a search on everyone. That must have been how they found his tattoo."

A tattoo with my words, Ren thought bleakly. If he had never written that essay, then Jay could still be here. If he had never become the Viper, then both Jay and Daisy Montgomery might be alive.

No, Ren told himself swiftly. *Don't go down that path.* But it was too late for that. The guilt he felt made it hard to breathe.

"What will happen to Jay's family?" Ren asked.

"I'm sure your cousin will help them with food and rent."

"Money won't be enough." He knew what Jay's mother and sisters would face. The shock. The grief. The rage that they would have to swallow because there would never be any justice for Jay as long as the Empire ruled. It was the same thing he had gone through after his mom was executed, and he wished he could tell them that eventually everything would be all right if they simply hung on. But he couldn't tell them that — because it would be a lie. He knew first-hand that nothing would feel normal again.

Plank pinched the button on a dress jacket between her fingers, tugging to ensure it had been fastened properly. "We'll mourn him when the mission is done. Do I have to remind you that the ball is less than forty-eight hours away?"

Ren wrestled the jacket from her grip before she popped off the button that he would need to mend. "Do you even care that he's dead?"

Her eyes went frigidly cold. "You think that I don't?"

"Could've fooled me," countered Ren.

She pushed her glasses up the bridge of her nose, her movements sharp and rigid. "Jay and I had been working together for months before you came on board." Her voice had lowered into a growl. "But I can't let what happened to him stop me from completing this mission. Go ahead and sulk if you want."

"Do you see me quitting?" Ren's fury doubled inside him, and his tone turned mocking. "I'm sorry for worrying about Jay's family. I'm sorry that I can't stop thinking about how he died."

"Don't lecture me," Plank warned. "I've lost far more than you can ever imagine."

That set Ren off. "You're a Nazi citizen. Have you ever gone to bed hungry? Has your house ever been ransacked because the soldiers got bored? What have you lost aside from your best friend?" Ren knew that he should cool off, but his rage was boiling over and he was too raw to stop it. So he let it ignite; he let it burst. And he let Plank bear the brunt of it all. "I watched my own mother get executed in front of me, and I live in constant fear that the Empire will do the same thing to my dad because he was married to a so-called traitor. So forgive me if I don't believe you, *Fräulein*."

Plank's chest heaved at his tirade, but she didn't meet his fire with her own. With her hands clenched, she said, "You don't want to play this game with me. I've lost every single person I love. Every single one. But getting angry and yelling about it won't get me anywhere — it'll get me arrested." There was a threat in her voice, but it was calculated and restrained. "You know, I told Marty that I don't think you're cut out for this job, and you're proving me right."

Ren exploded. Years of tamped-down fury demanded an outlet. With his cheeks burning, he grabbed his chair and threw it against the wall. But it didn't make him feel any better. All his life he had struggled for breath in the Empire's noose — bowing to the soldiers and swallowing his humiliation and saying nothing at all when his mother was ripped out of his life. Or when his dad let their home be ransacked again and again. All the while the royal family lived in luxury, throwing their parties while millions suffered beyond their gilded windows. He turned his attention to the crown princess's dress forms. If only he could destroy them the way that they had destroyed his family.

But as he neared the crown princess's banquet gown, Plank

yanked his wrist with surprising strength, forcing Ren to turn around and face her. She clamped down tighter and stepped dangerously close to him. "Pack your bags," she said, looking him dead in the eye. "Go home. Obviously that's where you'd rather be."

"Don't tell me what I want," Ren seethed. "You can't pull off this mission without me."

Plank glared at him again. "You're not worth the risk. You almost tore the crown princess's wardrobe to pieces just because you couldn't control your temper."

Ren's rage deflated at the steel in her voice. She was right. He had been seconds away from destroying it — but what would that have accomplished? Shame painted Ren's cheeks red. If Plank hadn't stopped him, he would have gotten himself fired and jeopardized the mission. Maybe annihilated it entirely.

Grudglingly, Ren stepped back.

No amount of screaming would bring Jay back to life. The only thing left for Ren to do was to finish what Jay had helped start — and he needed a level head to accomplish that.

"Sorry," Ren said to Plank through clenched teeth. "I . . . I messed up."

Her mouth puckered at his apology, as if she had tasted something sour. But she nodded once and adjusted her glasses. "You can't let that happen again."

"I won't," Ren said, picking up his chair. It was a miracle no one had run into the sewing room to find out what was going on.

"You'd better not," Plank said doubtfully. "We have to focus on the ball, and we need a new escape route."

Ren leaned against the door, exhaustion seeping into his bones.

His anger had quieted and lurked away to its corner, but he could still feel it there. He didn't know if he would ever get rid of it. He could only lock it away or channel it into his essays, which he couldn't do inside the Fortress. Ren sighed.

"I don't know if we can find a new route," he said wearily. "I found a possible lead last night but —"

"I know. Jay filled me in, and I think I may have a lead, too."

Ren stared at her. "You do?"

"I was going to tell you before you started throwing things," she sniffed. "I've never heard about a Stairwell Fifteen, but I have seen a Stairwell Eleven."

The muscles in Ren's jaw slowly eased. He'd always thought he had decent control over his emotions, but it appeared that Plank could teach him a thing or two. "Where is this Stairwell Eleven?"

"I'll show you."

"Now?"

She tapped her finger on her watch. "When else? Come on, you should see this."

16

Ren followed Plank's lead. She strode out of the workers' wing, across the lobby, and toward the cluster of classrooms where the cadets learned arithmetic, studied the sciences, and spouted rhetoric that pledged their loyalty to the Chrysanthemum Throne. Plank stepped inside what looked like a chemistry laboratory and zigzagged through the tables toward the storage closet in the back.

With a flip of the light, Plank revealed a cramped room crammed with metal bookshelves, each shelf piled high with beakers, goggles, papers, and aprons. A white wall peeked through the open shelves, and Plank pointed to some faded lettering there.

"See?" She nudged aside a pile of worksheets and trailed a finger along the words. *Stairwell 11.* "It's in English. It must date back to when the hotel was first built."

Ren scanned the rest of the wall and saw the faint outline of a doorway next to the letters. "I think there's an old door here."

Together, they shimmied the heavy bookshelf forward, just far enough for Plank to stick her head in the gap. "I see it. There's a handle, but it's locked." She popped her head back out and pointed to the closet corner. "Hand me that fire extinguisher. I'll try to break the lock."

Ren handed her the extinguisher, and Plank got to work, giving the lock a few strong smacks until he heard it give way. Once they moved the shelf even farther, they squeezed into the gap and Plank switched on the small flashlight on her key ring.

Yanking the door open, she said, "I see a staircase. Watch your step."

Plank led the way down a creaky set of metal stairs, some of which had gone missing, and that made Ren clutch the rusted railing. They plunged into a thick darkness and an eerie silence, punctuated only by their footsteps and the soft drip of water pinging somewhere down below. Step by step, they trudged down a flight of stairs until their soles hit solid ground again. Plank swept the flashlight around them, but the dark swallowed most of the feeble light.

"I should've brought three of these lights," she muttered.

They found themselves standing in an open space, about the size of the classroom they had left behind, with two tunnels to their left and right, both of them wide enough and tall enough for Ren to walk through.

"Wonder what these tunnels were built for," he said.

Plank's flashlight hovered over an ancient-looking sign that had been nailed to the tunnel's wall. A green sludge dripped from its corners, but Ren could make out the worn characters.

"I think it says, 'Attention, students.'" He continued reading, translating from the Japanese. "'Your radios will not work underground. If you get lost, stay where you are and an instructor will locate you after the training run.'" He glanced over to Plank. "Maybe the cadets did drills down here, but for some reason they stopped."

"Tunnel collapse?" Plank said bluntly.

"Don't joke about that."

"I was being serious. We'd better be careful."

With that thought haunting him, Ren gingerly moved into a tunnel. It stank of ripening rot, and Ren's shoes became coated with a slick slime. The farther they ventured, the more his hope dimmed. The laundry chute escape route had been much simpler — grab Aiko, rappel down the chute, crawl through a vent system that led outside, and hop away in the getaway car that Plank would be driving. Even if he could find an exit point somewhere in this sublevel, Ren would have a tough time bringing Aiko down here and through the tunnels, all without getting caught. But he would have to figure something out.

"There's a light up there," said Ren, squinting. Not far ahead, he saw a shaft of moonlight, so faint that he'd nearly missed it.

"I see it, too," said Plank.

Ren upped his pace, then slowed again when he neared the circle of light. He craned his head back to find its source and found himself staring up a narrow shaft that climbed up toward a street grate.

"That," said Ren, pointing skyward, "could be promising. If we can get up there."

Fräulein Plank craned her head back, too. "We have to find out where that grate leads. Do you see those rungs on the inside of the shaft? I might be able to grab the lowest one, but I'll need a boost."

True enough, Ren spotted a column of iron bars that were bolted to the side of the shaft — a makeshift ladder that looked dangerous on a good day and deadly on every other. Yet the shaft had to be explored. "I can climb it."

"This isn't the time to be chivalrous," retorted Plank. "*I'll* go up. I don't have the strength to hoist you that far anyway." She didn't wait for him to agree; she just placed her hands on his shoulders. "Boost me."

Ren decided not to fight her on this. Stooping down, he laced his fingers together for Plank's foot and slowly straightened his knees to his full height. After a few tries, she grasped the lowest iron bar and made a grab for the next rung. With a few winces and grunts, Ren lifted her up higher until she found her footing and climbed into the shadows.

"See anything?" Ren said, the sound echoing up the shaft.

"Let me come down and we'll talk." Plank made her way back down, and Ren guided her to the floor. "There's a rain grate that goes over this shaft. It looks like we're right next to one of the new barracks under construction, which is good news because the video cameras haven't been installed there yet."

Ren realized that he had been holding his breath. "Do you think this could be our new escape route?"

"We can make it work. I can take Kato's car around to meet you here on the night of the ball. We'll use the same plan as before. Once Aiko gets sick, I'll let you into the apartment and we'll move her into the laundry cart. From there, we'll split up. I'll go get Kato's car while you get her through the tunnels."

"I'll have to carry her here and get her up the shaft," Ren said, mostly to himself. That would have been much more doable with Jay's help, but obviously, Jay wouldn't be around to lend a hand.

"You can hoist her over your shoulders to carry her. Take a couple of breaks if you need to." She sounded more confident in Ren's abilities than he was. It wasn't like he carried royal princesses from point A to point B on a regular basis, but he was taller than Aiko by at least a foot, so he did have a height advantage. "But getting her up the shaft will be tricky. I could throw down a couple of ropes to you after I pry open the grate. You can wrap one around Aiko's waist, and I'll pull you up first. Then we'll both get Aiko up and out."

"What if she falls?"

Plank glared at him. "She won't because we won't drop her."

"Just trying to cover our bases. I mean —"

Suddenly, Plank clamped a hand over Ren's mouth and clicked off her flashlight. Ren choked down the rest of his sentence, and his head whipped around in the darkness. Had someone followed them?

Plank switched the flashlight on again. "I heard something!" she whispered.

Ren caught her by the elbow. "We should head back. We found what we came for."

"It sounded like someone was crying for help — in *English*." She tugged her elbow from his grasp and disappeared down the tunnel, taking their lone light source with her.

"Plank!" Ren hissed, but she didn't turn around and he didn't want to get trapped in the darkness. Groaning, he began running, too.

They veered left, then right, then right again, but Plank wouldn't stop. Ren was about to tell her that this was useless, but then he heard something, too.

"*Please.*" The voice was faint and hazy. And female.

Plank beckoned to Ren. "Cabot! Come see this."

Ren stumbled in the dark, groping the slick walls for support. The tunnel narrowed and forced him into a crawl, but soon the tunnel's surface changed — from old rusted metal to dry concrete. The concrete scratched Ren's palms, and he realized the Fortress's sublevel was much bigger than he had ever imagined. Up ahead, Plank had climbed inside an even smaller tunnel, barely big enough to fit Ren's body if he slithered on his stomach.

Plank whispered, "Look."

"We shouldn't be here," Ren whispered back.

"There's someone down there." She stared down an air vent and into a darkened room. "It looks like a prison cell."

That definitely got Ren's attention. The hairs on the back of his neck prickled as he inched forward. He heard the voice again.

"Is anyone there? You have to help me —" The girl fell silent as footsteps approached her cell.

A door swung open and lights illuminated the cell, giving Ren a good look around. It was a metal box, not much wider than the span of his arms. The filthy floors looked like they hadn't been mopped in a decade, a striking contrast to the shiny metal rails of the hospital bed that occupied the majority of the cell. A prisoner lay upon that bed. She wore gray coveralls, like the ones that Daisy and Jay had been wearing when they were executed. One of her sleeves had been rolled up to accommodate an IV needle in the crook of her arm.

Ren tried to get a closer look at the prisoner. She was a slip of a thing, all bones and sickly pale skin. Her dark hair covered her face as she whispered again, "Send . . . help."

A doctor in a white coat approached the bed and changed out the IV bag before he checked the girl's vitals, ignoring her pleas while he listened to her heartbeat and flashed a light down her throat.

The girl tried to pull away from his touch, but her wrists and ankles had been anchored with metal restraints. A large leather belt ran across her stomach, too, securing her in place, but the girl fought against it anyway.

"Relax!" the doctor commanded.

A strange breeze suddenly whipped through the cell and scratched Ren's forehead with ice-cold fingers. He touched his cheek. That breeze had come out of nowhere.

When the girl kept thrashing, the doctor sank a syringe into her IV. The bag's clear liquid soon swirled with black tendrils, as dark as octopus ink. The girl whimpered. Her hands fell slack and her legs went still. The doctor scribbled notes onto a pad from his pocket, mumbling to himself before he left the room and turned the locks on the door one by one.

At last, the girl's head lolled back. Her eyes were closed and her hair covered half her face, but Ren didn't need to see any more to realize who was lying on that bed.

His breath abandoned him.

"Is that . . . is that her?" whispered Plank.

Ren could only nod. There lay the one person more famous than even the Viper.

The Empire had captured Zara St. James.

17

Ren tilted his head toward Plank. "Zara St. James?" he mouthed.

She nodded shakily, without speaking. Ren had never seen her look so startled. "How did they find her?"

Ren didn't know. Deputy Führer Forst had told the crown prince that the Nazis were tracking Zara's movements along the border, but Ren never thought that Zara would get caught. Let alone by Imperial Japan.

Staring through the grate again, Ren flinched at how helpless Zara looked, strapped down and unconscious. He grimly considered what the Empire had planned for her. Zara was one of the most powerful Anomalies in both territories, possessing two terrifying powers — the ability to manipulate the air and create lighting bolts in her hands. So it was strange that Crown Prince Katsura had kept Zara at the Fortress instead of locking her up in Alcatraz or turning her over to the Nazis. The Empire knew how desperate the Nazis were to find her, but the crown prince might have kept her as a political pawn. After all, he had bargained off his daughter to seal the V2 deal with the Germans and he needed a new piece of leverage — and maybe that was Zara.

A sick feeling roiled in Ren's stomach. Did Crown Prince Katsura plan on experimenting on her, too?

Plank bumped shoulders with Ren. "We have to go. We can't get caught here."

"What about Zara, though?"

"We can't exactly take her with us."

Ren didn't move. How could they leave her like this? "We need to talk."

Plank pursed her lips into a flat line. "Fine, but not here."

Together, they wound their way back the way they came, with their lone flashlight leading every move. They climbed the staircase to the main floor and slipped back into the storage closet. Once Ren pushed the bookshelf back into place, he sat down on a pile of textbooks, right there in the closet. He didn't want to wait any longer to discuss what they had seen.

"What are we going to do about Zara St. James?" he said.

Shutting the closet door, Plank hushed him even though he had whispered. "It isn't our job to save her. Our mission is to kidnap Aiko. Period." She refused to sit down next to him, opting to use the time to straighten her blouse and reposition the bobby pins in her hair, repairing her professional armor.

"Who says we can't do both — kidnap Aiko and rescue Zara? We can't leave her in that room to rot, and we don't know if the Empire will move her to another facility. This could be our only chance."

Plank tackled her glasses next, wiping the lenses with a handkerchief from her pocket. "Think about what you're proposing. There are only two of us embedded inside the Fortress, and even if Jay were alive, our chances of kidnapping Aiko and making it out of the hotel have always been middling. And I can guarantee you that our chances will go down to nothing if we decide to break out Zara, too. It'll be suicide." She slipped her glasses back on and a sanctimonious tone to go with it. "Look, Cabot. We have a job to do. I can relay what we saw tonight to your cousin, and she can alert the Revolutionary Alliance that we know Zara's whereabouts. We have to leave it up to the Alliance to free her."

"It could take weeks for them to put a plan together. Probably months," said Ren, wishing she would at least see his point.

Plank rolled her eyes. "You're welcome to have a go at saving Zara — but only *after* you help me get the princess to the getaway car. You can do whatever you want after that."

"You could be sentencing Zara to death."

"And *you're* forgetting why we're here. Do you want to help the Resistance to break into Alcatraz or not?" Before he could protest, she held up a hand. "I'm not picking a fight with you. Think about the lives on the line."

Her words felt like a slap, but she was right, even though he wasn't ready to say that out loud. They didn't have the manpower or resources to break Zara out from her cell — and they definitely couldn't jeopardize their mission to kidnap Aiko. The princess was the key to infiltrating Alcatraz, freeing the prisoners, and finding out about Ren's mom. Zara may have ignited a revolution, but in this moment, it was her life weighed against a hundred others.

"Fine," Ren said at last. Plank raised her chin in a very I-told-you-so way, but he pressed on. "But you have to tell Marty what we saw here tonight."

"I'll try to meet with her tomorrow when I'm out running errands," Plank conceded. "It's getting late. We'd better go." With that, she rolled her neck back and forth and opened the door, clearly ready for bed.

Ren was a step behind her, but distracted. He could only hope that Zara was strong enough to survive until her Alliance could arrive. She was one of the most powerful Anomalies in the territories, but she was up against the Empire.

They were halfway across the room when Plank froze in front of him. "Get down!" she whispered.

It was too late.

The classroom door swung open, and Ren's pulse took off running. The beam of a flashlight blinded both of their eyes.

"Arms up!" ordered a male voice in Japanese.

Panic choked Ren as his arms flew up over his head. He tried to map out an escape plan — knock the soldier down, make a run for the closest exit — but his gut told him that they'd never get far. They wouldn't get past the first checkpoint.

Plank placed herself between Ren and the flashlight, her own hands lifted high in the air. "Sasaki-sama! It's me. Greta."

Ren's face went white. Of all the soldiers who could have discovered them, it had to be Sasaki.

Sasaki lowered his flashlight but didn't turn it off. "Fräulein Plank? What are you doing here after hours?" His lips curled when he noticed Ren. "And with him?"

"We were discussing the cadet uniforms in my office, and on our way out I thought I heard something in this classroom," Plank said with a nervous laugh. "It must've been some old pipes."

Sasaki regarded her doubtfully. "Why didn't you turn on a light?"

"I — I," Plank stammered. "We were about to leave when you

came in. I know it's a little after curfew, so we'll be on our way." She straightened and smiled. "Thank you for your concern, though. I'm grateful that we have such excellent security at the fort, and I'll be sure to let your superior know."

For a second, Sasaki's chest puffed with pride, and Ren thought that he might let them go. But then Sasaki frowned. "I have to bring you both in for questioning, especially *him*. His mother was a Chinese traitor."

"Sasaki-sama, *please*. This was all a misunderstanding," Plank said, even though Ren figured this was a lost cause. "Look at me. There's no need to bring us in. This was all an innocent mistake."

"It's protocol —"

She stepped forward again, never breaking eye contact with the soldier. "Let us go. You don't want to trouble your commanding officer with such a trivial thing. Don't you agree?" Sasaki tried to look away, but Plank matched his movement to keep their eyes level. "Go back the way you came and forget all of this happened."

Ren's pulse pedaled faster and faster. He wasn't sure what Plank was playing at, and he was pretty sure that she was only making things worse. But then something strange happened.

Sasaki's voice went monotone. "Go back . . . forget this happened . . ."

"You won't mention this to your commanding officer."

"I won't mention this to Sergeant Abe," Sasaki repeated in the same deadened voice.

Plank gave an encouraging smile. "You'd better finish your rounds."

Sasaki blinked sleepily and murmured, "Yes, that sounds right. Good-bye, *Fräulein*." He broke eye contact and turned, swinging his flashlight around and shuffling out the door.

As soon as Sasaki was gone, Ren pulled his arms down slowly, completely unsure of what had happened. All he knew was that what he had seen wasn't natural. It was almost as if . . .

Ren stared at Plank's back. "What did you do to Sasaki?"

"I got him to leave us alone." She didn't turn around to look at him. "You're welcome, by the way."

Ren tried to mutter a thanks, but he was confused.

"His mom is Chinese, too, you know," Plank added, her voice weak. "That's why he has it out for you."

Ren nodded slowly. So that was why Sasaki had taken such an interest in Ren. If Sasaki was half Japanese and half Chinese, then he had probably been taunted ever since he was a kid. Sasaki had probably tried to prove over and over that he was just as Japanese as his schoolmates and his fellow soldiers, but his mother's heritage had dogged him wherever he went.

"But wait, *how* did you get him to back off? It was like —" Ren didn't even know how to formulate what to say next, but before he could try, Fräulein Plank stumbled backward and slumped against him. He grunted as he caught her. "What's wrong?"

"We can't talk here. Let's go" — she was panting now — "to my office. It's down the hall. Fifth door on the right."

Ren struggled to keep her standing. "You should lie down."

"No! What if Sasaki comes back? I can't . . . I can't convince him to leave us alone again when I'm like this."

"Like what? What happened —"

"I said that we can't talk here!" she repeated, sounding desperate. "We have to go to my office. Right now."

Her words came out in staccato, and Ren thought that she might actually faint, but she refused to lie down. Using Ren as a crutch, she pointed him toward her office, unlocked the door, and sank into her desk chair, as if she had run for miles in the searing summer heat.

"Water," she whispered.

Ren unscrewed the glass bottle of water on her desk and held it up to her lips while she gulped down a couple of sips. He had never seen her so vulnerable. The Greta Plank he had come to know always had her hair perfectly pinned into place, could never tolerate a wrinkle in her shirt, and spat out orders as easily as breathing air. But now her bun had unraveled and her makeup had smudged. Her armor had been stripped down, and she was laid bare.

Having no place else to sit, Ren leaned against the desk. There was nothing for him to clear off from the surface — the tabletop was empty aside from a day planner and a pen. Plank obviously kept her workspace impeccably neat and devoid of anything personal. It struck Ren that he knew next to nothing about her — and that was made even more apparent tonight.

"What happened back there?" he said softly.

She swallowed another sip of water and shut her eyes.

"Did you hear me?" Ren pressed.

Her eyes fluttered open, but she wouldn't look at him.

"You need to tell me what's going on." When she still said nothing, Ren bent down toward her. "Are you okay? Plank?"

Finally, she met his gaze. She whispered, "My name isn't Greta Plank."

18

Ren launched to his feet. Out of all the things she could have said, he had never expected *that*. "If you aren't Greta Plank, then who are you?"

Plank rubbed her temples and rummaged through her desk drawer for a bottle of aspirin. "We've actually met before."

"When? I think I'd remember something like that." But a thought niggled at the back of Ren's mind. He remembered thinking that Plank looked familiar during his first job interview, but he had figured he was mixing her up with someone else.

"We were in school at the same time." She tapped out two pills from the aspirin bottle and swallowed them. "You and my little sister, Hannah, sometimes played together at recess."

Neurons fired in Ren's head, connecting dot to dot until it formed a memory. Then the air abandoned his lungs. "Hannah Quirk," he whispered. The family had had three daughters — the youngest was Hannah and the oldest was Sophie. Which left the middle sister. "Tessa?"

She gave a slight nod.

Ren studied her face, and now he remembered. Her nose, her sharp chin — like her father's. The set of her eyes, like her sisters'. But a lot had changed about Tessa, too. The girl that he had known had dark hair instead of blond. She giggled a lot, too, so often that the teachers would paddle her for it. Fräulein Plank, however, had never laughed in front of Ren.

"How . . . what . . ." Ren didn't even know where to start.

So Tessa did it for him. "How did I end up here? What happened to my sisters and me?"

"And —"

"And how did I get Sasaki to back off?" she added bluntly, sounding so much like Tessa.

Ren had to wonder about where Tessa ended and Plank began. It had been years since he and Tessa crossed paths, and somewhere along the line she had gone undercover as a Nazi to work for the Resistance. There was a lot she needed to tell him.

"After our dad was killed and our mom died inside Alcatraz, my sisters and I were sent off to an orphanage on the Oregon coast." Her tone flatlined as she mentioned the execution and she stared at her water bottle, watching a bead drip from the lip. "Sophie didn't survive the trip."

"The fever?" asked Ren. The same one that had nearly killed him.

"Hannah and I gave her our rations, but it wasn't enough. We needed medicine." She laced her fingers together around the bottle, clutching it tight. "When we got to the orphanage, Sophie's lips were blue. The soldiers took her out of the bus, and that was the last time we saw her."

Ren leaned back against the wall with his shoulders slumped. He hadn't known Sophie well, but she had always been kind to him, the sort of girl who would share her lunch with you even if she was starving. "I'm sorry."

"It was years ago now. I'm fine," Plank replied. But she didn't sound like it.

"How long were you at the orphanage?"

"Not long. We were old enough to work, so they farmed us out for work in a hotel on the coast. We did housekeeping there for years. The pay was next to nothing, but Hannah and I pooled our money together." Pain threaded through her words. "We were planning on running away to the colonies in South America. Start over fresh."

That made sense to Ren. Decades prior, the Axis powers had invaded, defeated, and divided the southern continent among themselves to exploit the resources there, like lumber and gold and the fertile fields that grew coffee and cocoa. But the colonies weren't well policed, making them places where you could shed your old identity and slip on a new one.

Tessa's gaze moved from her bottle to a water stain on the wall, a large brown spot opposite her desk, which marred the surrounding white paint. "But after Hannah turned thirteen, she started sneaking out at night after I was asleep. She wouldn't tell me what she was up to, either, which drove me crazy. I thought she had a secret boyfriend or something." She paused. "I wish that had been the case."

"Where was she going?" asked Ren, almost afraid to hear the answer.

"To Resistance meetings. I followed her one night. There was a new cell getting organized, and they were recruiting members. We got into a huge fight after that, but she kept going." Tessa's voice grew thick with emotion. "One night, the soldiers raided the Resistance meeting. Hannah was arrested and sent to an internment camp." She laughed bitterly. "Or a 'reeducation center,' according to the crown prince.'"

"Is she still at the camp?" Ren said grimly.

Tessa shook her head quickly. "She didn't last a month. She tried to make a run for the fence, and you know what happens to people like that. I didn't find out until six weeks later." Anger sliced through her words and she said nothing for a minute. Then she sighed. "A few days after that, I manifested my ability."

Ren could only stare. Tessa Quirk was an Anomaly? He had a hunch that this was coming, but hearing her say it, hearing her admit it, still knocked the air out of his lungs. "How old were you?"

"Sixteen."

"That's how you flew under the Empire's radar," Ren murmured. "So what exactly is your power? Persuasion?"

"Yes, but it's not that simple —"

"Does Marty know what you can do?" The questions were crammed inside Ren's mouth, fighting to be uttered next. "If you can talk people into doing what you want, then can you talk Aiko into coming with us willingly? We could be done with the mission tonight."

"It doesn't work like that!" Tessa blurted as she rubbed her temples harder. She eyed the aspirin bottle and took one more pill. "If I could make the Empire do whatever I wanted, do you really think that we'd be sitting here? I could be talking my way into the royal apartment and telling Crown Prince Katsura to slit his own throat."

"But you told Sasaki to leave us alone and forget what he saw. That's not nothing."

"And you see what it took out of me." She shot him a glare. "I don't have any formal training, remember? If I had teachers like the Ronin cadets, then I could probably do a lot more with my power. But because I've had to learn on my own, my abilities are limited.

"I couldn't tell Sasaki to step off a cliff or drink a cup of poison. I can only convince people to do something that they're inclined to do on their own."

"I doubt Sasaki really wanted to let us go," Ren said, not understanding her.

"No, but it helped that I made eye contact with him. That amplifies my ability, but to be honest, we got lucky that Sasaki found us instead of someone else. He has been hounding me to grab tea or lunch for weeks. That made it a lot easier to convince him to leave because he *wanted* to believe me."

It took Ren a moment to process her explanation. A part of him was disappointed — Tessa's power had so much potential to help them on this mission, but it could only go so far. But it was still a huge asset to have in their arsenal, and it had certainly saved their necks tonight. "I don't think I thanked you for getting Sasaki to back off," he said.

"That might be the first nice thing you've said to me," she said dryly, but her cheeks had flushed with color. She swiftly glanced down at her desk. "Where was I?"

"You were talking about when you first manifested your ability."

"Right." She gathered her thoughts and continued. "I ran away from the hotel to San Francisco. There was nothing left for me there. I scraped by with odd jobs for a while. Saved money. Practiced my ability whenever I could. Dyed my hair." Her fingertips absently touched a stray piece of pale hair that had wiggled itself out of her bun. "I used my savings to buy a fake identity with the name Greta Plank because German citizens can travel around easier. Then I started south."

"But you didn't make it to South America."

Tessa hugged her arms around herself, looking far younger than Plank. "I stopped in White Crescent Bay first. I wanted to see my old house, one last time. It sounds silly, I know."

"No it doesn't," Ren said softly. He hadn't been gone from his apartment for even a week, but he missed everything about it, from the scent of oatmeal simmering on the stove to the loud pipes that jolted him awake at night. Mostly, though, he missed his dad.

"There was a new family at the house," Tessa said, sounding far away, lost in the memory. "They had two little kids. Both girls. I watched them walk together to school, holding hands, like Sophie and Hannah and I used to do. And for the first time in a long time, I let myself remember what it was like to be part of a family, before the Empire took it all away." She took off her glasses to clean the lenses again, but Ren noticed her wiping her tears away, too. "My bus wasn't leaving until that evening, so I walked around town to fill up the time. I passed by our old school and I walked by your shop." She looked up at him. "I'm sorry about your mom. I always liked her. One time Hannah got the flu and she brought over a big pot of rice porridge."

His mother's congee, Ren realized. The recipe had been passed down through her family for generations, and his mom used to make it whenever Ren or his dad got sick. He could almost smell the dish now, creamy and salty and easy on the stomach. He hadn't eaten it in years, not since his mom died. Her death had created a crater in Ren's chest, but he couldn't imagine what Tessa had lost. Her parents. Her sisters. Her home. Everything. If that had happened to him, Ren probably would have given up. But something had pushed Tessa to keep fighting, or else she wouldn't be sitting here in front of him.

"Why didn't you keep going south?" he asked.

"I'd planned to. But before my bus pulled up, I got a copy of the newspaper to check the forecast, but something was tucked inside the pages. An essay."

Ren shifted uncomfortably. He knew the Viper had a wide readership, but it was still weird for him when people he knew — Marty, Jay, and now Tessa — broached the topic. He always felt like he was lying to them somehow, and in a way he was.

"It was by the Viper. The one that talked about how we can't remain complacent."

"I remember that one," murmured Ren.

"The bus pulled up and I couldn't make myself get on board," Tessa continued, staring off at the water stain again as she recited something from memory. *"Every American needs to ask ourselves these questions. What do you do when your neighbors get arrested? What do you say when the patrols pillage the house down the street? How many times have you said to yourself, 'But they deserved to be punished. They knew the rules.' Complacency comes with a price — in the form of internment camps, of comfort women, of live executions up on the cliffs. Complacency fuels the Empire."*

Ren knew those words well. He had spent days revising the essay again and again, switching out one noun for another and frowning at the syntax. He had wanted to get the piece just right — it was yet another nod to his mother.

"I was mad at my parents for so long," Tessa said, her eyes bright with new tears. "If they had followed the rules, then they'd be alive and we'd all be together. But they wanted a better world for my sisters and me, and they lost their lives because they refused to be complacent. Now I'm the only one left, and the only one who remembers what they fought for." She had to pause to calm herself. "I knew right then I had to find my way into the Resistance. I got a room at a boardinghouse on West Palm Road, and I used my German name to get a part-time position in the Fortress's mail room. Eventually, word got around that Kato was looking for a new assistant, so I applied for that slot. Kato-sama is actually not a bad boss to work for, but I gave him a bowl of the same breakfast soup that Jay had poisoned to knock out the sewing staff. I couldn't have him looking over my shoulder while we moved everything in place."

Ren hadn't known about Kato getting poisoned, too. He had to give it to Tessa for thinking ahead. "How long did it take to get in touch with the Resistance?"

"It took a while to get my foot in the door," she admitted. "I had to do some digging to figure out that Jay was the person to talk to, so I made sure to bump into him and drop hints whenever I could. And I . . ." Her head dipped down. "I may have used my ability on him a little, and I may have done the same with Marty. Don't tell her, okay? But she wasn't quite buying my cover story about how my best friend was killed by her soldier boyfriend."

Ren slowly crossed his arms. "So Marty doesn't know about your power?"

"I haven't told her yet. I should but . . ."

"I understand. I won't say anything." Tessa's secret wasn't Ren's to divulge, and he could see why she hadn't wanted to disclose it. It was the same reason why he had said nothing about moonlighting as the Viper. With a secret that big, where do you even start? You want to keep those around you safe, so you say nothing.

"Thanks," Tessa whispered. "Maybe now you can understand why I'm putting everything into this mission. It's what the Quirks do. It's what my family died for."

"I get it. One of the reasons I signed on to this mission was because of my family, too." He wasn't sure how much Marty had told Tessa about the intel she had discovered about Jenny Tsai. So Ren took a breath and said, "My mom might be alive."

Tessa gaped at him. "Alive? How?"

"There's a chance she survived her execution and was taken to Alcatraz. The Resistance found a partial prisoner list, and my mom's initials were on it."

"I had no idea," she whispered. "I wondered why you signed on to the mission after your dad got hurt."

"I have to find out what happened to her," Ren said quietly.

"Then it's even more important that we focus on getting Aiko. We can't add more variables to the equation."

Ren nodded. They couldn't risk the lives of those American prisoners — including his mom's — to possibly save Zara St. James. He wasn't a gambler like Jay was. "You'll tell Marty, though, about Zara?"

"I will," Tessa said, standing to tuck her blouse into her skirt until it looked perfect. "We should get going. I'll walk you back to the sewing room in case anyone gives you trouble. Stay a few paces behind me." Her lips twitched into the briefest of smiles. "Out of respect for the good *Fräulein*."

They returned to the workers' quarters, but on the way Ren couldn't help but glance at the classroom that led down to the sublevel below. He thought again about Zara, locked away in her cell, pumped full of drugs and begging for help.

With no one coming to save her.

Guilt gnawed at Ren, but he walked on. He hated to admit it, but there was no way he could save Zara St. James.

19

The next day and a half zoomed by in a blur of preparations, and soon the morning of the Joint Prosperity Ball arrived.

Delivery trucks packed the hotel's rear parking lot and were alternately filled with fresh squid on ice, maroon-colored cuts of beef, and embroidered hand towels for each guest to take home. The pastry chefs prepared a buffet of traditional *wagashi* sweets, like crystal sugar candy and steamed cakes shaped into intricate flowers, while the floral team placed fresh arrangements on every flat surface in the hotel — on side tables and antique chests and even the grand piano in the music room. The fresh scent of lilies and roses perfumed the hallways, whose floors had been waxed to a high shine.

Ren, however, didn't have time to enjoy the flowers. His head was still crowded with questions about Fräulein Plank — *Tessa Quirk*, he had to keep reminding himself. He had thought about the Quirk girls once or twice over the years, but he never could've imagined that one of them would become a Resistance spy disguised as a Nazi — and an illegal Anomaly on top of all that. When he managed to stop thinking about Tessa's powers, his mind would inevitably shift to Zara St. James. He kept seeing her hooked up to an IV that pumped strange chemicals into her body. And the guilt hit him all over again.

But Ren forced himself to focus on his duties, not only to the Resistance but to his job and to Aiko. He had staved off sleep to complete her secret commission, but even then the finished product had been far from perfect. There was some puckering along the neckline — his father would've clucked his tongue and told him to start all over again — and he wasn't sure if choosing a Hong Kong seam had been the right choice for the bodice, but the dress was passable and he left it at the drop-off point as Aiko instructed. Yet Ren had to wonder again what she planned on doing with the dress, but he was soon hit with another tornado of alterations and he had to abandon his questions.

As the Joint Prosperity Ball ticked ever closer, Ren squeezed in a few minutes right before lunch to stop by Tessa's office for one last meeting. He found the room mobbed with people — a florist inquiring about a shipment of hydrangea, the band leader asking about where to store the tubas, and a frantic chef panicking over the wilted state of the cucumbers — and Ren had to wait until Tessa could clear the place out.

"Close the door and shut the lights," Tessa said wearily as soon as they were alone. "Or someone else will barge in."

"That busy?" Ren said.

"Since six-thirty this morning." She was looking the part of Fräulein Plank again, and she redid her bun with the usual precision, combing out the bumps and pinning each strand in place. To complete the look, she slid her glasses back on. Ren almost asked if she really needed them to see, but he bit his tongue as she pulled a slim spray bottle from her desk drawer. It was labeled *Starch*. "This is for you. Marty sends her best."

Ren took the bottle from her, handling it with care. It held the liquid sleeping drug that he needed to apply to Aiko's wardrobe. "Will this be enough?"

"It's a full dose, so be sure to use it up. Also, Marty told me to tell you a couple of things. First, she's moving your dad and herself to a safe house today. That's where they'll be waiting for us once we get out tonight. Second, memorize this address." She rattled off a street number and road, in a little town fifteen miles north of White Crescent Bay that Ren had never heard of before. "It's where we're supposed to meet. Head there if we get separated."

Ren repeated the address until he had committed it to memory. The more details he memorized the better, but he hoped that he and Tessa wouldn't be forced to split up.

"Will you be able to lay low until the ball begins?" Tessa asked, checking her makeup in the mirror of her compact. She would be interacting with dignitaries throughout the day and needed to look her best. Her usual blouse-and-pencil-skirt combination had been swapped out for a black dress suit. The vulnerability she had shown to Ren the night before was nowhere to be found.

"I'll be busy in the sewing room for a while," replied Ren. "Then I'll switch over to the janitorial team for the ball." Ren needed a reason to remain at the Fortress through the night because his tailoring duties were nearly finished, and it just so happened that the janitors needed an extra hand to fill the hole that Jay had left. So Ren had volunteered his services even though he hated the idea that he was "replacing" Jay for the night. "I can apply the sleeping drug without much trouble, but the rest won't be as cut and dry."

The whole mission rested on some shaky legs. Once Ren and

Tessa smuggled Aiko out of the Fortress and to the safe house, Marty would take over from there. Her rebels would drive Aiko to San Francisco, where they would board the stolen Coast Guard ship and speed across the winter waters toward Alcatraz. Then, after scanning Aiko's retinas and fingerprints to gain access to the Rock, they would fight their way into the main prison building and shut down the island's electricity, plunging everything into darkness and neutralizing the underwater bombs.

That was when the rest of the Resistance forces would join the fight, crammed onto stolen boats and ships that would skim past the dead bombs and land at Alcatraz. Hundreds of rebels had pledged themselves to the mission, hailing from cells up and down the western coast and a few from the Rockies. They had been split into groups — some would take on the prison guards while others would free the prisoners and escort them back to the boats. Meanwhile, the leaders of each cell would search for the V2, scouring every outbuilding on Alcatraz if necessary.

And then came Marty's main job for the night. She would look for Ren's mom and, if Jenny Tsai was alive, she would personally help her aunt get out of the prison.

Ren had decided that he would go with Marty, even if she didn't know that yet. He wasn't exactly commando material — and he was sure that Marty would tell him to remain at the safe house — but he couldn't stay behind and twiddle his thumbs until he got word about what was happening. Ever since Marty sparked the hope that Ren's mom might be alive, that small flame had flickered and grown. Ren couldn't stop thinking about finding his mother and folding his arms around her. Of becoming a family again. Maybe he would get his dad back, too — the version of Mr. Cabot who had died along with his wife — and the three of them would have a new start. They would have to go into hiding, and Ren would have to say good-bye to his press. But that didn't mean he would stop writing. Once his mother was healthy, they could start up her newspaper again, working side by side as they went to print. He hoped that she would be proud of him.

But a tiny misstep could snuff out Ren's flicker of hope and send the mission crashing down.

Unlike Ren, however, Tessa didn't look fazed at what lay ahead of them. "Stick to the plan. That's all we can do at this point."

Ren wouldn't have minded a more enthusiastic pep talk because his nerves were already multiplying. When he wrote as the Viper, he could revise and rewrite an essay until he was happy with every sentence, but there would be no redos when it came to kidnapping Aiko. He and Tessa had one chance to get this right — and that was it.

Ren turned toward the door, figuring that they were finished. "I'll see you tonight? I should be mopping up in the workers' wing when you come to get me." Tessa was supposed to retrieve Ren as soon as she got word that Aiko had retreated to her bedroom to rest. It was Ren's job to stay out of trouble until then.

"Don't worry, I'll find you, but there's one more thing we have to talk about," Tessa said before he could leave. "In case we get caught tonight."

"What's there to talk about?" Ren said, slightly anxious.

She rose from her desk and strode toward him, which only made Ren more nervous. "I've been thinking about this a lot, and I don't want to be paraded across the cliffs like my dad was if I get caught tonight. That's why I asked Marty to get me this." She reached into her blazer pocket and retrieved an unassuming white pill. "Allied spies used to carry these during the war. If they knew they were going to get tortured and killed, they'd bite into it. It's a quick and painless way to go."

Ren stared at the simple capsule in her palm. "These are suicide pills?"

"Basically," she said matter-of-factly, as if she were holding some aspirin. "I can't speak for your last wishes, but I got you a pill in case you might want it." She offered it to Ren.

Ren hesitated. The thought had crossed his mind more than once that they might not make it out of the Fortress alive, but he clearly hadn't been as prepared as Tessa.

Growing impatient, Tessa took Ren's hand and deposited the pill there. "Just in case." She looked up at him, completely clear-eyed. "My dad didn't have a say in how he died and neither did your mom. But we do. Keep this if you want or throw it away. I figure it's smart to have the choice."

Ren's tongue felt rubbery, so he closed his fingers over the pill. It barely weighed a thing, and yet it represented his worst fears for the night: the mission failing, the soldiers arresting him and torturing him. He'd never see his father or Marty again. What would he tell them if he could see them one last time? He hadn't even thought about that, but he would tell them how much they meant to him. He would also ask them to find out if his mother was really alive. And he'd tell them that he was the Viper, too. He realized now that he didn't want to take that secret to the grave — he would want them to know that he had fought the Empire however he could and he would want them to find someone else to take up what his mother had started.

Ren shifted his gaze to Tessa. He could give her a message to relay to his family — he could reveal himself as the Viper. It might have been worth it if their mission went south.

But just as Ren tried to form the words in his mouth, the phone rang.

"I'd better get that," Tessa said quickly, picking up the call. "Good luck."

"Right," Ren said as he pocketed the pill. The moment was gone, and he found himself leaving Tessa's office and weaving his way back, telling himself that he would have time later to fill Tessa in on everything.

Until then, there was work to finish.

Back in the sewing room, the hours whooshed by in a rush of last-minute hemming and patching and adjustments. Ren was grateful to keep his hands busy, and before long it was four o'clock. By then, the rest of the recent hires had already vacated their workstations, and the regular staff was busy upstairs, assisting an Italian princess who had spilled red wine all over her champagne-colored gown and couldn't be comforted. Only Ren and Ms. Clarke remained, along with the crown princess's and Aiko's wardrobes. Ms. Clarke was steaming one last skirt before the royal workers arrived to retrieve the six outfits.

"Why don't you let me finish that?" Ren offered from his side of the room. He had drawn out packing up his workstation for as long as he could. "I don't think you had lunch, and you should get some food before everything's picked clean."

It took some back and forth until Ms. Clarke gave in to her hunger and vacated the room, wheeling the steamer over to Ren before she departed. Ren had never shut the door so quickly. Finally, he was alone — and he would set out to finish what he came to the Fortress to do.

After giving Aiko's banquet kimono a swift steaming, he gently removed each outfit from its dress form and hung it on a rolling dress rack. Then, angling his back toward the security camera, he grabbed the starch bottle that Tessa had given him and began spraying the collars, his hands shaking the entire time. Ms. Clarke could return at any minute and demand to know what he was doing, or the royal workers could arrive early and botch everything up. So Ren hurried, dousing the collars generously before he ran the steamer wand over them to dry the fabric.

As Ren zipped the last gown into its garment bag, the royal workers were hurrying down the hallway. By then, Ms. Clarke had returned, too, and she grabbed a sewing kit to accompany the workers back to the penthouse, in case Aiko or her mother required assistance. It was all over within minutes, and as soon as they left, Ren plunked into his chair.

He almost laughed. He'd spent nearly a week inside the Fortress just to spend two minutes spraying a clear liquid onto three fancy dresses. But that laugh died in Ren's throat when he reminded himself that his real work had yet to begin.

With a few hours before the rest of the mission was to begin, Ren packed up his few possessions in his bunkroom and reported to the head janitor, who rattled off a checklist and sent Ren on his way, with a cleaning kit and a mop in tow.

Ren dove into his duties, starting first with bleaching the servants' bathrooms, mopping a few bunkrooms, and then sweeping the hallway that led to the hotel lobby. Other workers rushed around him — waiters tying their ties, maids holding clean towels, and a couple of maintenance workers heading outside to light candles on the cocktail tables.

Eventually, Ren felt brave enough to peek into the lobby, where the first guests had gathered. Military officers sipped from glasses of champagne while their wives complimented one another on their jeweled necklaces or delicate gold bracelets. Ren had never seen an event like this before, which flowed with wine and top-shelf liquor, with tuxedos and ballgowns, and with the very upper crust of both empires. Taking all this in, he couldn't help but think about his life in White Crescent Bay and how it differed from this glittering ball. How many times had he gone to bed hungry? Or shook with fear when the soldiers ransacked his apartment?

While the Empire downs its wine and dresses in jewels, the rest of us starve and clothe our children in scraps. How long will we let them grind their boots against our throats? Ask yourselves — at what point will you say enough is enough?

A snippet of an essay floated into Ren's thoughts, and he saved it for later use. He wasn't sure when he'd be able to publish again, but whenever he did, he had a wealth of new experiences to draw upon.

Now he just had to survive the night.

20

The evening charged onward. The cocktail hour concluded, leaving behind a trail of champagne flutes and empty hors d'oeuvres trays, and the formal dinner began in the banquet hall, where the guests dined on their choice of locally raised steak or freshly caught Pacific halibut, or braised root vegetables with an arrangement of delicately assembled greens.

Ren, however, was too nervous to even think about food. Once the clock on the wall ticked past nine, he began mopping the halls of the workers' quarters and counting down the minutes. Aiko and her mother had already changed into their third outfits for the night. Plenty of time had passed for the sleeping drug to seep into Aiko's skin, and she should have already felt the first effects of the drug: a headache, a churning stomach, the trickles of exhaustion. It was nearly time.

"Looks like you got a side job," someone said behind Ren.

Ren groaned. He knew that voice too well. Gripping on to the mop handle, he mumbled, "May I be of assistance, Sasaki-sama?"

Sasaki responded by shoving Ren against the wall. "There's something shifty about you." Ren could smell the faint smell of wine on his breath, but Sasaki wasn't drunk. He simply seemed angry. "I don't know how you got a job at the fort, but I'm going to get to the bottom of it. A criminal's son never should have been hired."

Ren's heart thudded hard. He hadn't seen Sasaki since Tessa used her power on him, and now Ren wondered if Sasaki had remembered some of that encounter. Hadn't Tessa said that her abilities were limited?

"I'm not my mother, Sasaki-sama," Ren forced himself to say. "I'm loyal to the emperor."

Sasaki laughed. "You expect me to believe you? The son of a Chinese traitor?"

Ren clutched his mop even tighter. He had to shake off Sasaki and keep a low profile until Tessa came to find him. He had to make an excuse and get away, but he had a feeling that Sasaki was relishing this moment.

Then, to Ren's surprise, Sasaki backed off and turned around. But that relief was short-lived.

"Come with me and bring that mop," Sasaki said, motioning at Ren. "I've got a job for you."

Once again, Ren didn't have much of a choice but to obey.

They entered the hotel lobby, where Ren got his second glimpse of the Joint Prosperity Ball. The glass doors to the courtyard had been thrown open, and about half the guests — hundreds of people — had already wandered outside, wine glasses in hand. Dozens of heat lamps were spread out over the patio to keep the air warm, and the band had started up their first set. Ren could see the swimming pool down the way, filled with lilies and floating candles, a scene straight from an Old World fairy tale.

The other guests remained in the banquet hall, lingering over plates of miniature apple strudels and small *taiyaki* cakes, which were sculpted into the shape of a fish and stuffed with red bean paste.

Most of the cadets had been sent up to bed, but the senior class had been given permission to remain. Ren spotted a few of them trying to steal liquor bottles from the bar.

"Stop gawking," Sasaki hissed. He elbowed Ren in the ribs and shoved him toward the reception desk. "One of the guests was sick, and you get to clean it up."

Ren flinched as soon as he spotted the large pool of vomit, not far from the elevators and the front doors of the hotel. A server had propped the doors open to air out the smell, and Ren saw a security checkpoint outside on the hotel's circular drive. Metal detectors had been set up by a majestic fountain, while a flock of suited security guards kept watch for late arrivals. Even a helicopter circled above the hotel, yet another line of defense for the evening. The chop of its propellers kept Ren company as he approached the vomit and began to clean.

Sasaki hovered over him. "Hurry up. There's another mess after you finish this one."

Ren mopped faster and said nothing. The sooner he finished, the sooner he could retreat to the workers' quarters. That was where Tessa expected to find him, and he wasn't about to let Sasaki or a pile of throw-up get in the way of the mission.

As Ren mopped, Sasaki's attention shifted toward the checkpoint outside. A group of latecomers had approached the metal detectors — a white-haired woman in her seventies, flanked by four younger women in bell skirts, likely her daughters or other family members. One of them interpreted for her from German to Japanese.

"I am Baroness Augusta of Saxe-Lauenburg," the woman announced, walking up to the first security guard while leaning on an ivory cane. She wore a velvet maroon gown with a grand poufed skirt that looked like something that had been plucked out of a Victorian painting. It almost resembled a costume.

The security guards had some trouble tracking down the baroness on their records, and the old woman appeared none too pleased. She began rattling off names of military officers whom she knew, but the guards still wouldn't let her inside the hotel. Sasaki curiously watched the proceedings unfold, ready to insert himself with a puffed-up chest.

But then, everyone's attention in the foyer was drawn elsewhere.

One of the elevators pinged open and out stepped Aiko, newly changed for the dancing portion of the ball. Her cheeks were freshly powdered and her lips had been painted pink and glossed over. Ren, however, wasn't looking at her face.

He was staring at her outfit. Aiko wasn't wearing the gown that the sewing team had spent months preparing. She was wearing a completely different dress — it was the A-line one that Ren had sewn for her. Except Aiko had made alterations to it.

The ivory fabric had been painted with sweeping black brushstrokes that stretched over the bodice and down to the skirt, forming a bold modern pattern. But as Aiko walked past Ren — she didn't even notice him — he saw that the brushstrokes didn't form a pattern at all. The strokes looked like words, written in beautiful Japanese kanji.

Liberty.

Freedom.

Power.

Ren's mouth dropped open. Over in the lounge area of the lobby, conversation all but hushed. Guests began tilting their heads in Aiko's direction, with their eyebrows arched at sharp angles. Soon, the whispering started.

Right then, Crown Princess Katsura stepped out of the banquet hall, already dressed in her third kimono for the evening and with the swell of her belly pushing out the delicate fabric. Her gaze traveled toward the elevator, where she spotted her daughter, and her face turned ghostly white.

Moving hastily, the crown princess pinned a frozen smile to her lips and hurried to take her daughter by the arm. Ren pretended to keep mopping but could hear pieces of their argument.

"What are you wearing? What *is* this?" the crown princess whispered frantically. She tried to nudge Aiko to the elevator, but Aiko refused to move. In fact, Aiko looked determined to join her father and her fiancé out on the patio.

"Let go," Aiko muttered. Somehow her features remained placid despite everyone staring at her.

"You should be grateful that your father hasn't seen you yet. How could you do this to him?"

"How could he marry me off to that old man?" Aiko said, hurt tearing through each syllable. "Forst is nearly Father's age."

"You're making a scene," the crown princess said through gritted teeth. She tried to jab a finger at the elevator buttons, but she needed a security card to swipe her in. Her servants must have held on to her ID on her behalf, but now they were nowhere to be seen.

"Our guests are waiting," Aiko said, triumph in her tone.

Her mother's voice lowered. "Don't insult your father like this, in front of all of these people."

"He didn't even tell me about the engagement until —"

"It's for the best."

"Best for who, exactly?" Aiko said, defiant.

The crown princess glanced back to the lobby and noticed everyone staring at them. Flushing, her eyes went wet with tears. "Don't do this. Not here."

At that, Aiko hesitated. She was probaby expecting a fight, but she hadn't been ready to watch her mother cry. Ren saw the warring emotions on Aiko's face. As a princess, she was expected to follow a life's plan that she never had any say in — to accept, to conform, to swallow her dreams and do it with grace. But Ren realized that Aiko's dreams wouldn't be banished so easily. She wanted to fight for them, and yet doing that would come with a price — humiliating her parents, disgracing her station, and shaming her own name.

But right as Ren thought Aiko would back down, she stood even straighter.

"I won't marry him," Aiko said. Her voice wobbled a step, but she steadied it. "I can't."

It took a few seconds for the crown princess to reply. "Is this about art school again?"

"It's not only —"

"Then what is it?"

Color rose up Aiko's neck as she searched for words. "It's about . . . it's about *everything!*" she said, echoing what she had said to Ren on the balcony of the royal penthouse.

The crown princess, however, refused to hear any of it. "We're going upstairs to change before your father sees you." She took her daughter by the arm again while she searched for one of their servants.

Again, Aiko tried to pull away. "For once, will you listen —"

But Ren would never hear what Aiko intended to say.

Sudden gunfire popped at the checkpoint outside, blasting into his eardrums and echoing inside the lobby. At first, Ren thought maybe a soldier's gun had misfired, but then more bullets sprayed and the soldiers began shouting orders. This wasn't an accident, Ren realized. This was an attack. With his pulse racing into a gallop, Ren hit the floor fast and crawled behind the reception desk, blinking to figure out what was going on.

Outside, just beyond the hotel's front doors, Ren watched the soldiers squaring off against Baroness Augusta and the four women accompanying her. But these women were no longer prim and proper blue-blooded ladies. Each one had pulled a pistol or rifle from under her skirt and had killed off most of the security team already. As they reloaded their weapons to fight an incoming wave of soldiers, Baroness Augusta revealed a grenade launcher strapped to her right leg.

"Take cover!" she shouted in perfect American English to her comrades. And then she launched the first bomb straight at the helicopter hovering over the hotel, clipping the aircraft's tail.

Everything flashed bright. A metallic roar sounded in the sky, and the helicopter came crashing down, a hot smear of red against the night. It landed right outside the hotel, shaking the walls, shuddering across the floor, and hurling debris and smoke into the lobby.

Ren buried his head under his arms as chunks of marble flew past him. Screams erupted from every direction as Baroness Augusta launched another grenade outside, turning the bubbling fountain into a boiling explosion.

Inside the lobby, the soldiers ordered everyone to get down and not to panic.

No one listened. The screams ratcheted louder, while the ceiling cracked and moaned.

Ren had no idea who the baroness was or why she was here.

All he knew was that the Fortress was under attack.

And his mission was turning to dust in front of his eyes.

21

Smoke billowed in the hotel lobby, invading people's lungs and conquering every inch of clean air. The fire alarms blared and the emergency sprinklers turned on, showering Ren with freezing-cold water.

Ren huddled into a ball as another spray of bullets popped somewhere outside. Anarchy had taken hold in the hotel, despite all the security measures. Soldiers lay dead while others stood dazed, unsure of where to go. Meanwhile, the guests were crying and stumbling around. No one knew what they should do — head outside where the fires blazed, or remain inside and risk the hotel collapsing? — so they resorted to spinning around in circles.

Ren coughed out a mouthful of dirt, still shell-shocked at what had happened. This couldn't have been a Resistance attack — Marty wouldn't have jeopardized the mission. So who was Baroness Augusta and why had she come? Ren doubted that she was a Soviet operative; the Russians had been itching for a fight against the Nazis, not the Empire.

It doesn't matter. You have to move, Ren told himself. What mattered was salvaging the mission if he could. Not to mention staying alive.

Another shudder rippled across the hotel floor, and Ren scuttled to his feet. He didn't see Sasaki anywhere, thankfully, but he couldn't find Aiko, either. But even if he did locate the princess, he still needed Tessa. There would be no getaway car without her.

Smoke wafted into Ren's nose and he coughed again, just as a chilling thought struck him. Were Aiko and Tessa even alive?

Ren picked his way over the debris and the puddles. The sprinklers kept spewing water onto the lobby, extinguishing the flames but turning the marble floors into a slippery mess. Ren was nearly knocked over by a couple of Nazi colonels sprinting for the front door, and as he staggered to gain his balance, he bumped into a girl behind him. He swung around and grabbed on to her shoulders to steady himself and was about to move on, but the girl clutched his hands.

"Ren!" she shouted over the fire.

Ren blinked, the pandemonium around him quieting as he realized who was standing in front of him. He couldn't believe it. "Tessa —" He stopped himself. "Fräulein Plank?"

"I was coming to find you when the bomb went off! I'd just gotten to the lobby before the first explosion," she shouted over the mayhem. Her hair was drenched, and her fist was coiled tightly around a key ring.

Ren fixated on the keys. "Are those —"

"For the car, yes," she yelled.

Somewhere outside, another grenade went off and both of them ducked for cover. A line of cadets poured out of an emergency stairwell, some of them still dressed in their uniforms while others were in their pajamas and barefoot. Their instructors shouted for them to get outside quickly. It was the start of an evacuation.

"We have to get out of the Fortress," Ren said, and grabbed

Tessa's hand. "Can you drive us?" Ren repeated himself twice more, but Tessa wasn't listening. She wasn't looking at him, either. Her gaze had fixed on a pile of rubble by one of the elevators. The ceiling had crumbled there, cracking the marble beneath, but she ran toward it.

"Plank!" Ren called out.

Tessa sank to her knees next to the debris and started tossing ceiling tiles and rubble over her shoulder. "Help me!"

Ren thought she might have gotten a knock to the head. "What are you doing?"

"*Help me.* I think Aiko is under here." She tugged at a piece of dusty fabric from the rubble, a square of dirty silk with bold black brushstrokes. The princess's last dress.

That was all the evidence Ren needed. Joining Tessa, he helped remove half the pile until he unearthed a dust-covered face, but it wasn't Aiko. It was her mother. Ren lifted a big hunk of marble from her body to reveal that she'd been pierced with a sharp piece of concrete, buried so deeply that he had to look away. Grimacing, Ren checked her pulse but felt nothing. She was gone.

"Ren!" Tessa said. "I think I found Aiko."

Ren's attention jolted back to the pile of rubble, and he pushed aside a heavy ceiling tile while Tessa freed Aiko from the wreckage. The fabric of Aiko's gown had turned gray with dust, while blood dripped from a long gash on her arm. Her eyes were shut, but Ren didn't know if she was unconscious from a blow to the head or from the sleeping drug that he'd given her.

"She's alive." Tessa caught Ren's eye, and a silent understanding passed between them.

They had Aiko in their hands.

The mission could still be a go.

"Let's head to the car from here," Ren said, making the decision abundantly clear. He pulled Aiko into his arms and stumbled to his feet. "We can't go through the sublevel. The hotel might collapse. If anyone gives us trouble, can you talk us out of it?"

Tessa began smoothing her hair out of nervous habit before she forced her hands to her sides. She nodded at him. "I'll take the lead. Stay close."

They fled from the hotel, exiting the smoke and entering the madness outside.

A hungry fire lapped at the hotel's façade, erupting from the helicopter wreckage. Ren could hear the fire trucks wailing somewhere inside the Fortress, but until they arrived the fire leapt higher and spread its arms farther out.

It was chaos. Sobs and screams filled the smoky air. Dozens of cadets and guests poured out of the hotel and into the chilly winter wind, and more than once Ren was knocked from behind by a frantic ambassador or a uniformed officer. Soldiers tried to shout orders, steering the injured toward the Fortress's health clinics and pointing everyone else to a nearby training field to be accounted for. One of the soldiers grabbed Ren by the shoulder and zeroed in on Aiko. Ren thought that they might be done for.

But Tessa stepped in. "You have to let us go! We need to get to the hospital," she shouted, forcing him to look her in her eyes. She repeated herself, "You have to let us go right now."

The soldier stared at her, looking confused, and that was all she needed to push Ren onward. They hurried away from the hotel until the smoke thinned out, with Tessa out front to run interference. They made a sharp right into a narrow alleyway that separated the Mission Hotel from a darkened office building. Ren had no idea how much farther they had to run, but his arms were groaning under Aiko's weight.

"The car's over there!" Tessa said.

Looking ahead, Ren noticed a parking garage adjacent to the office building. Not much farther.

Tessa headed for a gold-colored sedan, her feet bare because she had long abandoned her heels. She popped the trunk and removed the bottom panel to reveal a shallow niche below, which the Resistance had helped her hollow out a week prior. Ren nestled Aiko into the niche, tucking her arms in front of her and drawing her knees toward her chest, but she never stirred once. The sleeping drug had done its job and had done it well, but Ren wasn't looking forward to when Aiko woke up. Her world had been flipped inside out, and her mom had been killed. That wasn't Ren's fault, but he was taking her away from her home. From all that she knew.

But this was war, wasn't it? There were no happy choices, merely decisions that were a means to an end. That's what Ren told himself anyway.

Tessa placed the panel over Aiko's body and then covered that with a blanket and a box of jumper cables. Ren was about to tell her to start up the car when he heard footsteps running toward them, heavy yet fast.

"Stop right there!" someone shouted in Japanese before barreling into Ren's back, knocking both Ren and Tessa onto the hard garage pavement.

Dazed, Ren blinked up to find Sasaki standing over them, pointing a gun at their heads. Out of instinct, Ren raised his hands, but Tessa had other ideas.

"Sasaki-sama —" she started.

But Sasaki wasn't having it. With the gun aimed at her forehead, he spewed, "Shut up! What are you two doing?"

"We're trying to get somewhere safe!" Tessa replied. She kept trying to make eye contact with Sasaki, but he kept flicking glances in Ren's direction and breaking the connection.

"What's in the trunk?" With one hand still pointing the pistol at Tessa, Sasaki reached inside the trunk, but Ren was already moving. Ren kicked out his leg and swept Sasaki onto the concrete. It worked even better than Ren had planned, and the gun clattered out of Sasaki's hand. Ren made a dive for it.

"Get in the car!" Ren said to Tessa as his fingers curled around the pistol handle. But before he could aim the gun, Sasaki recovered and knocked it out of Ren's grasp. The gun flew deeper into the garage, and Sasaki used the chance to kick Ren in the ribs, stunning him. While Sasaki hurried to retrieve his pistol, he wrestled his radio from his belt.

Sasaki shouted into the black device. "Headquarters, come in! I need backup over in Garage 230. I'm calling in an arrest warrant for a Fortress employee named Cabot. That's C-A-B-O-T. His accomplice is —"

Ren sprang to his feet and tackled Sasaki from behind. Together they careened back to the pavement. As Ren landed hard, he groaned as something sharp jabbed his hip — the pistol.

Twisting around, Ren reached for the weapon but accidentally sent it skidding into a puddle and out of reach. That was when

Sasaki began pummeling Ren hard. A punch to the jaw. An elbow to the windpipe. Agony exploded on every part of Ren's body, but the blows only came faster. Sasaki readied another fist toward Ren's nose, when a shot rang out.

Sasaki made a gurgling sound. Blood spurted out of his neck, and he collapsed to the ground, clutching the spewing wound.

Stunned, Ren saw Tessa standing over them, pistol in hand. Ren shoved Sasaki off him and watched grimly as the soldier gasped and stared helplessly up at Tessa.

She fired at him again.

This time Sasaki went still.

Tessa's eyes were enormous. Her hands were shaking, but she wouldn't let go of the gun.

Ren swallowed a choppy breath and wobbled to his feet. "Are you okay?"

She didn't answer. She couldn't stop staring at Sasaki's body.

"We need to get out of here." Because Tessa was too shocked to move, Ren guided her gently into the car. "Listen. Do you still have the keys?"

It took her a few seconds to reply. "Front seat."

Ren started the car for her and gingerly pried the pistol from her grip, tucking it into the glove compartment. "In case you need it," he explained. "You have to start driving."

The fog seemed to clear from her eyes a little. She stared at the steering wheel, then up at Ren. "Why aren't you getting in?"

"I can't," Ren said, his voice cracking. "Sasaki radioed in my name. You'll never get out of this place if I go with you."

Her brows pulled together. "I can use my power to get us past the checkpoints. Get in."

Ren made no move to climb into the car. He saw the slump in her shoulders and the exhaustion on her face. She had pushed herself to the limit already, and what little strength remained she needed to save for the escape.

Ren shut the car door. "The mission comes first." He was probably signing his own death warrant by doing this, but he couldn't jeopardize the operation. "Tell my cousin good luck tonight. Tell my dad that I love him." His throat throbbed with emotion. "And if my mom is alive at Alcatraz, you have to get her out."

Tessa tried to get out of the car, but Ren wouldn't let her. "You don't have to do this!" she argued.

"Tell them all that I was the Viper," Ren forced out before he lost his nerve.

She blinked at him with new eyes. "Ren . . ."

"Everything I wrote was for my mom. I wanted to make her proud."

Before Tessa could say anything, Ren took off. He made the choice for her to leave him behind, even though he had no idea what he should do. He just ran. He bolted through the parking garage and past a block of quiet buildings, and he only let himself stop when he nearly doubled over from exhaustion. Huddling in the shadows of a half-constructed barrack, Ren tried to get his bearing. The hotel was far behind him, but its towering height made it easy to spot, standing tall and proud even as bright orange flames climbed up its exterior.

Ren went over his options, which weren't many. He had to get out of the Fortress fast, but he didn't know how without getting caught. He'd get shot dead if he tried to scale the fence that enveloped the Fortress, and he'd get interrogated if he tried to leave through a checkpoint. Once they demanded to see his ID and read his name, he'd be done for. But he had to make a decision soon. The longer he waited, the chances of survival dimmed more and more.

Ren forced himself to keep going, moving from shadow to shadow until he saw a small service checkpoint ahead. A handful of soldiers stood there, guarding a barrier that blocked anyone from coming in or going out. Ren could never slip past all of them. He would have to find another way.

But then came a sliver of an opportunity. Ren stood on tiptoe, watching, as two ambulances raced toward a checkpoint that led from White Crescent Bay. The soldiers stationed there hurried to open the barrier they had erected to block the road. A couple of them had even shed their rifles to work unencumbered while the rest of the team disappeared into a tiny building next to the checkpoint, maybe to call the Mission Hotel to say that medical assistance was on its way.

The guards were distracted.

The ambulances might offer some cover.

Ren shut off his thoughts and made a run for it.

The wail of the ambulances hid his thumping footsteps. The security guards hadn't spotted him yet, so he upped his pace, breathing hard, breathing fast. The first vehicle blazed through the checkpoint, its alarm blasting into Ren's head but he shook it off. He was nearly there.

"Stop!" a soldier cried.

Ren ignored him and sprinted like he'd never done before.

"I said stop!"

The second vehicle drove past the checkpoint, just as Ren cleared it, too. He had made it, but it was the smallest of victories. The soldiers were coming after him now, screaming at him and popping off shots. Ren ran in a zigzag to make himself a tougher target, and unbelievably, it seemed to be working. As the gravel road stretched before him, hope rose in his chest. Just a little farther and he might step into the clear.

But then the pain overcame him. It exploded on his right arm where a bullet grazed his skin from elbow to wrist, splitting the flesh open. Ren stumbled but managed to right himself. He could deal with a flesh wound.

Then the pain doubled, even tripled. This time it hit him in his side, right about his hip bone. Ren cried out and fell. Hot blood blossomed onto his shirt.

This one wasn't a flesh wound.

Another bullet had taken out a knuckle-size chunk of flesh from Ren's waist. He tried to get up — he had to push through the agony — but he just couldn't. The pain was too much.

But the soldiers caught up to him and hurled him onto his back. Ren gasped as one of them pointed a pistol in his face, straight at his nose. Another soldier arrived and yanked the bloodied work badge clipped to Ren's lapel.

"His name's Cabot!" the soldier shouted to his comrades. While they spoke in rapid Japanese, Ren tried to flip himself over and drag himself out of reach. He would crawl if he had to.

"Grab him!" someone yelled.

Ren forced himself to go faster, but his body protested and his vision had already blurred. The soldiers took him by the shoulders and dragged him onto his feet.

Ren thought about the suicide pill in his pocket. Too late.

One of them lifted his rifle. The blow came quick and sharp, and the darkness soon followed.

22

Ren sank in and out of consciousness, drifting between darkness and harsh light.

The first time he came to, he found himself lying on a cot and being carried into a small health clinic on base. The wail of ambulance sirens filled his ears, prodding Ren more awake.

The soldiers carrying Ren's cot halted at the clinic's white doors, where a harried nurse was directing orders. "We're full," she told them. "You'll have to bring him to the makeshift clinic on the training fields."

"He could bleed out before then, and we have to keep him alive," one of the soldiers said crisply. "We think he has information about the attack."

The nurse paused and murmured something into her radio. "A bed opened up in Station Twelve. Take him inside."

Pain thrummed through every corner of Ren's body and he nearly blacked out again — he would have welcomed it gladly — but the jolt of the cot kept Ren awake. Around him, he saw nurses dashing along the corridor, their arms holding IV bags, while guests from the ball, covered in blood and dust, lined up against the wall for the next available doctor.

The soldiers deposited Ren inside what looked like an employee lounge, where a white-coated doctor had set up a makeshift medical station. He spoke to the soldiers in rapid Japanese and ordered them to move Ren from the cot and onto the hospital bed.

The doctor was going to save him, but Ren didn't want to be saved, not like this. He tried to reach for the small white pill in his pocket. The end would be painless, Tessa had said.

But the doctor batted Ren's hand away as he assessed the gunshot wound in Ren's side. Ren's back arched in agony, and a scream tore out of his mouth. But strong hands held him down, and a needle slid into Ren's skin, making his vision go foggy.

Ren thought again about his pill, but the darkness entered the corners of his vision and dragged him under.

A part of him wished that he would never wake up again. He didn't want to find out what would await him there.

Hours passed, or maybe it was a day or two. Ren lived in snatches of consciousness — the sharpest of pains before another needle bit into his body and sent him sinking back to sleep. Every time his eyes cracked open, he saw something new. A nurse checking his pulse. A doctor scribbling notes. A soldier standing guard beside him. One time, he thought he saw Sasaki at his bedside, a smirk on his chapped lips, but it must have been a dream. Sasaki was dead, wasn't he? Ren couldn't remember.

A harsh slap on the cheek brought Ren fully awake for the first time since the Joint Prosperity Ball. Ren gasped for air as his whole body throbbed. His gunshot wounds had been stitched up and dressed, but he could feel those stitches stretching with every breath.

Ren's head whipped around, unsure of where he was. One thing was for certain — he wasn't in the health clinic anymore. Walls of concrete surrounded him, and a sole lightbulb swung above his head. This must have been a prison cell. Or an interrogation room.

Ren had been propped up on a wooden chair, and a large mirror hung opposite him. He grimaced at the mirror, his face unrecognizable between the bruises and swelling that had overtaken it. He also grimly wondered if this was a two-way mirror and who was sitting on the other side of it.

Another slap came swift and hard. When Ren's eyes refocused, he found a soldier at his side, wearing the uniform of the Ronin Elite. His blood froze at the sight of her.

Major Endo.

She leaned toward Ren, and he flinched at their closeness. He could see the pores on her nose and the mole that rested on her left cheek.

Her face remained calm as she spoke, but he heard daggers in her voice. "Where is the princess?"

Ren pressed his lips together.

The next blow came quick. She punched him in the jaw. "Where is she?"

Ren tasted blood, but before he could spit it out, she hit him again, this time in the temple. "We know you helped kidnap her. Who are your accomplices?"

Ren still said nothing, but he winced when he saw the new punch coming. It hit him square in the stomach and he fell backward in the chair, sprawling onto the concrete floor.

"Tell me their names!" Major Endo kicked aside the chair, leaving Ren vulnerable on the ground.

Ren drew his knees against his chest, his only defense, but Endo stomped a boot into the gunshot wound at his side. The pain was blinding, but somehow Ren kept his mouth shut. He wouldn't betray Marty or Tessa. He would die here, taking their names to his grave.

But when Major Endo's boot landed against his groin, Ren's vision went sideways and he almost let something slip, just to make all of this stop. That temptation doubled as Endo knelt beside Ren's quivering body and placed her fingertips on his skull. Ren had watched her do this before, on Daisy and Jay, but that never could have prepared him for what came next.

"Tell us where your people took the princess," she said softly.

Ren began to shake. Sweat coated his forehead as a wave of heat surged through his muscles, like a fire unleashed in his veins.

She was going to boil him from the inside out.

"I don't know!" Ren said.

The heat rose. He vomited bile.

"Don't lie to us." Major Endo slid her gaze to the mirror, and somehow Ren knew that Crown Prince Katsura was watching them. Waiting for Ren to crack. "Where did you take the princess?"

Every inch of Ren burned, and he knew he was dying. Memories flashed through his mind, snapshots from his last sixteen years: the shop, the cliffs, his dad, and his mom. He held on to the picture of her inside his head. He would never know if she was in Alcatraz or not, but he had given the Resistance the key to find out.

That would have to be enough.

When the pain exploded a hundredfold, Ren felt himself go, floating above the room, above the Fortress, above White Crescent Bay, and higher still.

He hoped that this was the end.

• • •

Ren's eyes fluttered open.

He wasn't dead. The pain told him that he was still alive.

But he had no idea where he was, either.

Lying on his back, he found himself in a world of mist and wind. Sheets of dark gray clouds covered the sky, and a cold drizzle fell onto his cheeks, sliding down his face and rolling onto his neck. Water lapped close by, and his body rocked slowly back and forth.

He was on a boat.

Ren tried to sit up but couldn't. It hurt too much. So he lay there while his head pounded and his throat begged for water and his shriveled stomach hungered for some soup or rice. He felt wrung dry and exhausted, but Major Endo wasn't hitting him or kicking him and, for that, he never wanted to leave this place.

Fingers of darkness crept into the corners of Ren's vision, and he teetered again on the edges of consciousness. But before his eyelids fell, he saw something in the distance — a massive bridge, so long that it took up his whole line of vision and so high that the top of it was obscured by the clouds. He had seen it before on his visits to San Francisco. The Golden Gate Bridge.

Sea spray misted Ren's cheeks, and the cry of gulls echoed in his ears. The water rolled beneath him in a steady rhythm, and Ren thought that he was dreaming. When the blackness beckoned him again, he fell into it without putting up a fight.

The next time Ren woke up, he wasn't sure how long he had been out. He only recognized the coldness that made his teeth chatter and his body shiver all over. He was lying on yet another cot, stripped down to a thin T-shirt and boxers, the same pair he had been wearing the night that he was shot. The clothes stank of blood and filth, and if that wasn't bad enough, his limbs and stomach had been bound to his bed with thick leather straps. Ren had no choice but to lie flat on his back, staring up at the fluorescent lights on the dripping ceiling.

Shuddering from the damp, Ren grimaced as a new wave of pain crashed over his body. It had dulled around the edges, but not by much. His gunshot wounds had been haphazardly re-stitched after Major Endo had split them open. He closed his eyes at that awful memory, but Endo wouldn't be banished so easily. He could still feel her fingertips on his head, and he could still see the small smile resting at the corners of her lips whenever he screamed. She had wanted to kill him, but someone must have ordered her to stop. The Empire must have had more plans for Ren.

More questions?

More torture?

Panic seized him. He couldn't face Endo again and whatever else the Empire had planned for him: needles in his veins, surgery without anesthesia, or chemicals pumped through his body until he couldn't take any more. The Empire had probably patched him up just to break him again.

But there was no way for Ren to wriggle out of his straps. He didn't even know where he was. He found himself in a large concrete cube of a room. Dozens of cots were lined up next to his own, some of them occupied, others empty. A strange stench hung in the air — a mixture of bleach and ammonia that covered up a third scent, which hovered underneath Ren's nose, smelling sour and foul and wrong. It smelled of death.

Ren's head jerked to one side when a silver-haired Japanese woman approached his cot. She was wearing a crisp white nurse's uniform and matching white shoes. Ren's breath felt trapped in his throat. Should he pretend that he was asleep? But the nurse had noticed that he was awake and had already grabbed the clipboard at the foot of his bed.

She approached him with a frown and stuck a thermometer into Ren's mouth, nearly gagging him. Then she gave his wounds a passing glance before jotting something on the clipboard and mumbling, "Patient may be dispatched tomorrow or the next day."

"Dispatched? Where am I?" The words tumbled out around the thermometer. Ren's pulse had doubled speed. Would he turn into a laboratory mouse that soon?

The nurse didn't reply. Instead, she glanced over her shoulder and called out, "Bring him some water and rations but not too much. We have orders to get him as strong as possible, but we're not a charity."

The nurse removed the thermometer, made another notation, and stomped away to attend to another patient who had started thrashing and screaming. A handful of seconds passed before a different nurse swung by Ren's cot, pushing a rickety metal cart. She looked younger, perhaps in her early twenties, but her face seemed drained of color, as if she hadn't stepped into sunlight for months.

Pulling a stool to Ren's bedside, the nurse poured water into a paper cup and some of the liquid spilled out because her hands were shaking, which was strange. She held the cup to Ren's lips while he took a few timid sips of the gritty-tasting liquid. Then the nurse removed the lid of a metal pot and ladled a single scoop of rice gruel into a bowl as her fingers kept trembling. She brought the bowl to Ren's lips, and he sniffed at it. A few spots of mold floated on the gruel's surface, but his starving stomach won out and he slurped it hungrily.

"Slowly," the nurse said, her voice pitched high.

Ren was halfway finished when he almost choked on something sharp. He coughed it out to find a folded-up piece of paper.

The nurse seemed to have been expecting this. She angled her body to obscure the paper from the other medical attendants scattered around the room, and she pressed the note into Ren's open hand. "Read it."

"What —"

She shook her head to silence him. "Hurry. Please."

Bewildered, Ren tried to open the paper with one hand, but he could barely move his arm and the note kept slipping out of reach. Finally, the nurse did it for him and placed the paper flat into his palm. Ren scanned the faint writing and his eyes bulged at what he saw.

Callipepla californica. I am a friend of your cousin's. She knows me as Bluefin.

Ren fought to steady his breathing. Marty had mentioned a source within Alcatraz code-named Bluefin, and this nurse had also known Marty's code phrase. He read on.

You're in a medical facility on Alcatraz Island. You were brought here not long after the Joint Prosperity Ball. The Revolutionary Alliance attacked the Fortress during the ball to free Zara St. James, but they failed. The Fortress is on lockdown, and Zara was transferred to Alcatraz along with you. I believe she's being held at the main prison.

A chill snuck down Ren's back. The Empire must have moved Zara to Alcatraz after her Alliance failed to rescue her. Now both he and Zara were locked up on this island, with thick walls surrounding them and only frigid seas beyond.

I've been in touch with your cousin via radio. She and your father are safe, but the Resistance canceled their operation on the prison. Tessa and Aiko didn't show up at the safe house. We don't know their whereabouts. Until they arrive, we have to wait.

Ren's chest hurt reading that — in relief and in pain. Marty and his dad were alive and breathing free air, and he was grateful for that, but now he worried about Tessa. Had she gotten caught? He didn't want to think about that, and he didn't want to think about what this meant for the mission. If Tessa and Aiko had been captured or killed, then there was no way for the Resistance to land their forces on Alcatraz. They wouldn't be able to free the prisoners being held here. Including Zara. Including himself.

Hopelessness descended over Ren like a cloak. The mission had collapsed — he had gambled and lost, and now he was trapped in Alcatraz. Amid the darkness, though, Ren found one jagged shred of light.

If his mom was alive, then she was somewhere nearby. Somewhere close.

Suddenly, Bluefin grasped the paper, plunked it back into the rice bowl, and urged Ren to down the contents. Wincing, Ren managed to swallow the gruel and destroy the evidence of the note's existence. As soon as he was finished, Bluefin's radio chirped in her pocket and she scuttled to her feet, nearly knocking the stool over in the process.

"I have to go," she whispered. "I've stayed too long."

"Wait!" Ren's fingers grabbed the back of her uniform. There was so much more that they needed to discuss, about Zara's whereabouts, about what Crown Prince Katsura had planned for him — and about one thing in particular. "Is my mom alive? Her name is Jenny Tsai."

But Bluefin was already wheeling the cart away from him and out of the room entirely.

Ren stared after her, awaiting a response that wouldn't come. It killed him that his mother could be so close but there was no way for him to search for her. He was stuck on this cot, deep in the Empire's lair, with little hope and no way out.

The Viper was trapped.

23

Ren dreamed of dark and twisted things. He was back at the Fortress, and the base was in flames. Screams shattered Ren's eardrums while he tried to escape the inferno. He stumbled over moaning bodies that clawed at his shoes with burnt fingertips. One of the bodies clutched Ren's pant leg, and he looked down to find Jay staring up at him. Then the face shifted into Marty's. Then Mr. Cabot's.

Help me, Ren, his father whispered. *Help me get home.*

But the smoke thickened, and Ren could no longer see his father. He shouted his dad's name until his throat was scratched raw. *Don't leave me, Dad. Come back, come back, come back.*

Somebody shook Ren out of his dream, and he jerked awake into a different nightmare entirely. He was still in the medical clinic at Alcatraz and was still strapped to his cot. Bluefin hovered over him, and she looked worried.

"Wake up," she said, slapping his cheek as a show to the other nurses. "You need to eat and drink. You have a long day ahead." Just like their last encounter, she held up a cup of water to his lips and then a bowl of rice gruel.

With sleep clinging to his eyelids, Ren managed to gulp some water, but even such a small act pulled at his swollen stitches. Then he took in the gruel sip by sip until he discovered a new note from

Bluefin. He slid it out of his mouth, and she helped him unfold it before placing it into his hand.

Good news: Tessa and Aiko have been found, but the attack is stalled. There's no way inside. Alcatraz has ordered that all incoming ships must have the correct passcode. No exceptions for fingerprint and retina scans.

Ren felt something being crushed inside him. His heart, maybe. Or his last wisps of hope. He wasn't surprised that the Empire had taken these precautions, but having his suspicions confirmed felt like another kick to his gut. The Resistance may have put together a huge army of fighters, but what good was that if there was no way of accessing the prison?

Your cousin has been talking to Zara's Alliance. Her uncle has sent troops across the border to help the Resistance and to retrieve his niece. Both the Alliance and the Resistance may attempt a prisoner exchange — Aiko for you, Zara, and the other detainees.

Ren blinked at this development. A part of him was skeptical that the Empire would accept a prisoner exchange of this magnitude. Trading Aiko for over a hundred American prisoners, including Zara, himself, *and* all of the Anomalies? That was too much to ask, but such a deal *could* work if the crown prince was desperate enough to get his daughter back, especially now that his wife and unborn son had been killed. The Empire needed Aiko to cement the upcoming deal with the Nazis. If she wasn't in the picture, there would be no engagement — and possibly no more V2.

The note continued, but Ren had to ask something first. He had been turning the thought over and over since he last saw Bluefin, and he couldn't hold it back any longer.

"Is my mother alive?" he whispered. "Is she here?"

Bluefin gave a small nod. "Yes, she's here."

Ren forgot how to breathe. Joy surged through him, dulling the pain that clung to his wounds. "Is she . . . is she all right?"

Bluefin looked away, which dampened Ren's relief.

Before she could say anything, though, the head nurse called to Bluefin from the front of the room. "Get the prisoner ready! The guards are coming for him."

"*Hai,*" Bluefin replied to her superior.

"The guards?" Ren whispered, the questions about his mother silenced for now.

Bluefin nodded and motioned at the note, and Ren hurriedly finished the rest of it.

Unfortunately, the bad news. Now that you've recovered enough, they're sending you back to interrogation. I'm very sorry, but there's nothing I can do.

Sweat broke along Ren's hairline. He couldn't go through another round of torture. He couldn't go back to that place. As his pulse went erratic, Ren pulled hard against his restraints. He would rather die trying to escape than with Endo's hands on his skull again, his blood raging hotter and hotter.

"Let me out!" Ren rasped at Bluefin.

She looked stricken, but she pursed her lips and held down Ren's shoulders with a surprisingly strong grip. With one hand, she dropped her note into the gruel and forced him to drink it. Ren wouldn't open his mouth.

"You'll get us both killed if you don't!" she whispered back to him. "And you need to eat to keep up your strength. Open up."

Ren choked down the slippery rice, but that was all the complacency he would give her.

"I can't go back!" Ren knew he sounded desperate, but he didn't care. "Kill me. Give me an overdose of something. *Please!*"

Just then, the doors to the clinic were flung open. Two prison guards strode inside, searching over each bed-strapped patient until they landed upon Ren. Bluefin grasped the handle of her cart.

"Stay strong," she said, regarding him with pity before she retreated into the shadows.

Ren wanted to call her back, but he couldn't. Even now, he knew better than to reveal their connection, but he couldn't stop the panic that flooded him. He yanked again at the restraints, his feeble muscles straining as far as they would go, but the prison guards overpowered him easily. One of them pressed him down while the other undid Ren's straps. Working together, they dragged Ren from the cot. Ren's bare feet hit the floor and his knees buckled immediately from days without use, but the guards simply flanked him and carried him out of the clinic and onto the gravel path outside, not bothering to cover his feet.

Once they were out in the open, Ren flinched in the daylight, even though a layer of thick clouds stretched across the sky, smearing the sun and shielding the city from sight. A biting breeze sent shivers down Ren's skin. He was wearing a worn prisoner's jumpsuit, pocked with holes and old blood — it might have been his or it might have been someone else's — and he trembled in the chilly weather.

Wisps of fog curled around Alcatraz, but Ren finally managed to get his first lucid glimpse of the place. It was an enormous rock plunked into the middle of a bay, with a lone road that circled the island and a half dozen buildings that branched out from that path.

Most of those buildings — like the water tower and the medical facility that Ren had left behind — were situated close to shore, but the main prison rose above the rest, built at the very center and the very pinnacle of Alcatraz.

The main prison seemed to watch Ren's approach with its security cameras twisting and turning their metal necks to follow him. Truth be told, the building looked rather ordinary to Ren, merely three stories tall and with a plain façade. But he knew what he feared most lay within those walls, not without.

The guards yanked Ren to the prison entrance, where they passed through the heavily locked main door and the inside gate. The soles of Ren's feet slid over cool concrete as they entered the cellblock. Each cell was squished against the next like matches in a matchbox, and they were stacked on top of one another, three levels high. The rooms were tiny, too, with barely enough space to cram in a bed, a toilet, a sink, and the prisoners themselves.

That's when Ren dug his heels against the floor — he saw his own future etched on those lifeless faces. Some of the prisoners lay on bare mattresses, hooked to an IV bag of bright orange or neon-yellow liquid. If they heard Ren coming, they didn't seem to care; they simply gazed up at the ceiling. Other prisoners sat on the cell floor, hugging their knees to their chests and knocking their heads against the bars. And still there were more, a few with missing limbs or eyes, a couple with no teeth or hair. An old man was scratching so desperately at his arms that his skin had turned into a bloodied mess. Yet he wouldn't stop. He just kept whispering, "It's in my blood. I have to get it out. It's inside me."

Despite the gruesomeness surrounding him, Ren kept looking into every cell that they passed. His mother might be close. Ren tried shouting her name, but one of the guards thrust his elbow into Ren's gut and that was enough to silence him.

The guards strode by the last cell in the block and headed into the cavernous room at the back of the building. Every window had been blacked out, and the fluorescent lights overhead offered a flickering and unreliable light source. A long, thick curtain had been strung along the ceiling, cutting the room down the middle and obscuring the other half from Ren's view. But the curtain couldn't block the sounds drifting through the fabric, groans and cries and a growl. Ren shivered. He didn't want to think about what was beyond.

The guards deposited Ren at the center of the space, pushing him onto a metal folding chair that dug into his spine. The area around Ren was empty, aside from a lone standing spotlight. One of the guards switched on the light, and it flooded Ren's face with its hot brightness. When he managed to pry open his eyes, the guards had taken a few steps back, their arms at their sides. They hadn't bothered to restrain Ren to the seat.

Soon Ren discovered why.

The curtain parted slightly and out stepped Major Endo. Ren tried to run, even though he knew how useless that would be. Within seconds, the guards had thrown him back into the chair and that's where Major Endo joined them. She punched Ren in the cheekbone, and Ren went flying backward. Then she hit him again, this time with an elbow to his windpipe.

Ren gasped for air, but it wouldn't come. He clawed at his throat and managed to choke down a breath before Endo was on top of him, yanking his hair back until their gazes clashed.

"What did you do to Aiko?" she said, her voice surprisingly soft. "Is she alive?"

Ren couldn't speak even if he wanted to spill all of his secrets. The truth was, he didn't know what was happening to Aiko, but Major Endo seemed convinced that Ren knew the princess's exact location.

"Who are your accomplices?" she breathed into his face. Their noses were inches apart, and he could smell her mint gum. It was a jarring scent. *Tell us.*

Ren shook his head. He wouldn't give up Marty or Tessa, and he'd never give up his dad, even if it had been years since his father had been in the Resistance.

And the cycle began again.

Major Endo tossed him around the room, hitting Ren with her fists and her feet, with her head, and even with her fingers. Ren had never thought that a thumb could inflict so much pain, but as she dug a fingernail against his stitches and then into the gunshot wound in his side, he almost blacked out.

But he wouldn't say his family's names, and he wouldn't reveal Tessa's, either.

Ren lay curled on the floor, his cheek pressed against the concrete, his whole body on fire. Blood poured out of his stitches, hot and sticky against his skin. He didn't even have the strength to close his eyes. He was focused only on the next punch, the next blow, the next surge of agony.

It didn't come.

The curtain parted again, and the strike of boots hit the concrete. Soon, one of those boots nudged him from his side onto his back. Ren's chest heaved as he stared at the man standing over him.

It was Crown Prince Katsura.

He looked down at Ren. The spotlight lit him from behind, haloing his body and giving him an ethereal look, which only made Ren grimace.

"Where is my daughter?" said Crown Prince Katsura. He wasn't wearing his usual gold-framed glasses. Maybe they had gotten broken on the night of the ball. "Is she alive?"

A trickle of blood dribbled from Ren's mouth as he blinked at the crown prince. He looked different from his on-camera self. He lacked his caked-on makeup and his hair looked unwashed. There were also frown lines tugging at his mouth, making him look older — and ordinary. The crown prince was just a man, after all, a mere mortal made of muscle and bone.

In any other situation, Ren might have laughed. This situation was so absurd, how one human being could inflict so much suffering on another. Wasn't Ren made of muscle and bone, too? And yet in the WAT, the crown prince's life was considered far more important and precious than Ren's. This idea would have made for a thought-provoking essay, but Ren doubted he would ever get a chance to write it.

Crown Prince Katsura held up a yellow envelope that Major Endo handed to him, but he didn't open it. Instead, he took a seat on Ren's folding chair. "You won't believe me, but I don't like causing pain."

Ren coughed out. Obviously, he saw things differently. Maybe the crown prince had meant that he didn't like witnessing the pain he had inflicted. How uncomfortable it must have made him.

"I've tried to help your people: I've built schools. I've erected clinics. I've paved new roads. The Empire has paid for all of these amenities." The crown prince started to tick the items off on his fingers. "But it's never enough. Rebels like you have only upped your attacks. You've killed innocent civilians, sometimes your fellow Americans who've gotten caught in the cross fire, the very people you say you fight for." He shook his head. "And you call your cause just."

Ren spat out blood where one of his teeth had shaken loose. He could pick apart the crown prince's reasoning so easily — he could've written whole essays about it. Crown Prince Katsura may have viewed himself as a reformer, but he had never believed in real change. He had built schools and roads to "benefit" his subjects, but mostly they benefited the Empire itself. He may have thought that he cared for the American people, but only if they gladly worked for pennies and humbly accepted their downcast lives. As soon as they called for higher wages or organized strikes, the crown prince had been quick to open more internment camps. And when the Viper had gotten underneath the crown prince's skin, he had used the same scare tactics as his predecessors. New curfews. More patrols. Executions on the cliff.

"It's obvious that inflicting pain has yet to work on you." Crown Prince Katsura took a handkerchief from his jacket pocket to clean the blood droplets that had sprayed his cheeks. "My men would advise me to keep questioning you until you're ready to kiss the imperial flag, but I'm a practical man and I want to locate my daughter.

She's . . . she's very important to me." His voice thickened, and Ren wondered what he had meant by "important." Did he truly love Aiko? Or did he want her back to marry her off? Perhaps it was both. The crown prince's mouth twisted and he spat out, "Rebels like you killed her mother and brother."

The crown prince may have called himself practical, but his grief over his dead wife and son won out in the end. With a murmur to Endo, she began the beatings again. She kicked Ren in the shoulder, then smashed her boot against his back. Ren didn't know how long it lasted. He was too delirious to even whimper.

When Major Endo was finished, Crown Prince Katsura approached Ren's shuddering body and sighed. "Like I mentioned, physical pain seems to have little effect on you," the crown prince said, which was the most ridiculous thing Ren had ever heard. "But perhaps emotional manipulation will." Finally, he opened the yellow envelope and emptied its contents into his open palm, catching several black-and-white photos.

"This picture was taken shortly after your mother arrived in Alcatraz," Crown Prince Katsura began. He held aloft the first photo, dangling it in front of Ren's swollen eyes. In it, a woman lay unconscious on a hospital cot, with her abdomen bandaged and a tube down her throat. Her head had been shaved, but Ren would recognize that face anywhere.

"Mom," he whispered before he could stop himself. He tried to lift his fingers to take the photo, but Crown Prince Katsura snatched his hand away.

"Her body was supposed to be tossed into the ocean after her execution, like all other traitors," the crown prince explained, "but she survived her ordeal, so she was sent to Alcatraz. If she was hearty enough to live through a sword in the stomach, then her body could likely take on more."

Fury spiked through Ren. He hated how he hung on every one of the crown prince's words, desperate to learn more about his mother's fate. He hated, too, how the crown prince spoke of her, like she was a sturdy mule ready to serve the Empire. It made him want to explode.

But all Ren could do was cough up blood and try not pass out, and doing that was a feat.

Crown Prince Katsura showed the next photo to Ren, this one displaying his mother in a jail cell like the ones he had walked past earlier. She was sitting on her mattress with her arms lying limply at her sides, while a doctor and nurse checked her over.

"Where is she?" Ren rasped.

The crown prince replied by holding up the last photo of the bunch. This one was blurred and showed a close-up of Jenny Tsai. Her skin looked too pale and stretched too tautly over her cheekbones. Her lips were pressed shut, as if she was hiding something in her mouth. A web of dark veins fanned across her forehead, which didn't look natural.

"Where is she?" repeated Ren. "What did you do to her?"

The crown prince didn't acknowledge Ren's questions. "What matters is that your mother is alive. As you can see, that photo was dated four days ago."

Photographs could easily be doctored. Ren wasn't buying it. "Let me see her."

Crown Prince Katsura leaned in toward Ren. "If you'd like to be reunited with your mother, then I want to know what happened to my daughter."

So that's what the crown prince had meant by "emotional manipulation." For a few seconds, Ren was tempted in his bleeding and haggard state. He wanted to see his mom as much as he needed air. But Ren clung onto his last scraps of rationality. He couldn't give in.

"Give me your intelligence," the crown prince pressed, dangling the photograph of Ren's mother in front of Ren. "I want names of Resistance leaders. Coordinates to your safe houses. Once your information is verified, I'll bring you to your mother."

"I'm supposed to trust your word?" Ren said through swollen lips and broken teeth. He had to buy himself a little time. It was hard enough to keep breathing, much less formulate a full thought in his head, but he had to play this game somehow. He wanted to save his mother and the other prisoners, but to do that the Resistance needed access to Alcatraz. And to accomplish *that*, Ren would have to pass the island's authorization codes on to Marty.

But maybe there was another option. What if Ren could convince the crown prince to willingly turn off Alcatraz's defensive perimeter? It sounded crazy, but the idea glowed bright in Ren's dizzy head.

"Look around you," said Crown Prince Katsura, motioning to the solid walls and the prison guards. "You don't have much of a choice but to take me at my word." His lips twitched with irritation. "I'm not a patient man. Should I order Major Endo to do what she does best?"

"No," Ren said, far too quickly. *Think, think,* he told himself. What would make the crown prince lower Alcatraz's defenses? Aiko, maybe? He seemed desperate enough to find her.

Ren tried to piece together a strategy, using the few neurons he had left. The crown prince had dangled Ren's mother to manipulate Ren. Now Ren would have to dangle something in front of him.

Ren started talking. "Offer the Resistance a prisoner exchange."

The crown prince frowned. "That isn't —"

"If you want to see your daughter again, then listen. It would be a two-to-one exchange. Aiko for my mother and me," Ren said quickly.

"You expect me to believe that your Resistance would trade for you and your mother?"

"No, they'd never do that for Ren Cabot." Ren's pulse was fluttering so quickly that he became light-headed. Doubt hounded him. Did he really want to do this? If he did, there would be no going back. And he would have to confront every consequence that would come with this decision. But Ren had to go all in — with every single one of his chips, even though he was holding a pair of sixes. He had to hope that the crown prince wouldn't call his bluff.

"But they *would* trade for the Viper."

Ren heard an intake of breath. The crown prince's face shifted quickly with emotion, from bafflement to realization to plain shock.

"You can't be saying...," the crown prince murmured. He squinted at Ren.

"I have proof. You want to know where I do my work? Go to 4890 Cliffside Lane, north of White Crescent Bay." Ren couldn't believe he was giving away his identity, but he was probably going to die anyway. He might as well use everything in his arsenal. So many lives depended on it. "Send your soldiers to the gardening shed out back. There's a room hidden below it. You'll find a printing press there."

The crown prince fell silent, and Ren grew worried. This was his main concern about revealing his identity — that the crown prince would rather keep the Viper in his clutches than give Ren up.

"If you want to see your daughter again — alive — then you'll offer a prisoner exchange," Ren continued, hoping this would remind the crown prince what was at stake. "We'll rendezvous here at Alcatraz. The Resistance will hand over Her Imperial Highness, and you'll let my mother and me go." *And then the Resistance will launch a larger attack to free the rest of the prisoners,* Ren thought. That was his delirious plan anyway.

Crown Prince Katusra said nothing. His face had closed, unreadable, and he stood to speak to Major Endo. They whispered to each other, and soon Major Endo snapped orders to the guards to get a boat readied. Ren's heart thumped.

Before the crown prince departed, however, he stopped and stood over Ren. Then he glanced again at Major Endo.

"I don't believe the two of you have been properly introduced. Ren, this is Major Endo. Major, this boy claims to be the Viper."

Major Endo took two steps forward, and Ren's stomach took a deep dive. Fear forced his voice higher.

"The Resistance will want me alive!" Ren coughed out desperately.

"Noted," replied the crown prince. He turned to leave but said over his shoulder, "Make sure that he stays alive, Major." Then he was gone, leaving Ren alone again with one of the most deadly Ronin Elite in the Empire.

Rolling her neck, Major Endo approached Ren slowly to draw out his anxiety, circling him twice before kneeling at his side.

"No," Ren whimpered. "Please."

She placed her fingertips on his scalp.

"No!" Ren screamed. "I'm not the Viper — I'm not the Viper!" He hated the sounds coming out of his mouth. They were the words of a coward, but as he felt his blood heating up, he began to beg Major Endo for mercy.

It didn't matter. She didn't listen.

24

By the time Major Endo was dismissed, Ren couldn't remember his last name. All he knew was pain. It gnawed through every limb, every muscle; it throbbed down to the last cell. Even breathing hurt. Blinking hurt. Simply *existing* hurt.

Ren didn't know how long the torture had lasted. Hours, probably, although it had felt like weeks. He couldn't recall when it had stopped, either, only that one minute he was screaming and the next he was hauled out of the interrogation room and shoved into a prison cell and left there, utterly broken.

Bloodied and bone-weary, Ren had lacked the strength to even pull himself onto the cot. So he lay on the dirty floor and waited for the darkness to come.

When he woke up, the pain greeted him once again. Ren looked down at himself. Someone had moved him from the floor and onto his cot when he was unconscious. Probably a nurse, judging by the new bandages crisscrossing his body. There were too many wounds to count — his old gunshot injuries, his tender ribs, the cuts and gashes and bruises that Endo had left in her wake. She was the artist, and Ren had been her canvas. He was sure that he would wear her scars on his body and inside his mind for years, if he lived that long.

Ren tried to sit up, hoping to find a cup of water, but his head went dizzy and bile rose in his throat. He moaned and shivered instead. He was naked from the waist up, and the prison was damp and chilly. He hadn't been given a blanket, so he gingerly wrapped his arms around himself, not that they offered him much warmth. He used his tongue to probe the two empty sockets where he had lost teeth.

He didn't think he could sink much lower.

But then he remembered what he had told the crown prince.

He had revealed his deepest secret, and now he thought about if he had made a mistake. Would the crown prince make Ren rot inside Alcatraz for the rest of his life? Would he get pumped full of injections or wheeled into experimental surgery? Or would he get marched across the cliffs and made an example of? That would have been a good punishment for the Viper, Ren thought bitterly.

Footsteps shuffled toward the cell, and fear rose fast in Ren's chest. He couldn't face Endo again. But thankfully, Endo didn't walk into Ren's view. It was Bluefin and another nurse, pushing a cart that held water and food and medical kits. A prison guard joined them, keeping a sharp eye on the prisoners while the nurses fanned out to care for their charges.

Unlocking Ren's cell, Bluefin shuffled inside with a medical bag in tow. Their gazes locked, and Ren saw the shock in her eyes. He knew how he must have looked. Busted lip. Swollen face. Crusted blood under his nose and at the corners of his lips. But maybe she had seen worse, considering that she worked at Alcatraz.

"Can you open your mouth?" she said. She slid a thermometer through Ren's lips, treating him as gingerly as possible, and waited for the prison guard to pace away from the cell before she pushed a note into Ren's palm. While he opened the paper she continued his checkup, marking his temperature and pulse, flashing a light up his nose and into his ears.

The crown prince is arranging a prisoner exchange. Aiko for you and your mother. No time or date set. Is it true that you're the Viper?

Ren lifted his eyes and nodded at Bluefin before he continued reading.

Your mother is being held in the room where you were interrogated. Behind the curtain.

"Thank you," Ren mouthed to her, realizing he would never be able to repay her. Because of her, the Resistance had learned about what was happening at Alcatraz; and because of her intel, Marty had discovered that Ren's mom might still be alive. And now Ren knew where Jenny Tsai was being kept. His mom was so close, just steps beyond where he was interrogated. And maybe, if his plan worked, then he could still get his mother off this island.

But if Ren wanted to make that a reality, he had preparations to make.

"I need your help," he whispered to Bluefin. "I've come up with —"

She silenced him by pushing a cup of water at him. "We can't talk. Too risky," she whispered, sliding a glance over her shoulder. She ladled Ren another round of rice gruel, gestured for him to swallow her note, and surreptitiously slid him a pencil and palm-size piece of paper from the medical kit.

"Don't let anyone find these," she said quietly as she forced him to finish the gruel. "Understand?"

Ren could read between the lines. If a guard or another nurse discovered his note, both he and Bluefin would be done for. He would have to keep the paper and pencil very carefully hidden. He nodded.

After Bluefin and the prison guard departed, Ren grimaced and slid back onto the floor. His joints protested his every move, but he needed a hard surface to write on. Pretending to be nauseous, Ren curled his body around the metal toilet — in case another guard walked by — and got to work, grasping the pencil between his swollen fingers and scribbling the plan he had been plotting in his head. Forming each letter was a labor; every sentence made him breathless. But he forced himself to keep writing. He had to finish this note before Bluefin returned or before he went dizzy again and slipped into unconsciousness.

Relay this to Marty ASAP.

This is what I think will happen: The crown prince will turn off the bombs surrounding Alcatraz in order for Aiko's boat to come through. Then the prisoner exchange will start. I have a feeling that the crown prince will turn on the bombs again, trapping our ship and arresting the Resistance members inside. He'll think that we're swimming right into his trap. But he'll be wrong.

While the boat carrying Aiko comes ashore, I need Bluefin to shut off the electricity on the island. The island's security will be focused on saving Aiko, so Bluefin should be able to slip away. Once the lights are cut, the bombs will go dead. That's when our full forces will swoop in, and the mission will go on as we planned before.

Ren set the pencil down, exhausted. Marty should be able to piece the rest of the operation from there. They would free the prisoners, including Zara. They would search for V2. And they would locate Ren's mother. The Alcatraz experiments would come to an end, and the Resistance would let the entire WAT know what the Empire had been doing to American prisoners.

When he was finished, Ren read over his writing and made a few changes, but his instructions would have to do. Folding the note into a small square, Ren shoved it into his pants pocket and hid the pencil under his cot. He was completely out of breath by then, but a spark of hope managed to flare in his heart. He held on to the little flame, clinging to it desperately, until he gave in to the abyss.

Two days passed, and Ren slipped in and out of sleep. As promised, Bluefin had returned and retrieved the note. She had read over it quickly as Ren swallowed a cup of water. He had watched her cheeks drain of color as she read each line, and her fingers had clutched the note tightly when she was finished. Ren didn't even know if what he was asking of her was possible — maybe she didn't know how to turn off the island's power or if she even had access to the panels — but Bluefin hadn't protested.

"I know what I'm asking of you," Ren had whispered as she handed him some rice.

She had responded by nodding. "I can do it. I know where the panels are."

But Ren saw the fear in her eyes. He knew she could get killed if she was caught. "What's your name? Your real name?"

She shook her head. "I should go."

"Please. I owe you my life."

Her mouth opened hesitatingly. Then she murmured, "Midori."

"Thank you, Midori," rasped Ren. He hated that those words would never be enough. She was a Japanese citizen and she owed nothing to him or the Resistance, yet she was risking her life for him and for this cause.

Midori's fingers trembled as she readied her cart. With one last glance, she whispered, "In the darkest of nights."

And she had left it at that.

Midori was in. Ren was ready. But still, they had to wait. The prisoner exchange had been set for Thursday night, not even a week since the Joint Prosperity Ball had come to a bloody end. Ren could only hope that it would be enough time for Marty to put the mission back together. This would probably be their only shot.

Finally, the hour arrived. A prison guard approached Ren's cell, a hulking man with a bulldog face and a neck even thicker than Ren's thigh. He said nothing to Ren as he shoved three items through the bars: a clean jumpsuit, a wet sponge, a thin pair of slippers.

"Get yourself cleaned up and dressed," the guard ordered. He held up one hand and splayed out his fingers. "Five minutes."

Ren nodded. Moving as fast as he could (which wasn't fast at all), he slid out of his soiled garments and wiped himself down with the cold, wet sponge, scrubbing at the dried blood and dirt that he had worn for a week. By the time he was scrubbed, the sponge had turned a dark brown color.

Next, Ren forced his tired limbs into the jumpsuit, zipping it closed. He had barely raked his fingers through his greasy hair when the prison guard unlocked the door and yanked Ren toward him.

Ren almost blacked out from the sudden movement, but the guard slapped his cheek and dragged him down the hallway. A few forlorn faces stared at Ren from the cells, their deadened eyes unblinking. If all went well tonight, those prisoners would soon taste freedom, but Ren doubted that they could leave Alcatraz fully behind. Deep down, he knew that he would never forget his short time in the prison. The nightmares had already started, and more than once he'd woken up in a cold sweat, his throat sore from screaming and his mind swarming with memories of Major Endo. Alcatraz would haunt him for the rest of his life. He knew that in his bones.

The guard thrust the main prison door open and thrust Ren into a cloudy night. The last remnants of muted sunlight were leaching across the sky, and the lights of Alcatraz had been switched on to full blast. But even those searing searchlights couldn't push through the thick fog that rolled in from the water.

Ren took small comfort in the weather. He couldn't have asked for better conditions.

The prison guard steered Ren over the uneven earth, leading him down the winding path that led to a dock, which was used for receiving supplies. The prison looked ready for battle. Armed soldiers stood throughout the island — up on the rooftops, gathered outside every building, sprinkled over the paths. The crown prince wasn't taking any chances.

Ren's bare toes went numb in the cold as they approached the metal dock, which extended so far out into the water that the fog had swallowed over half of it. The prison guard shoved Ren onto his knees on the dock, and he planted his hands on Ren's shoulders to keep him from moving. But that wasn't necessary. Even if Ren had the strength to wrestle free and escape the inevitable bullets, he would have a long swim to safety in the dark hypothermic waters.

Seconds ticked by, then minutes. Ren drummed his fingers against his thigh to keep his hands busy because his anxiety felt close to suffocating. By now Marty should have been nearing the island on the stolen Coast Guard ship, and the rest of the Resistance forces should have been lurking in the waters, ready for Marty's signal to strike. Once the attack began, everything would move quickly from there, and he had to concentrate on his task — running to his mom and getting her to any Resistance ship.

Ren dared a glance up the path to find a new group of people clustered there. A troop of soldiers formed a shield around Major Endo and Crown Prince Katsura.

Ren's head snapped forward to the waves. The sight of Major Endo had made his stomach churn and revolt, and before long he was retching on the dock. The prison guard slapped him on the back of his head and ordered him to stop, but Ren couldn't do a thing until his belly emptied. He told himself he had to think about the mission instead of Endo's fingertips, but his whole body shivered. He would rather take his chances out at sea than ever face her again.

The hum of a boat engine pulled Ren out of his thoughts. The prisoner exchange should start any time now — but where was his mother? Ren had thought that she would have been brought out to the dock already.

But Ren saw no movement coming from the prison, and that made him go cold all over. Was the crown prince already reneging on the deal?

Just then, the nose of a sleek white boat pierced through the fog. It was the Resistance's Coast Guard ship. All of the lights on board had been turned off, and there were no Resistance members in sight. An eerie quiet settled over the dock and spread onto the shore. It looked like no one was aboard the boat at all.

Then a voice boomed from the ship's speakers. "Our trade was for the Viper and Jenny Tsai."

Major Endo lifted a bullhorn in her perch. "Give us the princess first."

The Resistance didn't hesitate to reply. "Bring Jenny Tsai to the dock *immediately.*"

"We'll bring the traitor to the beach, but *after* we get confirmation that Aiko is alive and on board your ship," Endo countered.

Ren gnashed his teeth together. He didn't know what the crown prince was doing — and he didn't like it.

A moment passed before a light switched on inside the ship's pilothouse. A solitary figure stood by the window, blindfolded and gagged and handcuffed. She wore a white T-shirt and men's trousers, but there was no mistaking who it was. Aiko.

She was the key to unlocking this mission.

She was the pawn both sides needed.

Ren had willingly put her on the chessboard, but this was the only way for the Resistance to strike back. Perhaps it was cruel, but fairness belonged to another world.

Major Endo's voice pitched higher at the sight of the princess. "Escort Her Imperial Highness onto the dock. Slowly."

"That wasn't the deal," the loudspeakers blared.

Ren couldn't see Endo behind him, but he could hear the smirk in her tone. "You have no other choice. As you can see, our soldiers outnumber yours and we've blocked your escape. We switched on the defensive perimeter as soon as you crossed over the bombs. If you don't send out the princess, then prepare to be boarded."

The Resistance, however, had been expecting this. Within seconds, the light switched off in the pilothouse, plunging the ship back into darkness. The loudspeakers crackled, and Ren heard a terrified scream.

"Father, please!" came Aiko's voice.

Then all went quiet.

The Resistance had tossed down its hand, making it clear that it wouldn't be cowed by the crown prince's games.

Tension multiplied across the shore, thickening the air with an electric bite. Major Endo didn't answer right away, and Ren guessed that she was conferring with Crown Prince Katsura on what to do next. They had probably thought that the rebels would have surrendered and crumbled.

"The crown prince will grant you mercy if you turn over the princess right now," Major Endo said into the bullhorn, her tone sharp as glass. "We'll send you to reeducation centers instead of slitting your throats. This will be the best offer you'll receive."

The silence stretched further. The Resistance said nothing.

Ren hummed with nerves. His knees had gone numb kneeling on the dock and his skin was frigid to the touch, and he wasn't sure how long he could keep still. What had happened to Midori? The Resistance *needed* her to shut the lights off — and fast. This standstill could soon turn bloody, and like Endo said, the Resistance had no way of escape. The entire mission now hinged on a single nurse.

As if on cue, darkness fell fast over Alcatraz. Every light was snuffed out, plummeting the soldiers into chaos. Midori had come through.

Confused shouts filled Ren's ears. Major Endo ordered everyone to keep calm, but then came a spray of gunfire. The prison guard next to Ren fell into a heap on the dock, clutching his throat, which had started spurting blood. Ren splayed himself on the ground to avoid getting caught in the blast, unsure of which side had discharged first.

"Hold your fire — the princess is aboard that ship!" shouted Major Endo to everyone onshore. "Get the crown prince to safety!"

The bullets drowned out her voice, popping off hot and fast. The Resistance was firing from the ship, blowing through their magazines to take out the soldiers before reinforcements could pour in.

Ren ignored the impulse to run, even when a bullet singed his hair. He had to lay low until the rest of the Resistance rebels arrived on their ships. It was suicide otherwise.

With a grimace, Ren crawled next to the dead prison guard and dragged his body onto the rocky shoreline, not far from the dock. Ren yanked the pistol from the guard's belt. He didn't have much experience with guns, but he didn't want to dive into battle unarmed and the cold metal gave him the smallest sliver of comfort. Then he huddled next to the guard's warm corpse, using it as a shield.

Suddenly, the soldiers' shouts multiplied along the shore.

"Open fire!" someone said.

"They're out on the water!"

Ren lifted his head high enough to make out the dark shapes moving toward Alcatraz. There were dozens of ships — speedboats and tugboats and more stolen military ships — of all colors and sizes. Their engines hummed in a mechanical chorus, and Ren had never heard such a beautiful sound.

The Resistance was here.

The battle unfurled in front of him. As the Resistance ships closed in on the island, the rebels got straight to work. Some of them fired rifles and machine guns from the deck of their ships, providing cover for their comrades who paddled ashore on rubber boats. Soon the water swarmed with Resistance forces, but the Empire struck back hard. Armed guards poured out from the prison buildings, and Ren was sure that the soldiers had already called in reinforcements from the city.

The first wave of rebels invaded the Rock, their pistols at the ready and their belts filled with grenades. They didn't have the armor or military-grade rifles that the prison guards had, but they made up for that in sheer numbers, dozens upon dozens arriving by the minute. They charged up the path toward the main prison, unleashing their bullets as the soldiers matched their fire. As soon as one rebel fell, another grabbed their weapons and took up their place. There was no time to call for the medics and no time to comfort the dying. The Resistance had been preparing for this moment for months — and it showed.

As the Resistance swept over Alcatraz, Ren made his own move at last. He crouched on shaky knees, pistol in hand, and followed a group of rebels onto the gravel path. His foot stepped on a dead body — ally or enemy, he wasn't sure — and he hunkered down as a grenade exploded behind them, the heat lashing against his forehead. But Ren had to keep going. He no longer felt the sting of his injuries, just a fresh rush of adrenaline that pumped through his body, propelling him forward.

Ren reached the prison and threw himself into the pandemonium inside. The first wave of rebels had already cleared the path for him. Bodies lay strewn on the floor, over a dozen prison guards along with a few dark-clothed rebels. A fire burned on the third story of the building — a grenade must have gone off up there — but the flames hadn't stopped the Resistance members from tackling their job.

Over fifty rebels had swarmed on all of the prison floors. Some of them fought the remaining guards while others were opening the cells. They moved like clockwork — as soon as one rebel unlocked a door, another one would help the prisoner inside to their feet and escort them out. They had to return quickly to the boats before the Empire flew in more soldiers and sent in the navy. That was why the Resistance had to rely on quickness — because they could never fight the full arsenal of the enemy. Ren had learned that once, and it was a lesson he would never need to learn again.

As Ren delved deeper into the prison, he kept an eye out for Marty. She was somewhere on Alcatraz, but he didn't see her yet and he had to focus on finding his mom. With each step that he took, he closed the distance between them. Ren crossed the threshold into the interrogation room to find that the curtain dividing the space had already been swept aside. He darted forward.

"Ren!"

Ren didn't turn around. He was focused on one thing only, and the voice calling for him had barely registered.

"Ren, wait!"

All of a sudden, Ren was spun around so fast that he lost his grip on his gun. He was about to retrieve it, thinking that a prison guard had disarmed him, but then he went absolutely still.

Ren stared at the man in front of him. "Dad?"

His father didn't answer. He simply opened his arms and crushed Ren to his chest. For a few seconds, Ren leaned into Mr. Cabot, too surprised to do anything else. The chances must have been tiny, but somehow his father had found him here on Alcatraz.

Mr. Cabot leaned back to look his son over. And his eyes filled with anguish as he took in the cuts on Ren's face and the holes where he was missing teeth. "My God."

"We have to find Mom," Ren said, cutting their reunion short. He would explain everything later. There was work to do first, like staying alive. "She's back here."

Mr. Cabot didn't ask any questions. He merely picked up Ren's pistol, pressed it into Ren's hand, and held his own gun in front of him. His right hand was still bandaged, so he had to hold his weapon in his left. "Stay behind me."

Together they parted the rest of the curtain and uncovered what the Empire had been hiding for years. Metal cages were spread throughout the space, each one about the size of a cramped prison cell. A few of the rebels had killed off the guards and scientists stationed there, and now they were unlocking each cage to release the Anomalies. But not all of the prisoners were rushing out.

Ren blinked from cage to cage, prisoner to prisoner. There were fifteen of them, all of them with shaved heads and wearing bright orange jumpsuits. *The fifteen Anomalies,* he realized. These prisoners had survived the very first testing of V2, and the Empire had locked them all in this room. For observation? For further experimentation? His jaw twitched. Probably both.

"Come on, Dad," Ren said hoarsely. "Mom should be in here."

The two of them hurried to the cages. A few of the prisoners had already left for the ships, guided by their rebel escorts, but others had shrunk into their cages, rocking back and forth. One of the women had formed tentacles of electricity around her body, like a protective shell. Another had gone invisible, but Ren could make out their body through the lines of their uniforms. There were more of them still, being coaxed gently by the rebels charged with getting them out to the boats.

"Ren, this way!" Mr. Cabot said, running toward a cage in the far corner. The door was already unlocked and flung open, but the prisoner inside had curled up next to her dirty mattress, clearly terrified. Her eyes flew between Ren and his father, looming large like twin moons.

Ren knew those eyes. He barreled past his dad.

"Not yet!" his father warned. "Give her some space."

But Ren couldn't wait, not after all of these years that had cruelly separated them.

Ren entered the cage and raised his hands slowly — he didn't want to scare her — and inched forward. His heart felt open and raw and hopeful.

"Mom?" he whispered.

25

As Ren focused on his mother, the world around them went quiet, leaving only the sound of his rapid heartbeat.

"Mom," Ren said again, a little louder this time. But his mother shrank farther away from him, murmuring a long string of numbers that made no sense. Her entire cage was covered in numbers as well, elaborate equations that Ren couldn't decipher. Some of them were written in marker, while others looked like they had been penned in blood.

"Jenny," Mr. Cabot said, joining Ren inside the cage. His voice cracked as he beckoned for his wife, but she pressed her hands against her ears.

"Three, five, six, nine, nine, zero, zero," she mumbled. "Four, one, two, two, eight."

Something broke inside Ren. What had the scientists done to her?

"We have to get her out," Ren said to his dad. They had years ahead of them to help his mother heal. Right now, however, they were losing time. "We'll have to carry her."

Mr. Cabot made the first move, opening his arms to grab his wife, but she darted to the other side of the cage, surprisingly fast. "Grab her, Ren!"

Ren wrapped his arms around his mother's waist and pulled her against him. She was rail-thin, all angles and bones, and Ren almost let her go because he thought he might crush her. But soon his father was there, taking his wife's right arm while Ren grasped her left, holding on tightly as Jenny twisted and thrashed and let out an animal-like scream.

"Five, five, zero!" she gasped. Ren had no idea what the V2 had done to her aside from make her lose her mind. Her equations may have unlocked riddles or propelled mathematics forward by a century, but all Ren knew was that she had suffered.

They forced her out of the cage, and Ren hated the look that she gave them. He wasn't sure what was worse — the fear in his mother's eyes or the lack of recognition. He had told himself that she might not remember him, but the reality of it had carved a hole in his heart. His mother had no idea who he was.

Just then, a bomb went off outside the prison. The walls shook, and the floors rumbled, almost knocking Ren off balance. Pieces of concrete were sloughed off from the ceiling, missing Mr. Cabot's head by mere inches.

"We have to get to the boats!" Mr. Cabot said to Ren. "Do you still have your pistol?"

Ren retrieved his gun from his jumpsuit pocket while another bomb went off. "Let's go."

With his mother balanced between them, Ren and his dad stepped over the fresh rubble and returned to the main hallway of the prison. The cells had been cleared out, their doors swinging wide open, and a handful of rebels escorted the last prisoners toward the exit.

"Is Marty here?" Ren asked his dad.

"She's searching for the V2. We'll meet up with her later. Right now, though, we have to —"

Another bomb silenced the remainder of his sentence. The walls groaned louder, and Ren tried to up their pace, but he tripped over a crack that had opened along the floor. Ren lost his hold on his mom as he fell forward, right on top of a female rebel's warm corpse. Shuddering, Ren was about to push himself up when he heard someone moaning. His gaze zeroed in on the sound.

It was one of the prisoners, dressed in a much too large orange jumpsuit that swallowed her slim frame. Her head had been shaved and she weighed next to nothing as Ren lifted her into his arms. She must have been trying to escape when one of the bombs struck her down, but she had managed to hold on to a small locked box. Her fingers were firmly gripped around it, even though she was only half conscious.

"Ren!" Mr. Cabot cried out after he had helped his wife to her feet. "Are you hurt?"

"I'm fine. Keep going!" Ren coughed out. He shifted the prisoner in his arms and hurried behind his parents toward the main door. As they neared, the prisoner's bald head lolled toward him, revealing her face. Ren almost dropped her.

It was Zara St. James. He was absolutely sure of it.

"Dad —" Ren started to say, but then Zara stirred in his arms and her eyes shot open when she realized a stranger was carrying her. She quickly began to squirm.

"I'm with the Resistance," Ren rushed to reassure her. "I don't know how much you remember, but you were captured and taken to

Alcatraz. We've infiltrated the island and now we're heading to the escape boats."

It was a whole lot to take in, but Zara had stopped struggling, at least. Despite the gash slicing her temple and the bruises on her cheeks, she croaked, "Let me down. I can walk."

Ren doubted that, but he set her onto her feet. She wobbled for a second and had to lean on Ren for support, but she managed to stand upright.

"The doctors . . . ," she said woozily, still holding on to the locked box. "They gave me something that makes me dizzy."

"Use me as a crutch if you have to, but we have to leave now," offered Ren.

Suddenly, Mr. Cabot recognized the prisoner next to his son. He had been so busy trying to calm his wife down that he hadn't given Zara a closer look. But now wasn't the time for handshakes or introductions. He simply nodded at her, and she returned the favor.

"Ren, come take your mom," said Mr. Cabot, tenderly shifting his wife's weight toward his son. "It isn't far to the boats and there will be rebels stationed along the path to give us cover, but we'll be easy targets." To Zara he said, "Stick close to us."

She nodded but her lips pursed in frustration. She held her right palm up, trying to ignite a lightning bolt, but only a few sparks went off. "Whatever chemicals they gave me muted my powers."

"We'll cover you," Mr. Cabot assured her. Then he rested his bandaged hand on Ren's shoulder. "I'll lead us out, but if I go down, you have to keep going. Head to the nearest ship. The fleet has to move out soon, so get on board as soon as possible. Okay?"

Ren didn't want to talk about this, even though it needed to be said. He didn't want to confront what waited for them on the other side of the door, either.

"Okay, Ren?" his father repeated. "Don't lose sight of the boats."

Ren forced a nod. "Okay, Dad."

Mr. Cabot kissed his son's forehead before he gripped the door handle. "On the count of three, then. One . . . two . . ."

Throwing the door open, Mr. Cabot ducked into the night. Ren and his mom went next, with Zara a step behind.

They entered a war zone. Imperial helicopters circled above the island while they dropped soldiers onto Alcatraz to replace the lost troops. Out on the water, it looked like over half of the Resistance fleet had departed, packed full of prisoners and fanning across the water toward different safe houses. But the other half of the fleet still bobbed by the island, awaiting the remaining rebels and prisoners to come aboard. Ren saw the mission in motion, how some of the rebels shepherded the feeble prisoners toward the ships while other rebels fought off the new wave of soldiers. The tide was turning in the Empire's favor as more reinforcements poured in, including a troop of Ronin Elite.

The Anomalies had arrived. One Ronin flew in circles over the island, mowing down rebels and prisoners with a sniper's precision. Another swam out toward a Resistance tugboat, evading the rebels' bullets with her impenetrable skin. And yet another Ronin used his superspeed to snatch pistols from the rebels' hands.

But the Resistance fought back. A handful of the freed Anomaly prisoners had joined in on the fight, still dressed in their jumpsuits but ready to release years of pent-up rage. One woman thrust her hands toward the sky, creating a sheath of fog to wrap itself around a helicopter and blind the pilots in the cockpit. Another stood ankle-deep in the water and used his power of manipulating liquid to help push the fleeing Resistance ships farther out to sea. Ren saw another man, too, just skin and bones and barely able to stand, yet somehow he lifted soldiers into the air with his mind and flung them out into the ocean.

"This way!" shouted Mr. Cabot, hurrying over the gravel path that led toward the dock.

Bullets whizzed by them, but Ren pushed down his fear and followed his father. Like his dad had promised, the rebels had been stationed all along the path, allowing the prisoners the safest escape route. But the casualties had already been racked up. Ren lost count of how many bodies he stumbled over, some of them still moaning.

"Seven point three. Zero point two," Ren's mother wailed. Her hands smashed over her ears, and Ren struggled to keep ahold of her.

About halfway down the way, a grenade exploded right behind Zara and she fell forward into Ren and his mom. With his face crushed against the gravel, Ren coughed and felt his neck, wet with blood. The wound, however, didn't feel deep.

"Are you okay?" Zara's voice sounded far away as Ren lay dazed, but he jolted awake when she yanked him up with the strength of someone triple her size.

"Where's my mom?" Ren yelled back. He spotted his dad trying to crawl toward them, but his mother was nowhere in sight. Ren twisted around, searching desperately for his mom's orange jumpsuit.

Then he found her. She was sprinting back up the road, back toward the prison that had been her home these last five years.

But someone was blocking the path.

Major Endo.

Ren didn't know where Endo had come from. He thought she had escaped with the crown prince, but apparently she had remained behind to pick off the rebels. Armed with a pistol in each hand, she popped off shots and reloaded.

Everything unraveled very quickly from there.

Ren's mother charged up the path, frantic, and Endo whirled around, firing twice.

Jenny Tsai staggered and fell.

But Ren was already running.

Fear ripped through him. *Let her be okay*, he thought desperately. Then that fear twisted into shock when he saw Endo firing again — this time into his mother's abdomen — and suddenly the shock grew into a hot and burning rage.

With his anger driving him, Ren grabbed his pistol and fired three rounds, his whole body humming with fury. Each one of his shots had flown wide, but they certainly got Major Endo's attention. She aimed and fired back, and Ren dove down to avoid the bullets. Once her magazine emptied, however, he was back on his feet and surging forward to his mom. Her jumpsuit was blooming with fresh blood, already soaking through the fabric.

Suddenly, someone tackled Ren from behind. "Get down!" Zara

said, rolling him to the side of the path to avoid Major Endo's reloaded pistols. Wrath filled her eyes and she thrust her right hand toward Endo, shooting a small but terrifying bolt of lightning out of her palm. The bolt sizzled through the air, and Endo tried to leap out of its way, but it hit her in the back of the head, fanning down her body in a spidery blue wave.

Ren scrambled to his mom's side and cradled her head as she struggled to breathe.

Dark blood pumped freely from the bullet hole in her stomach, pouring down the sides of her jumpsuit and seeping into the earth. Ren didn't know what to do. He couldn't lose her again. He looked around helplessly, but obviously there were no nurses or doctors to help them. Was it already too late for that?

"Ren! Oh God," said Mr. Cabot, hurtling up the path. He took his wife into his arms, nestling her against his chest while she moaned from the pain. "We have to get her to a ship."

Ren could only stare at his hands, now covered with his mother's blood. He had come this far; he had endured so much; only to watch his mother get shot again and again.

"Ren!" his father yelled. "Move out."

But there was one last thing Ren had to do.

"There's no time!" his father said.

Ren jerked away. He would *make* time for this. Rage consumed him, was unleashed inside him like a living thing. For so long he had ignored it and locked it away. For once, though, he would let it take over.

Ren hobbled to where Major Endo had fallen. Her face twitched.

Severe burns covered her neck, and Ren almost vomited at the smell of the cooked flesh. Zara was kneeling next to Endo and trying to call up another bolt of lighting, but every attempt sputtered out. Frustrated, she glanced at Ren.

"I'll do it," he said firmly. Ren curled his finger around the trigger.

Endo looked up at him. Her eyes had grown wide, panicked, and she tried to mumble something. Ren had never seen her so vulnerable, so afraid.

But his fury demanded justice, just this once.

He fired. And Endo went still.

It was finished within a split second, and Ren's arm fell heavily against his side. Exhaustion spread over his body like a sedative. He had killed someone. He had fired and taken a life. Strangely, though, he felt nothing but numbness, as if someone had depleted him of all feeling.

And the night was far from over.

"Come on!" Zara said, grabbing Ren by the hand. Ren was ready to let her guide him down the road, but she had other ideas. All of a sudden, Ren's feet left the earth. The two of them zoomed upward, their legs dangling in thin air as they soared over the path and the shore. She was flying them toward the Resistance ships.

But Zara's full power had yet to return, and she struggled to keep them upright. "I see your parents down there."

"Can you bring them with us?"

"Maybe." Squinting at the ground, she swooped an arm through the air, trying to call up a great gust of wind. Thankfully, it worked, and the wind picked up Ren's parents and sent them soaring over the waves. The four of them careened through the winter chill, leaving behind the beach and the dock and the prison on Alcatraz.

Glancing behind him, the island unfurled beneath Ren's feet. Smoke billowed from most of the buildings, some of them burning while others had been smashed to rubble. Bodies lay sprawled everywhere as the last of the rebels and prisoners fled to the boats. It looked like most of the prisoners had made it out, although no one could know the final tally until later. Ren wondered if the crown prince and Aiko had survived, and he especially worried about Marty, but right now he had to help his mom.

As Zara's breathing grew heavy, she guided them all toward the remaining fleet. She headed straight for the nearest ship, a sleek black yacht. Ren saw people on board raising their weapons, and he had to say something.

"We're on your side!" Ren shouted as loudly as he could.

The four of them crashed onto the back of the ship. Ren went first, crumpling onto the deck, and Zara landed on top of him. Ren's parents tumbled nearby and almost went overboard, but some of the rebels grabbed them before they fell into the bay.

Groaning, Ren tried to check on Zara, but she waved him off. "I'll be okay. I'm just c-cold." She tilted her head toward his parents. "Go."

Ren nodded gratefully and limped toward where his mother lay. The rebels had already brought out towels to sop up the blood, and Mr. Cabot used them to apply pressure to Jenny's wounds.

"Is there a nurse on board?" Ren pleaded. "Anyone with medical experience?"

Nobody came forward.

The next question tore out of Ren's throat. "Can *anyone* help us?"

Finally, one of the rebels spoke out. "There should be a nurse at the safe house."

"How long until we get there?" demanded Ren.

"An hour at least."

Ren's stomach exploded with nerves. Could his mother hang on for that long? He thought about asking Zara to fly them into the city, but she had curled up on the deck, utterly spent. She didn't look like she could walk, much less fly.

Ren knelt at his mother's side, helping his dad apply pressure while touching her cheek with the other hand. Her skin was freezing; her body trembled. Yet her eyes stayed wide open, blinking up at Ren but not quite seeing him.

Ren leaned in, hoping to find a flicker of his mother on her face. "You're going to be okay." His voice broke in half. "It's me. It's Ren."

"Zero, zero, zero," she whispered. "Zero, zero, zero."

Ren looked helplessly at his dad. "Is she going to make it?"

"We'll do everything we can," said his father, his throat raw. "She has survived this far. Don't forget that." But Ren heard the doubt in his father's voice.

Ren clutched his mother's hand. He pressed his cheek against hers, quietly begging her not to go. "Hang on, Mom. Just hang on."

His mother coughed up blood, and Ren had to release her hand to turn her onto her side, letting the liquid pour out of her mouth. His gaze snagged his father's.

"Is she dying?" Ren asked, his voice so small.

His dad stubbornly shook his head. "She's strong. She's going to make it."

Ren wished that he had his father's hope. Pain ripped through him from the deepest of wounds that even Major Endo had never reached. He wanted to believe that his mother would be okay, that with the right care and treatment she would become the woman she once was, the woman who stirred chicken congee on the stove and worked on her articles at night.

But Ren's dream was shrinking by the second.

Noises came out of Ren's mother's mouth. No longer numbers but nonsense. Soon, she stopped speaking at all. Every breath thickened as her lungs filled with blood. She was drowning.

"Mom!" Ren cried out. She was dying in front of him again and there was nothing he could do. He wanted to shake her. Scream at her. Plead with her not to go. It didn't matter if she never got her mind back, but Ren needed her here with him. He needed his heart and his family to be whole again.

His mother started to shake, and her eyes rolled back into her head. Mr. Cabot elbowed Ren aside and began administering CPR, pumping his wife's chest and breathing air into her lungs, but she made no sound. She only kept bleeding until her skin emptied of color.

"Mom," Ren said again. He squeezed her hand in his own, hoping to tether her to this life.

It didn't work.

His mother's chest stopped moving.

She was gone. This time for good.

Ren slumped forward, his forehead landing on his father's shoulder while his fingers gripped his mother's limp ones. Mr. Cabot wrapped an arm around his son and pulled him into his chest. Their tears fell fast and freely.

Their family had been severed yet again. The two of them were alone.

Ren clenched his father's shirt and wept.

26

An hour later, the boat slowed its speed and edged back toward the land. Ren watched vacantly as they approached the coast, seeing nothing but wilderness. A sandy shore curved in the distance and sloped steeply upward into a brush-covered hill. Ren didn't see a road, not that he cared. His whole body had gone numb, both from the cold and from losing his mother again. But he preferred the numbness to the pain. He knew the grief would come — it would crash into him like a tsunami and threaten to drown him. Just like the last time.

The boat pulled up to the pebbled coast. The passengers jumped out and sloshed through the knee-deep, frigid waters until they dragged their bodies onto land. For safety reasons, the group couldn't dock at the safe house in case they had been tailed, and so the captain would steer the vessel back out to sea while the rest of them traveled overland. One of the rebels had explained all of the details to Mr. Cabot and Ren, but Ren had only processed small fragments of it. All he knew was that there were miles to cross until they were safe and until they could find out what happenened to the rest of the prisoners and rebels. Every escape boat had splintered in different directions, heading toward safe houses spread up and down the coast and inland.

Ren stared at the hills along the coast that he would soon have to ascend. It wouldn't be an easy trek, but the Resistance members and the prisoners with him — about a dozen in all — didn't complain.

Shivering, Ren followed his father off the boat. His dad was limping badly from a bullet that had bitten off a piece of his calf, but he placed a firm hand on Ren's shoulder to draw him closer.

"You can lean on me," his father said. Softly, he added, "Don't look back."

But Ren didn't listen. After they climbed over the first hill, he glanced out to sea. Without any moonlight, Ren couldn't tell where the waters stopped and the sky began. He couldn't see much of anything, but that didn't stop his heart from cracking open all over again. His mother's body was out there somewhere, lifeless and alone. While they were still aboard the boat, his dad had told him that they wouldn't have time to bury her, so they slid her body into the ocean thirty minutes before landfall, whispering their last farewells as she disappeared into the deep.

A part of Ren had wanted to go with her. Instead, he had leaned on his father's shoulder and tried not to think about his mom's last moments.

The group moved silently up the next hill, but Ren and his father struggled with the incline. His dad's leg was bleeding freely, and Ren was too weak to get his father over the rise. Eventually, two Resistance members flanked Mr. Cabot, and they pulled him up together. Ren tried to follow them, but he lost his footing and almost slid halfway down the hilltop — until a small breath of wind caught his weight and held him aloft as he regained his balance. Soon, Zara joined him, panting hard herself, and together they made it the rest of the way.

"Thank you," Ren managed to say.

Zara waved him off while she bent over to rest. She was dressed like Ren in a prisoner's jumpsuit and bare feet, but that was where their similarities ended. She stood two heads shorter than him and probably topped off at half his weight, but she had more power in her pinky toe than Ren would ever possess. She was cradling in one hand the small locked box that she had carried from Alcatraz, which puzzled Ren.

"I should be the one thanking you," said Zara, coughing. Her hands were trembling, too, perhaps aftereffects of the Empire's chemicals. "You got me out of Alcatraz before the roof caved in. You didn't even know me." She studied him. "What's your name?"

"Ren Cabot."

Something dawned in her eyes. "Cabot. I think I heard one of the nurses talking about you. They said you were the Viper."

Ren didn't know what to do but nod. A few weeks ago, his life was completely different. He had worked in the shop by day and wrote his essays by moonlight. But here he was, standing somewhere along the Pacific coast and feeling like a lifetime had passed in a matter of days. The Viper felt like someone from his past. And could the Viper exist without his printing press, especially now that his identity had been revealed? Did he want it to?

Zara looked up to locate the others, who were taking a short rest. She spoke to Ren hesitantly. "I'm sorry about your mom."

Again, Ren nodded, and again he said nothing. Tears brimmed in his eyes, even though he had been sure that he had been wrung dry of them.

Zara avoided looking at him. "I lost my mom, too. The Nazis

killed her." She seemed to struggle with what she wanted to say, but she forced it out. "I know you don't know me, but I hope you keep fighting. We can't let another generation of Americans go through what we've been through, you know?" She chewed her lip hard. "This is coming out all wrong . . ."

"I get what you're saying," Ren said. Truth be told, he appreciated her honesty, and he was glad that she didn't try to pat him on the back or tell him everything would be okay. He knew what it felt like to lose his mom once — he just didn't know how to weather it twice.

"If there's anything you need — from me or the Alliance — let me know. We're fighting the same enemy, after all." She watched the others preparing to move out again. "We better go, but I should give you this first." She thrust the box at Ren.

Ren stared at the unexpected gift. "What is this?"

In reply, Zara opened the flaps of the box and slid out a piece of foam that hugged a glass vial of liquid. "When the Resistance attacked Alcatraz, the scientists started evacuating and I saw one of them clearing the shelves inside a locked cabinet. He was holding the boxes like they were newborns when he got shot in the back. Most of the vials had been smashed open, but I found this one intact. I figured if it was important to the Empire, then it might be important to the Resistance, too."

Ren couldn't believe it. This must have been a vial of V2. He delicately took the box from Zara, slid the vial back inside, and closed the flaps. To keep it safe, he tucked it inside the collar of his jumpsuit, letting it nestle between his chest and the fabric. He didn't know what the Resistance would do with the V2, but he knew what this vial represented, especially if the others had been destroyed.

With the group on the move, Ren and Zara soldiered up another hill and trudged forward step by step. Ren wasn't sure how far or how long they walked, but by the time they came upon a fish-processing plant, nestled among trees in a quiet inlet, he was ready to collapse.

The plant was shaped like an enormous old brick, square and sturdy and halfway to crumbling. The place must have been abandoned years ago, but then Ren caught the unmistakable whiff of recently caught fish, which meant the plant was still in use. They went in through a side entrance, and Zara had to help Ren over the steps because his knees threatened to give out, which was a little humiliating for him. Zara had spent much longer in the Empire's clutches than he had, but she insisted.

Once inside, they hobbled together across the plant's main floor, edging past the long metal tables where workers must have broken down each fish. The entire factory floor lay quiet since it was the middle of the night, leaving no witnesses. Ren stumbled up a set of wobbling steps with the rest of the group and onto the second floor of the factory.

A carpeted hallway greeted Ren's bleeding feet, and he saw a long line of doors flanking him on both sides. Ren snuck glances into them as he shuffled by — bunkrooms and lockers and an office space — and he walked into a large storage room in the back that had been cleared out and converted into a sick bay. Makeshift medical stations had been erected around the room — a cot here, a chair there, and each one assigned a nurse or medic. Ren tried to make his way toward his dad, whose leg was getting looked over, but both he and Zara were pulled toward their own exam chairs.

Ren bristled. "I'm fine," he said to a determined-looking nurse who stood toe to toe with him. "I have to see if my dad is okay."

But the nurse wouldn't let Ren leave. Placing her hands on his shoulders, she made him sit at the nearest station and opened her medical kit. Before Ren could sneak off, he heard someone walk up behind him.

"You ought to listen to Nurse Pine. She knows what she's doing," said a familiar voice.

Ren looked up and stammered, "Tessa?" He almost didn't recognize her. Her hair had been freed from its bun, her face had been scrubbed of makeup, and her glasses were gone. Gone, too, was her usual uniform of a blouse and skirt, replaced with a fitted gray T-shirt and camouflage pants. He couldn't find many traces of Fräulein Plank, but even if he had, it wouldn't have mattered. He was simply relieved to see her. "I didn't realize you'd be here."

"I hope that isn't a complaint," she said with a little smile as she scooted a stool next to Ren.

"Not at all. I'm just glad —" Emotion thickened in his throat. After everything he had gone through these last few days, it was overwhelming to see a friend. "I'm glad you made it out okay."

"I can say the same about you." Her smile widened, only to break when she took in the bruises on his cheeks and the dried blood covering his jumpsuit. The nurse started to cut open Ren's clothing and he told Tessa to look away.

"I'm not going anywhere," Tessa said frankly, sounding a lot like the *Fräulein*. But her expression grew more grim as Ren's jumpsuit opened to reveal bloodied gashes and torn-apart stitches. As the nurse removed more fabric, Ren felt the box of V2 shift and he caught it before it fell, cradling it against his chest.

Tessa looked confused. "What's in the box?"

"V2," whispered Ren. He nodded toward Zara's exam station. "*She* found it."

Tessa looked over her shoulder and her jaw went slack. "Is that . . . ?"

"Zara St. James. We escaped from Alcatraz together."

"You'll have to introduce me later," Tessa said, unable to stop sneaking glances at Zara, the symbol of the Second American Revolutionary War and one of the most wanted criminals. "But there's a lot we should talk about first."

Ren leaned back, flinching as the nurse applied a local anesthetic and began cleaning his injuries. He didn't like feeling so vulnerable in front of Tessa, but her presence did take his mind off the nurse's poking and prodding.

"I want to hear everything," said Ren. "What happened after I left you? Have you heard from Marty or Midori? What about Aiko and the crown prince — did they escape?"

Tessa told him to slow down and tried to tackle each point one by one. "We're still getting updates about the attack because everyone scattered to different safe houses around San Francisco. I'd say overall that we accomplished what we set out to do. We infiltrated the prison — thanks to you — and freed the prisoners and Anomalies. We won't have a final tally of survivors until tomorrow or the next day, but getting our hands on V2 is a very big deal." She eyed the box again. "Marty will be ecstatic. We got a radio message from her about twenty minutes ago. She has been routed to another safe house down the coast, but she's alive."

Ren let the relief wash over him. He knew Marty wasn't in the clear yet — none of them were — but he needed to hear some good news after losing so much.

She went on, and Ren noticed that she sounded different — less clipped, more casual. Less Plank, more Tessa. It was like speaking to a new person. "Midori did make it out" — Ren heard this and sighed in relief again — "but the crown prince's helicopter crashed during its escape."

Ren choked. "Is he dead?"

"Intel is sparse, but I'm assuming so. Apparently, one of our grenade launchers clipped the propellers of his helicopter on its way to the city. The whole thing went down in the bay, and you know how cold those waters are."

Ren went speechless. With the crown prince and his male heir both dead, the line of succession would be thrown into chaos. Crown Prince Katsura was the only living son of the emperor, and the emperor himself was already old and frail. Which left Aiko.

"What about Aiko? Was she on board?" Ren asked. He assumed that the Empire had retrieved her during the prisoner exchange.

A smile curved on Tessa's mouth. "No. The Resistance managed to keep her from the Empire. She's on her way to a safe house north of here." But her smile was quick to dim. "From the radio messages I've heard, we lost a lot of good men and women getting her back out to sea, but they did it. We'll probably have to move her from safe house to safe house every week to stay ahead of the Empire. They're going to do whatever they can to get their hands on her."

For good reason, too, thought Ren. Not only was Aiko the potential heir to the Chrysanthemum Throne, she was a key figure in the treaty between the Empire and the Nazis. Without Aiko, the Nazis might withhold sending more vials of V2.

The Resistance's attack had been a success in that light — they now had V2 *and* Aiko. This brought Ren a little comfort after what he had gone through, but it was a comfort laced with guilt. Ren was responsible for kidnapping Aiko and letting the Resistance use her like a chess piece just as her family had done. But when Ren thought about this more, weren't all of them pawns under the Empire's regime and struggling to get off the game board?

A beat passed. "I've been meaning to ask . . . and you don't have to answer but . . . did you find your mom?" said Tessa.

Ren's face darkened. He didn't know if he could bring himself to share that yet. He could try, but he wouldn't be able to stop the tears and Ren had had enough of that. Though he felt he owed Tessa an answer. "I did find her, but . . . she didn't make it."

"Oh." Her gaze slinked toward the floor. "I'm sorry."

"So am I," Ren whispered. Someday he would tell Tessa the whole story, but not tonight. Not now.

Ren wanted to shift their conversation back to the mission and what would happen next, but Mr. Cabot hobbled toward them on a crutch. At the sight of him, Tessa got up and placed a hand on Ren's shoulder.

"We'll talk soon," she said.

"You should talk to my dad. He knew your parents."

A flash of pain overtook her features, and her hand slid down to her side. "There'll be time for that later."

Within seconds, Tessa made her exit, and Mr. Cabot did a double take as they crossed paths. He stared at Ren, confused. "I could've sworn that was —"

"Tessa Quirk. She was one of Marty's spies inside the Fortress," Ren explained. He wasn't sure if Marty had ever disclosed Beetle's real identity to his father, but there would be time later to delve into all of that. "You shouldn't be walking around, Dad. You should be resting."

His father plunked himself onto the stool that Tessa had vacated, groaning as he stretched out his injured leg. "I could say the same to you."

"You were shot a couple of hours ago."

"And you were imprisoned in Alcatraz for days," his father countered. He touched Ren's cheek and looked at his son with so much concern that Ren felt himself blush. "It kills me to think what they did to you."

"Please don't go down that road," Ren said quickly. He didn't want his father giving himself nightmares over what Ren had gone through. Major Endo would haunt Ren for the rest of his life, but he didn't want his dad to share that burden.

"How can I not think about it? You're my son. I haven't been able to sleep since you ran off to the Fortress. Marty kept telling me that you'd be fine, but then I heard you got arrested and then . . ." Tears pooled in his tired gray eyes. "Then we got word that you had outted yourself as the Viper. I couldn't believe it at first. I'm not even sure if I can believe it now."

"I didn't know how to tell you. I knew you'd be mad," whispered Ren. Even now, he could never regret writing his essays and publishing them, but he hated the hurt on his father's face. "But I wanted to carry on what Mom was doing." Ren waited for his dad to begin lecturing him, and he wouldn't let it bother him because he was just thankful that his father was alive. Only the lecture didn't come.

"I should have suspected something," his father said at last. "Because you write like her."

Ren looked up with a knot in his throat. "Really?"

"She was a little more direct and punchy, but yes, really."

The knot in Ren's throat doubled in size. "I didn't know you read my essays."

"I didn't at first, but after a while I wanted to see what all the customers were whispering about. So I got my hands on a few copies and burned them after I read them, which seems ridiculous, looking back, because you were the one who wrote them. You're grounded, by the way. For life." Mr. Cabot laughed a little and Ren couldn't help but join him. It was a little burst of levity amid the heartache of the night.

"All right, but I'm still going to write those essays," Ren said finally.

"It's going to be dangerous," his father warned grimly. "Especially now that you're exposed."

But Ren couldn't back down. "I can't stop now. The Empire is going to come after me anyway. And . . ." The lightness they had shared a few seconds ago felt miles away already. "I don't think Mom would want me to stop."

"I think you're underestimating your mother's protectiveness when it came to you." Emotions warred on Mr. Cabot's face: pain and sadness, followed by resignation. "She would never want you to risk your life. It would've destroyed her to know that you were interrogated and" — he couldn't quite bring himself to say *tortured* — "and hurt. Deep down, I think she hoped that the revolution would have started long before you grew up. She hoped that her work would give you a different world to live in." Bitterness slid into his words. "But we all know how it goes. The Empire tends to crush our hopes in front of our eyes."

Ren paused before he asked, "Do you still think that now?"

"In some ways, yes. Look at what they did to your mother. Turning her into something I hardly recognized."

Ren wondered if his dad had doubted the mission in its entirety. Did he regret the Resistance attempting to free their prisoners from Alcatraz? Did he think that they had risked too much? Ren was afraid to ask.

"But in other ways, no," his father continued, and Ren dared to glance up. "The Empire will do whatever it can to kill our dreams, but the choice is up to us whether we let those dreams wither and die. I can admit it now that I let my hopes shrivel up after your mother's execution. I put everything into keeping you safe, but maybe I took things too far."

Ren felt breathless. He and his father had never talked about this before, even though it had ruled their lives. It was like the wall between them was vanishing brick by brick — it was still there, still present, but dismantling slowly. "What now? Do you want to get that hope back?"

An eternity seemed to pass before his father spoke again. "I do, mostly because I don't want to see that hope die inside you. I might be old and beaten down, but you don't have to be."

Ren's lips broke into a smile. He didn't know until this moment how much he needed to hear these words. "You're not old or beaten down, Dad."

"I don't know. You might be helping me with my dentures in a few years."

They smiled and Mr. Cabot laughed, and Ren's heart relished the sound. He couldn't remember the last time his dad had laughed — probably before his mother was executed — but soon the laughter faded and their smiles vanished. They sank back into the aftermath of what had happened earlier that night.

"She's gone. Really gone this time," Ren said, an ache worming through his chest.

His father couldn't reply. His chin wobbled as his eyes swarmed with tears.

"I'm glad we got to see her again but . . ." Ren's grief gave way to the years-old anger that had kept him company. Putting an end to Major Endo's life hadn't chased that fury away. Ren doubted anything ever would until the Empire was defeated. And maybe not even then. "I just feel cheated. We had to watch her die twice."

"I wish I could take away the hurt," Mr. Cabot managed to choke out. "But we'll weather it together. And we're going to make the Empire regret what it's done, but at least your mom is no longer living in that cage — and she has you to thank for that. She would be so proud of what you've become." The tears fell fast down his cheeks.

Ren broke inside. "I can't do this again, Dad. I can't go through it."

Mr. Cabot wrapped his arms around his son and pulled Ren toward him until their cheeks touched.

"I know," his father whispered into his ear. "But I'll be right here with you. I can promise you that."

Their shoulders shook and their tears flowed together, and they mourned the woman they had lost all over again.

27

The news trickled in hour by hour, from safe houses across the WAT. Over a hundred rebels had lost their lives at the Battle of Alcatraz — some died infiltrating the prison, others drowned during their escape — but no one could deny their success. Of the one hundred and twelve prisoners freed, seventy-nine had escaped — including the fourteen Anomalies. Ren's mom was the only one who hadn't made it to a safe house.

Ren wished he could lay on his cot and wait until his grief didn't choke him, even if that took him years. But he had barely gotten a few hours' sleep when his dad shook him awake and thrust some clean clothes at him.

"Get dressed. There's a car waiting for us outside," said Mr. Cabot, who had already changed into an ill-fitting button-down shirt and a pair of jeans that hardly reached his ankles. Faint light filtered in through the nearest window, telling Ren that dawn was fast approaching.

"What?" Ren said, bleary-eyed. "Where are we going?"

"Another safe house farther east. We've gotten word that there might be inspectors coming to the plant this morning. All of the prisoners and Resistance members have to leave right now." His tone grew more urgent. "The Empire is searching for the Viper and Zara especially."

Within minutes, Ren was dressed and ushered down the factory steps, where he was swept into an unmarked van along with his dad, Zara, and Tessa. The remaining prisoners were escorted to other vans that split off in separate directions, some heading south while others traveled inland. There was no time for thank-yous or good-byes.

Ren's van bumped along rough roads for hours, twisting and turning over the mountains, and taking back roads to avoid the checkpoints. The driver kept the radio on at a low hum, and Ren listened to it as he drifted asleep, then back to consciousness. The reporter treated the day like business as usual, offering a weather report and traffic updates and an interview with an East African diplomat who heavily praised Crown Prince Katsura. The broadcast carefully sidestepped any mention of the prison — or the fact that the crown prince was dead. The Empire had no interest in admitting defeat and stoking public resistance.

The news about Alcatraz, however, would eventually leak out, and then the whispers would start. The rumors would travel across the WAT that *something* had happened at the Rock, and the Empire would have to scramble to arrest more people as they covered up the attack. And that's when a thought struck Ren inside the van.

The Resistance needed to insert itself into this narrative. It had to take ownership of the attack. The rebels may have won the battle, but their victory could be so much greater with the right publicity. And the world needed to know about the horrific human experimentation.

"Paper," Ren said, flinching when the van hit a rock that sent shock waves of agony through his wounds. The nurse had disinfected and sewed his body together, but the painkillers had long worn off and his bruises throbbed with every bump. Still, Ren propped himself onto his elbows. "Is there paper and a pen anywhere?"

Mr. Cabot quieted him. "You need to rest. It should be a while until we get to the next safe house."

"I can't sleep," Ren said gruffly. And he had to write down his thoughts before they slipped out from his fingertips. When inspiration struck, it struck hard.

"I can check," Zara offered, who was sitting right behind the driver. She fished a hand into the console next to the driver's seat and produced a scrap of paper and the nub of a pencil for Ren. Brightness alighted in her eyes as she passed them back to Ren. "What are you writing down? An essay?"

"Not quite sure." Ren licked his lips and started jotting down a few key words, which turned into phrases and then a handful of half sentences, using his bruised knee as a desk. He stared out the window, letting his thoughts scatter so he could pick through them. War wasn't only about soldiers and tanks. It included controlling words and dictating history, which was why Jenny Tsai had risked her life to write her newspaper. The Empire had published propaganda for years to prop itself up and to silence dissent. It was time for the Resistance to open a battlefield on this particular front. And that was something the Viper could help with.

Ren had filled up both sides of the paper by the time the van rumbled up to an old wooden cabin in the middle of a forested mountain range. In the distance, a crystal-blue lake twinkled in the sunlight. They had arrived at the safe house.

Glancing out the windshield, Ren had to admit that the cabin wasn't much to look at. Its paint had long been stripped off, and its frame sagged on its foundation, like a shelf groaning under the weight of too many books. The place looked abandoned, but the driver murmured into a handheld radio, and all of a sudden the cabin's front door popped open. Out spilled a pair of rebels armed with rifles, trailed close behind by a young woman with one black eye and one arm in a sling.

It was Marty.

Both Ren his and father clambered out of the van and hurried toward her while Marty pushed past the armed rebels to greet them. She kissed her uncle's cheek before hugging Ren gingerly, not wanting to hurt his bruises.

"Good to see you, Renny," she murmured into his ear. "Or are you going by the Viper now?" Marty asked, releasing him, grimacing as she looked over his wounds, but she hid her shock by ruffling his hair like he was five years old again. Ren let her do that for once. He was just grateful to see her. But then Marty became solemn. "I'm sorry about your mom. Your dad relayed to me what happened over the radio late last night."

Ren nodded, thankful that his father had broken the news so that he wouldn't have to. He wasn't ready to talk about what had happened, and the silence stretched between them.

"We'll have a memorial for Aunt Jenny and all the others we lost last night. I can't believe —" Marty stopped short and shook her head. "Let's get you all inside. There's tea on the stove and there's a lot to talk about."

Marty motioned for Ren and Mr. Cabot to head into the cabin while she greeted Tessa and introduced herself to Zara. Ren hobbled up the stone walk and into the cabin, ready to find it ancient and dilapidated, but he was surprised to find the interior painted a fresh white hue and cozy sofas begging for him to take a seat.

"This is the oldest safe house in the Resistance," Marty explained after she swept inside with the others and locked the door. "The same family had owned it for decades, and they gave it to the rebels not too long after the war." She gestured around the first floor. "Kitchen. Dining room. Sitting area. There are two bathrooms in the back and plenty of places to sleep." Then she walked into the tiny kitchen and pulled back a shabby-looking runner to reveal a trapdoor. "We carved out a little basement, too, in case we have to hide something or someone."

Someone? Ren wanted to ask her what she meant, but Zara took the reins of the conversation. "I'm sorry to sound impatient, but you mentioned outside that you've talked to my uncle Red," she said to Marty. It was still jarring for Ren to see her in front of him, the legendary Zara St. James. She had found a baseball cap back at the plant to cover her shaved head, but other than that she looked so much like her Wanted posters. Truth be told, he doubted that he and his dad would be alive if it hadn't been for her help. "What did my uncle say? What happened to my friends who tried to break me out of Fort Tomogashima?"

"No need to apologize. There *is* a lot we have to discuss," Marty said. She motioned for everyone to take a seat in the great room while she paced in front of a stone fireplace. An old map of California hung over the hearth — a fitting image of rebellion.

"Let's backtrack a little," Marty started off. Along with her broken arm and bruised face, she was also limping a little, but she wouldn't sit down. "Right before the Joint Prosperity Ball, I relayed a message to Zara's uncle that Zara was being held inside the Fortress. Redmond replied that he would send in a rescue team to break Zara out, but that was where our wires must have crossed. I told him that this rescue team needed to wait until just *after* the ball to let Ren and Tessa kidnap Aiko, but the team launched their attack too early."

Ren and Tessa exchanged a look. This explained Baroness Augusta affecting their mission in the Fortress.

"How many of the team members were killed?" Zara asked, scooting to the very edge of her chair.

"Your uncle sent in a team of eight. Five survived the ball and were sent to Alcatraz along with you. Out of that five, three made it out and are currently at different safe houses." Marty sighed at the bad news. "I'm sorry."

Zara nodded but said nothing. She simply crossed her arms as the news sunk in. "I'd like to see them if that can be arranged."

"Your uncle is on his way to get you and the rescue team. He wants to get all of you back to the Eastern American Territories before the Empire tightens security even more."

Zara blinked up at this development. "He's coming *here*?"

"He wanted to escort you home himself," said Marty, offering a small smile.

Zara went quiet again, but Ren saw her mouth silently shape the word *home*. Weeks had passed since her capture, and Zara must have been itching to return to her uncle and her friends. To go home.

Ren envied her. He didn't have a home anymore. There was no way for him to return to White Crescent Bay. It might take years before he could see it again. But at least he had his father and Marty with him. An apartment was just an apartment and a shop was just a shop, but family was family. They could find a new place to call home eventually.

Marty went on. "It should take Zara's uncle about a week to arrive, considering all of the checkpoints going up on the borders. Once he's here, he'll take a day or two to rest and talk about strategies looking forward."

Tessa chimed in next. She was seated on a plaid sofa next to Mr. Cabot, and every time Ren looked at her he saw less of Plank and more of someone new. After months of wearing the *Fräulein's* skin, the girl inside was reemerging. "What kind of strategies are we talking about?"

Marty's entire face brightened. "A union between the Resistance and the Revolutionary Alliance. Obviously, our two groups have been in close contact for decades, but Redmond and our Resistance leaders are in agreement that we need each other more than ever. We're fighting a common enemy. We can't topple one empire without toppling the other. We'll never get America whole again if either empire remains in our country."

Pride hummed through Marty's revelation, and a tingle shivered down Ren's arms.

A real revolution was starting in the WAT. The Resistance had taken out the crown prince and his heir, and they had captured Aiko as well, thus killing the marriage that would have unified the two empires even further. This new partnership between the Resistance and the Alliance only cemented the fact that the rebels finally had firm legs to stand on.

"Plans are already in the works," Marty said. "Redmond would like to launch a joint attack on the port of New Orleans. It's a big trading depot between the two empires, and hitting the city hard will have disastrous consequences. We still have to come up with a master strategy and hammer out the details, but we're aiming to be ready in three months' time. Until then, we'll continue launching guerilla attacks throughout the WAT, and we have to figure out what to do with the V2. Hopefully you brought it with you?"

Ren retrieved the vial while Marty explained to Zara what exactly V2 was. "What are you going to do with it? Sell it?"

Marty shook her head. "Selling it would be too risky. Our likeliest buyer would be the Soviets, and while we share a common enemy, we can't trust their government." She opened the box and stared at the vial therein, trailing a lone finger against the glass. "I'll admit that the Resistance leaders debated duplicating the V2 ourselves. The Empire has always had the upper hand because of the Ronin Elite and this little vial could help us bridge that gap, but we've nixed the idea. It's not only that we don't have the scientists or the facilities — but we *can't* cross that line."

"Right." Zara was quick to agree. "Where would you stop? Twenty volunteers? Fifty? I wasn't at Alcatraz long, but I saw how the Empire's experimentation destroyed those prisoners." Her gaze shot toward Ren, then lowered quickly. "Destroy the vial."

"I won't say no to that," murmured Marty, shoving the V2 back into its box.

"I'll talk things over with my uncle, too. Any laboratories making V2 need to be targeted and taken out, and I'm sure there a few in the Eastern American Territories and even more in Germany proper.

I'll get in touch with my sources over there," she added with a flush. "I know someone in Belgium who could help us as well."

"Sounds like a plan," Marty said. She passed the box with the V2 to Zara. "Let's go take care of that out back. As for the rest of you, I'm sure you wouldn't mind napping or showering. I left clean towels in each bathroom, and you'll find changes of clothes in each closet. Take your pick. I'll round everyone up for dinner in a few hours."

The group stretched and split off, but Ren caught Marty's arm before she could go. "Can I talk to you for a minute?" he asked.

Marty nodded and waved on Zara to head outside. "What's going on?" She sat down on the plaid sofa and patted the cushion next to her for Ren to take.

Ren declined and showed her the notes he had written on the long ride over. "The Resistance has to spread word about the Battle of Alcatraz. Give a detailed account, including photos if you have them. Print it out and distribute it across the WAT. Show everyone what the Resistance has done because the Empire will do everything to cover it up."

Marty scanned his notes and arched a dark brow. "Are you volunteering to write a new essay as the Viper?"

Ren shifted. He still hadn't wrapped his brain around the fact that the Empire knew his identity, but the secret was out and he couldn't stuff it back into its bottle. Sooner or later, the whole public would know who he was, too. So he had a choice to make: Either the Empire would get to dictate his story or he could do it himself.

"I'll start drafting right away," Ren said quietly, feeling the weight of those words pressing down on his shoulders. He was about to add that he didn't want to mention his mother — that was too close and his emotions were too raw — but then he heard the sound of tires crunching over the dirt road.

"Are you expecting someone?" Ren asked, ready to fight or flee if necessary.

His cousin didn't look fazed. "We're going to have some extra company for a few days."

Marty didn't elaborate while she unlocked the front door and walked up the path to meet another white van covered in dust. Ren followed her out uninvited, watching as two Resistance members jumped out of the front of the van and pulled out a young woman from the back. She had been blindfolded and her wrists had been tied together, and her head darted from side to side as she was escorted toward the cabin.

"Take her to the basement," Marty said to the rebels. "We'll need to guard her around the clock."

Ren said nothing. He could only stare.

Marty had told him that she was expecting company — she hadn't told him that this company would be Aiko.

28

Marty refused to let Ren speak with Aiko. *Precautions*, she reasoned.

"We have to be extra careful around her. The fewer people Aiko sees, the better," Marty had explained, and told him to keep busy by working on the new essay, which Ren did. He had missed writing and had dove into that piece, detailing the Battle of Alcatraz and what the Empire had been hiding inside the prison, but his thoughts kept circling back to the princess sleeping a floor beneath his feet.

The rebel guards took shifts to watch over Aiko, but that wasn't necessary. The basement resembled a small prison cell, with iron bars and thick stone walls and no way out. Even if Aiko managed to pick her lock, take out the guards, and break out of the safe house, she would have to walk miles to civilization. Aiko was trapped and she knew it, but that didn't mean she would make life easy on her captors.

She refused to eat. She refused to drink. She pounded on the walls until her hands were bloodied, and she shouted for help until her voice disappeared.

Marty and the guards managed to finally make her drink some water, but getting her to eat proved trickier. Every time Aiko was force-fed a spoonful of soup, she would make herself throw it up. Ren didn't think that she could be so stubborn, but then again, this was the girl who had worn a defiant gown to the Joint Prosperity Ball.

By the fourth day in the safe house, Ren had come up with a plan. He told Marty that his first draft was ready, but he would only show it to her if he could have five minutes alone with Aiko.

Marty arched a brow in the living room, where they were siting. "Why do you want to talk to her so badly? And why alone?"

Ren kept his face emotionless. "I have my reasons."

"Do you *like* her?"

"No," said Ren. That was the truth. He had admitted to himself that he respected her for fighting for her independence, for daring to reject what the Empire expected out of her. He had admitted, too, that he thought she was pretty. But when it came down to it, Ren barely knew the princess, and yet he felt — he *knew* — that they would always be connected. He was the one who had kidnapped her, after all, and who used her like a pawn. He was the reason why she was here in the safe house. "Five minutes, and you can have my draft."

Marty didn't look too happy, but she agreed to Ren's terms. She opened the trapdoor and told him that she would be watching the time. "Five minutes. Better talk fast."

Climbing down the ladder, Ren breathed in a lungful of dust and got his first glimpse of the basement. It was a shoe box of a space, divided in half by a sturdy set of iron bars. Ren stood in the half where the guards kept watch over Aiko, a lone folding chair and lamp in the corner. The other half was the cell itself. It was double in size from the one that Ren had occupied inside Alcatraz, and it had even come with a pillow and blanket. But a cell was still a cell, and Ren could sense the wrath and the fear emanating from Aiko, who sat on the floor next to the toilet.

Ren's tongue tied inside his mouth and he wished he had prepared a script. He wasn't sure what to say. Should he apologize? No. He couldn't regret what he had done, but he still felt bad for Aiko. She didn't deserve what had happened to her, losing her parents and her home. Everything she had known.

"Your Imperial Highness," Ren murmured. He didn't bow.

Aiko didn't get up, but she lifted her head an inch, her dirty hair parting to reveal tired eyes. She glared at him. "The Viper," was all she said.

"It's Ren."

"Have you come to gloat?"

He shook his head.

"Then why are you here?" Pain wove through her words. Judging by the redness in her eyes, she had been crying.

Ren emptied his pants pockets, revealing a few folded sheets of paper and an old blue crayon he had found at the back of a desk. He didn't want to give her a pen or a pencil because both could be turned into weapons, but a crayon seemed innocent enough. Slowly, he placed the gifts between the bars of the cell. "I thought you might want something to do."

Curiosity got the best of her and she looked at his offering. When she realized what he had given her, she flew toward the bars, grabbing a hold of the paper and shredding it to pieces, then taking the crayon and hurtling it at Ren's head. Her chest rose and fell rapidly. "Do you expect me to thank you or kiss your hand? My parents are dead because of the Resistance."

Ren watched her panting, her eyes filled with murder, and it reminded him of himself five years ago, not long after his mom's execution and he thought he'd lost her forever. He understood the girl in front of him now, even though they were enemies. Her father had overseen the death of thousands of Americans, like his mom and like Jay; and her father's lackey Major Endo had left scars from which Ren might never heal. His nightmares had already begun, coating him in sweat and waking him from the memory of his screams. And those bad dreams were just the beginning. His hands shook. He had flashbacks. He jumped whenever someone came up behind him. Major Endo was dead, but a part of her was very much alive in Ren's head.

Ren didn't blame Aiko for that, though. He should hate her for what her father and Major Endo had done to him, but he didn't. Mostly, he felt sad when he looked at her.

"I watched my mom die twice," he heard himself say. "Your father's regime executed her five years ago, but when she didn't die they took her to Alcatraz and experimented on her until she lost her mind. I tried to free her, but Major Endo killed her."

Aiko said nothing, so Ren went on.

"Both of us have lost people we loved. Both of us live in a world that we didn't create."

She gave a harsh laugh. "I used to think that your Resistance had merit — I know that the Empire has committed horrible crimes — but you're all hypocrites. You kill innocent people, and you do it in the name of justice. How does that make you any better?" Her shoulders rose and fell. "What do you want from me? Forgiveness? Redemption?"

Ren winced. He hadn't known that Aiko had some sympathy for the rebels, but then again, how far had that sympathy extended? Had she ever asked her father to stop the executions? To close the internment camps? Probably not. "I don't want anything from you. I just wanted to say that I don't think you deserve to be punished for your father's crimes."

"But I have, haven't I?" she spat out bitterly. "My parents were *murdered.*"

Ren dipped his head. "So was my mom."

There was a thump on the trapdoor. It was Marty's way of telling Ren that his time was up. Ren rubbed the back of his neck while his thoughts splintered in every direction. At one point Aiko may have been persuaded to help the Resistance. She had admired feminist thinkers and had tried to revolt against tradition. But that girl had been killed back at the Fortress, replaced with the Aiko standing opposite Ren right now. Any common ground they'd shared had been shattered the night of the ball. Any bridges built between them had been broken apart, leaving a gaping chasm that could never be crossed again. From here on out, they'd always stand on opposite sides and there was nothing Ren could do about it.

Ren grabbed the ladder, but that's when Aiko pressed herself against the bars, clutching the metal in her hands. "When I get free — and I will — know that I'll be coming for you."

Emotions warred inside Ren's heart, regret and resentment and resignation. "I can't say that I'm looking forward to it."

Then he climbed up the ladder, dusted himself off, and left behind the revenge-seeking princess whom he had created. He had used Aiko, just like her father had, but he needed her to ignite a revolution. He had to make the choice to help his people, even if that might have ruined Aiko's life — or at least severely scarred it.

And Ren had to be ready for the consequences.

Ten days after they arrived at the safe house, it was time again to depart. Marty didn't like staying in one place for too long, and she had gotten word that the Empire had sent out patrols to sweep the valley below, which meant they couldn't afford to linger.

In the middle of the night, three vans arrived at the safe house to split up the group and head in different directions — Aiko would go southeast, Zara and her uncle would go north, while Ren and the rest would forge inland toward Nevada. Ren was nervous at what lay ahead. For so long he had focused on the immediate targets — getting hired at the Fortress, kidnapping Aiko during the ball, then surviving the Battle of Alcatraz. But now a new map unfurled in front of him and the Resistance. There was no clear-cut way to defeat the Empire. There would be wrong turns and dead ends; there would be uncharted paths and a destination that would shift constantly, dangling out of grasp. Yet they had no other choice but to press forward into deadly territory.

Aiko's van left first. The guards had blindfolded her before escorting her to the waiting vehicle, and even though she couldn't see Ren, he could feel her wrath as she walked by him. He couldn't blame her for that, and he hadn't forgotten her last words to him, either. If she ever escaped from the Resistance, he knew without a doubt that she would place a huge bounty on his head and come for him herself. It was an unsettling thought, one that Ren would lose sleep over, but what was done was done.

Next, the St. Jameses said their good-byes. Zara's uncle Red had arrived two days prior with a handful of Alliance members, and they had spent the last forty-eight hours huddled around a table with

Marty to discuss next steps and future strategies. They had all taken turns shaking Ren's hand, too, telling him about their favorite essays and how much they looked forward to the next one. It had been a little too much for Ren, and he had flushed through the exchange.

As Marty wished Redmond a farewell — Zara's uncle protectively kept his niece within his eyeshot after their long separation — Zara guided Ren under a California scrub oak to speak with him privately. Ren breathed air into his bare hands to keep them warm, but Zara didn't seem to mind the chill. After spending weeks locked up in prison cells, she relished the fresh air.

"I'll see you in New Orleans?" she asked.

"Hopefully," Ren replied. "I'm not sure if Marty or my dad will want me so close to the action, but I'll work on them."

Zara grinned. "We'll need a war correspondent, so you can use that angle."

"Hadn't thought of that." Ren returned her smile but couldn't quite put much life into it. Three months was an eternity during a war, and anything could happen. The last few weeks had taught him that hard lesson, and he worried for Zara. "Take care of yourself out there."

Zara's grin, however, hadn't faded. "I will. It's hard to kill me. You won't have to write my obituary anytime soon." She studied him with her sharp stare, and Ren was glad that they were on the same side. He wouldn't want to face her on a battlefield or anywhere else. "You take care of yourself, too. You're already the most wanted criminal in the WAT and you're going to give me a run for my money out east."

Ren couldn't help but laugh and offered her his hand. "Fair enough."

Zara took her hand out of her pocket, but in the process a folded-up piece of paper fell out. Ren bent down to pick it up.

"Is that a telegram?" he asked curiously. He had heard that some Resistance or Alliance members used telegrams to communicate over long distances, but he had never seen one before.

Zara snatched the paper from him. "It's intel from inside Nazi borders. Compliments of a friend with the Widerstand resistance." She mumbled the last part, as if she had revealed too much, and she shoved the telegram back into her pocket. "Anyway..."

Ren swallowed a chuckle. "See you later, Zara St. James."

She bumped her shoulder into his. "See you soon, Ren Cabot. Write an essay about me, okay? I could use some good PR for once."

29

The days flowed by like a winter stream, with the weeks coursing past swiftly until the spring arrived. By then, the Resistance's rebellion had roamed outward from San Francisco Bay, up to the Canadian border, down through Arizona, and arcing across the plains, where it pushed against the mighty Mississippi River. War had arrived in the Western American Territories, joining with the clash already burning in the east. The Second Revolutionary War was now being fought from coast to coast.

As the spring pushed out the winter winds, Ren thought often about Zara's parting words. Her Alliance had overseen a string of successes upon her return, and now the Carolinas had declared independence and New England was close to following suit, all thanks to additional reinforcement from Zara's contact within the Widerstand resistance. The Nazis weren't giving up, but their resources were being spread thinner and thinner. Berlin was in chaos — Deputy Führer Forst had returned home to mutiny, with two generals competing against him for control of the Third Reich — and couldn't offer much help to the Empire, especially now that his wedding to Aiko had been indefinitely postponed. Ren considered how long it would take until the Nazis packed up their things and retreated across the Atlantic. Another year? Less? But more and more he realized that the Eastern American Territories had a real chance at independence.

That was still a ways off in the WAT, where the dream of freedom was still just that — a dream. Guerilla attacks had increased from Seattle to New Tokyo, from San Antonio to Billings, but the Empire had been quick to retaliate. Martial law had been declared. A general from Tokyo had been sent to oversee the territories, and so far he had ruled the land ruthlessly, keeping the strict curfew laws, opening additional internment camps, and broadcasting more executions on live television. It was a terrifying new age in the WAT.

Yet the Resistance hadn't taken any of that sitting down. They had ratcheted up their attacks, they had stolen more weapons, and they had upped their recruits. Not only that, they were nearly ready for the joint battle at New Orleans. The Empire had no idea what was soon coming, and this would only be the beginning. The Resistance and the Alliance had planned even more missions together — from New Orleans they would head to Biloxi and then over to Houston, claiming the south city by city.

And Ren had lent a hand wherever he could.

"Hey, you ready?" said Marty.

Ren glanced up from his typewriter, then looked over at the wall clock. Almost time. "Give me a second."

As Ren finished his last sentence, Marty leaned against her crutch. She had broken her left ankle a few weeks ago after a close shave escaping a patrol car, which had sidelined her from any missions. Ren had to admit that she was driving him a little batty hanging around the office all day. Technically, it wasn't an office, merely a desk and a typewriter shoved inside a pantry, but Ren didn't need anything fancy to get his job done.

For months they had been hopping from safe house to safe house — Ren, Marty, Mr. Cabot, and Tessa — moving up and down the coast, venturing inland and back again. A few weeks prior, they had traveled to a little town north of San Luis Obispo and been taken in by the local Resistance cell. They were living now in a bunker below a rancher's barn, on land so secluded that Ren could take walks at night and stare up at the winking constellations. Ren didn't know how long they would stay here, but this was home for now.

As soon as Ren finished typing, he released the essay from the machine and made a few copies, but it took him another minute before he handed a sheet to Marty. He had been publishing an essay a week for months, but this piece was different. More honest. More personal. He had worked on it bit by bit since he had left Alcatraz, and now it was ready for the WAT. Or so he hoped. "Can you give this to Tessa? I'd love for her to read the final copy before we go to press. She'll understand."

Marty saluted him. "Will do, Renny. She should be getting the horses ready now."

"Thanks, *Martine*," he replied with a smile.

Marty made a face that shifted into a grin as she walked away. Ren followed her out. The bunker was tiny, about half the size of the Cabots' apartment in White Crescent Bay, but they had made do. Ren passed by their bunkroom and the galley kitchen before he ascended the ladder that led into the barn. Moonlight greeted him as he dusted himself off. It was well past midnight, but the barn hummed with activity. Tessa stood by the old green tractor, speaking to Marty in whispers after she saddled up a gray mare. In her hand she held Ren's essay and she was marking it up with a pen, but she stopped when she saw Ren standing there.

"This is good," Tessa said, walking up to him. "I corrected a couple of typos, but it's ready for press." She wore her hair in a braid now and had let it grow out to its natural brown hue. But elements of Plank still managed to peek out now and then, like how she ordered Ren around. She thrust the essay back at him. "Can you hold that for me while I change?"

"Sure," replied Ren, taking it and offering her his free hand as she stepped onto the ladder. Soon, she and Mr. Cabot would ride to a neighboring farm, where an illegal printing press had been stowed away for years. That was one of the reasons why the Resistance had sent Ren to this isolated town — so that his essays could be printed with ease. Tessa had played a huge part in the distribution efforts, too; her power had definitely come in handy more than once. She had finally revealed her Anomaly status to Marty a month ago — Marty had admitted that she had had a hunch for much longer — and Tessa had slotted herself into Resistance missions like an old pro. She had seemed more relaxed now, too, considering she no longer had to pretend she was a Nazi citizen. Ren had caught her laughing with Marty more than once, and Ren would happily prefer Tessa to the *Fräulein*.

Tessa was about to disappear into the bunker before she looked up at Ren. "I liked the very end of the essay especially. Thank you for including his name."

"It's the least I could do," said Ren. He watched her smile a sad smile, and he returned it. They had both lost so much — her more so than him — and their lives since Alcatraz hadn't been easy by a long shot. But each day had a purpose, and Ren was glad that Tessa was here to share that with him.

Mr. Cabot came up behind Ren. "Once Tessa comes back, we'll head out. Do you have a copy for me?" He had already saddled his own horse — a brown mare named Peppa, with a soft nose and a strong bite — and he slid two pistols into the holsters on his belt in case they ran into trouble. Ren had watched his father change these last few months. He had grown leaner and stronger, thanks to all of the riding he did; and he had opened himself to the Resistance once again, insisting on talking details with Marty and volunteering for extra patrols at night. And he had changed as a father, too. He may never be the hug-it-out type of parent, but he was trying to rebuild his relationship with Ren. After dinner each evening, they would break out a deck of cards, and late at night, whenever Ren had another nightmare, his father would soothe him. Sometimes, Mr. Cabot would sleep on the floor next to Ren's cot, no questions asked, just to let his son know that he was there and that he cared. The two of them might always be a work in progress, but Ren was grateful that his dad was trying. Ren may have lost his mother all over again, but he had regained his father in so many ways.

Ren ignored his nerves and held out his essay to Mr. Cabot before he chickened out. For some reason, he didn't mind the thought of thousands of Americans reading it — but his dad? That scared him.

"Everything okay?" his dad said warily.

Ren motioned at the paper. "Just read it and you'll see." Then he thrust his hands behind his back and threaded his fingers together as he waited for his father to finish. He had worked on this piece for so long that he had memorized some parts of it.

Over two centuries ago, our colonial ancestors broke free from the powers of tyranny and established across these lands a new nation, called America. Our country was born upon the greatest of dreams — of freedom, of liberty, of inalienable rights.

But this newborn nation was birthed with imperfections. Its freedoms were not given to all, and its rights were never extended to everyone. As America grew, these imperfections grew with it, sometimes leading even to war.

And yet America persisted. Her children fought for change, for freedom, and for equality for all. As we must do now, in the face of the Empire's evil.

The Empire believes that it had long ago slaughtered the United States, but they've never understood that they cannot kill a dream. Only we Americans can do such a thing if we let that dream wither and perish, if we allow our rights to be stripped, and if we forget about our claim to liberty and justice for all.

If we wish to breathe life back into our country, then we must rise up and fight. We must aid the Resistance, and we must reclaim what we've lost.

We must not fear. For in the darkest of nights, we shall strike — and strike again.

The Viper, you see, is more than a boy named Ren Cabot.

The Viper is Jenny Tsai, who believed in a cause.

The Viper is Abel Quirk, who died for freedom.

The Viper is Jay Park, who fought for equality.

The Viper is not one person, but a rallying cry. The Viper is you and me and every American living under oppression.

And it is time that we awaken.

It was taking a long time for Mr. Cabot to finish the essay, and Ren began babbling. "I'm not sure if I got the tone right. It might be a little heavy-handed but I thought —"

Mr. Cabot looked up and wiped his shining eyes. "I wouldn't change a thing, Ren."

Ren grinned so wide that his lips hurt. He blushed and tried to shrug off the compliment. "Sorry I made you cry, old man."

"Cry? These aren't tears on my face. It must be raining or something." They shared a laugh before the silence trickled back in. Mr. Cabot said softly, "I'm proud of you. Your mom would be, too."

Ren felt his own eyes prickle with tears, and his father gave him a handkerchief from his pocket.

"See?" Mr. Cabot said. "It *is* raining."

When Tessa returned, it was time to depart. Ren helped his dad guide his mare out of the barn, drawing the process out for as long as possible because he always hated this part. His dad and Tessa would take every precaution, but Ren would keep worrying until they returned.

"Careful out there," Ren said. "Watch your back."

"We'll be home before you know it," replied his father. "See you soon."

With a click of their tongues, they entered the night and Ren watched them go, feeling a piece of his heart ride off with them.

Once Ren could no longer hear the hoofbeats, he returned to the bunker, retrieved a glass of water, and sat back down at his desk, where he set his fingertips against the worn keys.

He wasn't sure what to write, but he wasn't too worried. Every essay began this way, with a blank page and a fresh start. The words would come eventually, sometimes in a jolt of inspiration and other times with what felt like pliers. But the writing process was never meant to be easy. His mother had taught him that, and Ren thought about her as he typed a few words and then a few more.

In a lonely bunker, in the middle of nowhere, the Viper got back to work.

ACKNOWLEDGMENTS

Over the years I've heard dozens of writers talk about how hard it was to write their second book. *Sophomore slump*, they'd groan. *The second-book blues.* But much to my surprise this didn't happen to me. My second novel wasn't easy by any stretch, but the words flowed and I met my deadlines. I thought I had escaped the second-book curse!

But in the end the Writing Gods got the last laugh. *Live in Infamy* is my third novel, but it was the most colicky of my book children yet. The characters eluded me. The plot wouldn't cooperate. I wrote and re-wrote the last quarter of the manuscript three times. Yet through all of the turmoil, my editor, Jody Corbett, never gave up on me or my story. She spent hours on the phone dissecting plot points with me, and she never blinked an eye when I glumly asked for a deadline extension. Simply put, *Live in Infamy* wouldn't exist without Jody, which is why this book is dedicated to her. I'm so grateful and lucky to have her in my corner.

I also owe my agent, Jim McCarthy, a million thanks. We've worked together now for eight years, and I'm constantly amazed by his professionalism, his kindness, and his lightning-quick response times. He never seems to mind when I bombard him with neurotic emails (of which I've written many), and he remains the anchor of my writing career — always steady and stable and funny to boot.

Many thanks to the staff at Scholastic who are basically the kindest and most talented people on earth. I'm incredibly thankful for the Book Fair and

Book Club teams in particular who have been so supportive of my novels. I also must give a tip of the hat to Phil Falco, who designed the cover for both *Live in Infamy* and *The Only Thing to Fear*. You're amazing, Phil!

As a mom, I simply couldn't have finished this book without my wonderful childcare providers. To Lorena Aziz, thank you for welcoming my daughter into your home and treating her like your own. To the teachers at the Bluemont Community Center, thank you for always greeting my girl with a smile, for kissing her ouchies, and for surrounding her with love while I finished this book.

To Amanda Fein and Allison Young, thank you for always being there for me since our days at Herbert Hoover Middle School. I'm lucky to have such inspiring, smart, and hilarious best friends. To my little sister, Kristy Tung, thank you for making me laugh, for cheering me on, and for regaling me with *Game of Thrones* plot theories. You're the best sister ever.

Lastly, I owe my biggest thank-you to my family. My mother-in-law, Donna Richmond, provided countless hours of childcare so that I could write and revise and then revise some more. My husband, Justin Richmond, has long been the patron saint of my writing career and the very best friend that I could ever ask for — I love you very much. And to my daughter, Aimee Rose — light of my life, destroyer of my sleep — thank you for bringing me such joy, even when you're refusing to brush your teeth or hair. My dearest girl, it is an honor to be your mom.

ABOUT THE AUTHOR

Caroline Tung Richmond is the author of the alternative history novel *The Only Thing to Fear* (a companion to *Live in Infamy*), and the historical fiction novel *The Darkest Hour*.

A self-proclaimed history nerd and cookie connoisseur, Caroline lives in Virginia, with her family and their dog, Otto von Bismarck — named for the German chancellor (naturally).